A Spider in the Eye

A HANNIBAL SMYTH MISADVENTURE

MARK HAYES

Salthomle Publishing

Saltholme publishing
11 Saltholme Close
High Clarence
TS21TL

Book Layout © 2018 Saltholme publications

A Spider In The Eye:
Mark Hayes -- 1st ed.
ISBN 9781791832049

By the same author

The Hannibal Smyth Misadventures Series

A Spider In the Eye

From Russia With Tassels (coming summer 2019)

A Scar of Avarice (novella)

A Squid on the Shoulder (coming 2020)

Other Novels

Passing Place: Location Relative

Cider Lane: Of Silences and Stars

Also features in the following Anthologies

Harvey Duckman presents vol 1

As ever this novel is for my children;
Sarah Louise and Aaron James. Neither of whom are
children anymore.

This novel could not have been possible without the help
of A Hawley, C.G. Hatton and A Hatton, for all the alpha
readings, proofreadings, editing and importantly the
ceaseless encouragment and advice. So I offer my heart felt
thanks to all three of them, as well as all the Adamscon
geeks, the Thursday night writers and the readers who are
kind enough to keep asking for more.

Contents

PROLOGUE

I have seen the future of humanity, and it is war.

War on a scale unprecedented, consuming the world and leaving millions slaughtered in Europe's mud.

War in all its untold misery, as nation fights nation with all the might of the industrial age.

A mere generation will pass, the lessons of the first war unlearned, before the world is plunged once more into darkness. Conflict on a scale unreckoned by our nightmares, embroiling all in its embittered grip. Wrapping the world in choking hands and bring suffering to all it touches.

Locomotives will carry men, woman, even children, into the gaping maws of factories of death built by the dreams of madmen. Millions sent to chambers of slaughter for the systematic butchery of a race.

Machines will fill the air, raining down death upon the great cities of Europe leaving nothing but shells of former glories. Broken remains of civilisation scorched and charred by storms of fire.

Men will craft weapons that level whole cities in a single blast.

Weapons that leave invisible death and poisoned air in their wake. Weapon once conceived never forgotten, in a world waiting on the abyss for the press of a single button.

Ideologies of East and West will clash in a century of blood, ceaseless in its undertaking. Humanity master of its own annihilation. Tyrants will rule both overt and hidden. Until money becomes the foremost of all ideologies.

An ideology that will eat away at the earth itself. Burning it up to feed the ever-growing appetites of the few who extend their power over the many with the propaganda of technology. Feeding lies through invisible transmissions that saturate the minds of humanity and reducing them to cattle, ripe for the slaughter, to feed the voracious appetites of the elite.

All to keep the system of war and hate moving forward.

All the advancements of the ages, all the wonders of humanity's devising, all the ingenuity of man turned to one sole purpose. The slaughter of the weak, to feed the vanities of the strong.

H G Wells, 1895

Unpublished introduction to The Time Machine

CHAPTER 1

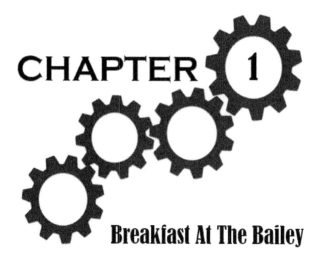

Breakfast At The Bailey

The cells of the New Bailey are not somewhere they take you to. Rather, they're a place they throw you, because once they put you there, they're finished with you.

It's the last stop but one on your life's road.

The last stop, the very last stop. Well, that's a mere hundred-yard walk across cold, damp flagstones through a tunnel into the small enclosed courtyard behind the Bailey.

There you climb up ten final steps to the scaffold before a short, sudden and very final drop. One which never quite reaches the ground.

The New Bailey is, you see, the highest court in the British Empire. So once your appeal fails there, they don't bother to take you anywhere else. They just throw you in a cell, to await that final journey.

That's it; you're done, finished.

That's all you get.

The cells of the New Bailey are the last place you ever go.

Well, except that is what's left of you afterwards, which they cram into a cheap pine box to be shipped off to your relatives, leastways if they are willing to pay for the body. Otherwise, it's the rendering plant. After all, the crown must recoup its costs somehow. Death and taxes are ever the only certainties, and the crown likes to get its due.

It should be said, therefore, that when I awoke to find myself flung into that dark, damp and foul-smelling cell, I wasn't entirely in my happy place. As such, when they threw me in that cell, I made some rather choice remarks to the court bailiffs.

There were also a few minor exclamations about injustice, protestations of my innocence and I shall admit, the odd observation in regards to the bailiff's parentage. These remarks I will admit, though without much in the way of regret, were somewhat less than gentlemanly. Considering my own parentage, the latter observation was also a tad out of character.

I've never been fond of those who use the word 'Bastard' as an insult. It is one that I've heard thrown at myself all too often, and for all its accuracy, it was seldom thrown at me for reasons other than abuse. Indeed, I doubt that most of those who'd called me such over the years were actually aware they spoke a literal truth. Not that many of them would've been surprised by this nugget, I am sure.

I, for my own part, swore never to use the term as an insult many years ago. Though I will admit that oath, like so many others I have sworn over the years, has been broken more than once. All the same, however, it's a rarity for me to throw that particular insult about. So, that I called the judge, the bailiffs and the jailors a 'Set of bastards' is perhaps an indication of my frame of mind at the moment of my incarceration. Though, in my meagre defence, I was at that juncture being condemned to dance the Tyburn jig.

Having your hanging, literally, hanging over you, does tend to prey on one's mind I have found, and leads you to forgo some of the niceties of polite conversation.

Questioning the parentage of those charged with marching you to the gallows may seem to be a measly recompense for such an indignity, but I am one who's been known to seek solace in the occasional small victory. Though as they go, it was a somewhat minuscule one at best.

However, before I go any further with my tale, so you don't begin to doubt my credence, let us have a moment of honesty between us. For I know exactly what it is you're thinking at this moment.

You're thinking that every condemned man protests his innocence, both to the court and elsewhere. Just as every condemned man will decry the injustice done to him. For that matter, I'm in little doubt every condemned man makes a remark or two in regards to the parentage of their jailors. But I am not claiming to be unique in this.

I'd suspect also, that you may hold true to that ever-popular view that the courts don't in point of fact 'get it wrong' very often, and the majority of the condemned deserve their fate. You may even subscribe to that other irascibly popular view expressed so often in the popular press… To wit, 'Hanging's too good for em…'

If not, then you are a better soul than I…

Indeed, had you asked me before my own dalliance with the courts of 'She who is seldom amused', I would have told you that a man who'd been through three appeals and still stands guilty before the crown is a man deserving of his punishment. For a man who has had his guilt weighed before the crown and been found wanting is just that, a guilty man.

You may, if somewhat grudgingly, also believe like most good English men that if, by chance, there is the rare occasion when that old blind girl on the Bailey's roof is miscarried, well, that is just the price that has to be paid for law and order. That too is an opinion I would have put forward myself in the past. One finds little solace in this if one is the miscarried I have come to believe.

I know there are some who consider themselves to hold to a higher moral philosophy. Those who say something along the lines of, 'Better a hundred guilty men walk free, than one innocent hang!' A view popularised by some important American or other before their nation fell apart, Franklin, I believe… But it's a view that's never proved popular with the British masses when they're braying for blood, and such high ideals did little to keep those states united after all. That said, it's a view I find myself with more sympathy for these days, all things considered. Certainly, right then, I was of the view that one less hanging could only be a good thing.

With that all in mind then let us be honest here. Why should you believe in my innocence? Even if I protested such as they slung me kicking and screaming into my last abode to await that longest of short strolls. I stood condemned by the court. I was, therefore, guilty. I'm sure nothing I say could convince you otherwise, any more than it convinced my jailors. But protest I did. Indeed, it would be fair to say, I protested loudly. I decried. I shouted. I ranted in anger. And I uttered my contempt for the judgement pronounced upon me. Most venomously in fact.

All of which elicited the response you'd expect from the bailiffs. A violent response involving a heartfelt kick to my rear end that sent me sprawling to the floor of the cell, followed by a few more swings of their Billy clubs than necessarily were required to subdue me. I'd stop my protests long before those blows stopped coming. Even in my anger, I knew they'd been futile before the first blow rained down, they were worse than futile once they struck. The blows, nevertheless, kept coming, along with kicks from iron-shod boots. Until, not as quickly as I would have liked, I finally slipped from consciousness, bruised, bloody and beaten on the stone floor of my new and final home, a stone-walled cell within dragging distance of the gallows.

There were probably a few kicks after I succumbed as well. Bailiffs are want to take their pleasures where they can, and in all honesty, who doesn't like kicking a man when he is down. It is right up there with fair play, high tea, and a stiff upper lip, as a good old English tradition after all.

If you don't believe me on that score, if indeed you hold some fanciful ideas about what it is to be English, you need only examine the treatment of any English sportsman in the tabloid press after the national team loses. Kicking men when they're down is one of the things we English truly excel at.

However, if, and I freely admit it is unlikely, you feel the bailiffs were perhaps too heavy-handed with their treatment, then I thank you for the thought.

In truth I don't blame them overly. In their position, I'd have done the same. Putting the boot into someone lying prone on the deck was always my favourite tactic in games lessons back at school. As long as it wasn't me who was the one prone on the ground, then all's fair in rugger as in life.

What care you, the bailiffs, or anyone else for that matter, if a prisoner taking the long walk has a black eye, barely healed cuts, fresh bruises, and a broken rib or three?

The bailiffs had no good reason to display a little kindness towards the condemned, and the job of death cell jailor isn't one that attracts the gentle-hearted. Being able to give their prisoner a good kicking, well I can see how men of a certain mind might consider that a perk of the job.

Thuggish jobs tend to attract thugs after all, because even thugs need to put food on the table. Some may even condone such wanton cruelty, as it gives said thugs an outlet for their rage. Better by far they get their 'kicks' in on the job, than say, brawling in the bars around Whitechapel. So my protests of innocence and for clemency were always doomed to fall on deaf ears.

Also, as we are being honest here, so there be no lie between us at so early a juncture in my tale, I was for all my protests, as guilty as the devil.

If indeed it had been I that sat in judgment that day, then I dare say I would have ordered my fine stiff neck to the noose just as readily as the bewigged one who pronounced sentence upon me.

I'd stood in that courtroom first accused and then roundly condemned for murder. Which as I am sure you're aware is a charge with a long established punishment.

Perhaps had I been a more honest man I may have just coughed up to the whole thing. Though such honesty would have seen me swing regardless, even were I to claim mitigating circumstances. At most, in honesty, I could claim a modicum of innocence on this charge, in that the man I killed was doing his best to kill me at the time. So it was an act of self-defence, as it were.

So, while I am far from honest, self-defence was what I claimed in court. A defence which was surprisingly truthful, as it held no lie to its construction, for I've no doubt that he had every intention to be the end of me that night.

"I saw it in his eyes, as plain as day, oh yes your honour, he had every intent to kill me and it was beholding on me to kill him first if I was to live through the night," as I claimed in court, and not one word of a lie was spoken in that claim I assure you, for all the court believed otherwise.

However, again to let the truth be our guide here, I did murder him. What I chose to omit from my feeble defence was a simple fact that paints me far from the innocence I claimed. That fact being that I had entered the gunnery bay that night with the fullest of intents to be the end of him also. That he pre-empted me and was reconciled to bring about my death is of slight regard in that respect. This fact I chose not to admit in court.

Shocking of me, I know…

I admit it now only so that you can give some credence to what I have further to tell in my tale. If it paints me black-hearted, well I see no reason to give lie to that here. So to be clear, it was with murderous intent that I was driven to act, and for that oldest and most human of reasons, that of fiscal gain.

Murder, I should mention, was also but one of the crimes for which I'd stood accused, been convicted and was now to face my demise.

There were other little matters like profiteering, black marketeering, conspiracy to defraud the crown, ungentlemanly conduct, arson of the queen's naval yards, and of course, treason.

Little matters as I say…

Matters for which I also have no defence, for of them I was also as guilty as sin. Though again, I claimed otherwise in court. With that in mind, I should probably add lying under oath and general perjury to the list of my perfidies.

I am, you see, as you may have surmised at this juncture, something of a villain. A man, it would be fair to say, whose word cannot be taken as true. So it is up to you, I guess, to decide if, given all that, you chose to believe a word of what I now impart. It is the truth, however, the whole truth and, allowing for the odd embellishment to save me looking a complete fool, nothing but the truth. So help me God, if you believe in that kind of thing, though I generally try to avoid such committed beliefs myself.

So as I was saying, I woke in one of the condemned cells beneath the New Bailey. I wasn't at my best.

My right eye was swollen, to the point my vision was blurred. Dried blood mingled with dirt on my face. I ached from head to toe, and I suspected that I had at least one if not three broken ribs from the Billy clubs the night before. I was, to put it mildly, in a bit of a state judging from the pain I felt.

The cell stank like someone had relieved themselves, and once I regained more of my faculties, much to my shame, I realised that was because I had. That it most likely happened after or while I was taking the beating did nothing to restore a sense of dignity.

It may seem a strange thing to worry about when all you are facing is the prospect of a short stroll to the gallows. But even with the certain conclusion that my life, such as it was, was drawing to a close, the fact I had lost control of my bladder and soiled myself brought with it the kind of shame a guilty verdict for murder never could.

It has to be said, therefore, that as I sat there still soaked in my own urine, in a cold, damp cell, battered and bruised, facing my imminent departure from the land of the living, I wasn't, in absolute truth, entirely happy about my current circumstances.

Beyond the cell, it was a beautiful May morning, and the sunlight was doing its best to stream through the single, very narrow and utterly unreachable window about ten foot above the cell floor. That stream was, however, little more than a trickle through the grim dirt of street-level London, so it did little to cheer my spirits. A feat that wasn't achieved either when one of my jailers arrived, carrying with him a tray containing breakfast for the condemned man. Which after he opened the cell door, he placed just within spitting distance of my hands.

You may be asking yourself how I knew it was spitting distance. Well, let's just say the guard demonstrated this fact with a certain distasteful flair.

I was, I should've probably mentioned, chained to the floor of the cell. Presumably, this was on the off chance I could've otherwise found a way through the bars, out of the cell block, through the New Bailey itself, past many armed and very motivated guards, through the upper courtyard and then over the wall to freedom. The guardians of the New Bailey had never lost a prisoner; they were taking no chances of doing so with me, sad to say.

At this point, I'd like to say I was considering my options, but in truth, I wasn't, for they looked as bleak as could be. The cell was robustly constructed, I was chained hand and foot to a steel eyelet within it, and even if I could in some way overcome this impediment, I would, as I mentioned, have to get past several locked doors and an array of guards. Also, time was a factor as I had only about two hours until my imminent appointment with the end of a rope, so tunnelling my way through the stone floor was somewhat unlikely.

Bribery, depressingly, was not going to be an option either. I wasn't, after all, locked up in some tiny despot kingdom where the guards might look the other way for a few Sheckles. This cell was in the very heart of Imperial London, itself the heart of the ever great and glorious British Empire. An Empire that may be considered at times a tad despotic, but tiny it certainly isn't.

That's not to say that there is no corruption to be found within the Empire's capital. If you are the sort to believe that, you are, sadly, very naïve. But if that is the case, then I invite you to play cards with me sometime.

Great and glorious though the Empire is, it remains corrupt to its rotten stinking heart. There'd, I'm sure, be little problem finding someone willing to take a bribe. Even in the highest court of the land. Finding a corrupt guard to slip me a file, or an equally corrupt judge who might change my sentence would probably be simple enough. The problem was more prosaic than that and of a fiscal nature. Or to put it another way, I was broke, and as such, I'd no means to pay said bribe. A bribe that would, after all, be far more than a few lousy Sheckles. Corrupt the Empire may be, but it is also very rich. So only the wealthy could afford the kind of bribes that neatly avoided those little inconveniences of a legal nature, and the larger the legal inconvenience, the greater the bribe required.

Lady Justice in London's courts wasn't exactly for sale, but she could be rented for a sizeable contribution to someone's retirement fund.

Sadly in my current straits, I couldn't have afforded the bribe in a tiny despot kingdom where they still considered a couple of Shillings a sizable amount. Besides, it would probably cost the wealth of said tiny despotic kingdom to gain clemency for one who had committed my sizable infractions. As it was, without funds, I was as equal in the eyes of the law as any other cash-strapped subject of 'Old Iron Knickers'. Equality of justice isn't just a dream for those who can't afford a better class of lawyer, but a stark reality. For the poor are always equal under the law.

Such equality with the common man was, as you may suspect, of little comfort to me at the time.

Breakfast had arrived, but my appetite was sadly lacking. Which was something the frankly inedible looking breakfast did little to alter. There is a lot of rubbish told about last meals for the condemned. I can testify it isn't the final treat that they make out.

The chef, if indeed it was prepared by someone to whom that title could be applied, seemed of the opinion that it was wasteful to make something edible for a condemned man. My stomach was, however, cramping for food all the same, so I made the best effort I could to eat it with the single spoon provided.

Life has taught me a few lessons over the years, eating whenever you've the chance being one of them. As an orphan raised under the care of the Empire, it's sometimes been a choice between eating the inedible or nothing at all, and nothing is never the better choice. In particular, if you don't know where the next inedible meal is coming from.

So, eat I did, somewhat unaware of my surroundings, as I found myself lost in thought.

Mostly the thoughts involved Gunnery Sergeant Hardacre falling to his death through the bomb bay doors after being the recipient of a good hard shove from yours truly. An image that I was sure at the time would stay with me for the rest of my life. The rest of my life being measurable in hours at this point.

I could remember the feeling of satisfaction I'd felt as I watched him fall, having finally put an end to the miserable swine. That and the look of panic in his eyes as he fell.

Sadly I could also remember the feeling that followed closely on the heels of that moment of satisfaction, the horrendous realisation that Petty Officer Maythorpe had been stood in the doorway watching it all as it happened.

Maythorpe, or 'Principal Witness for the Prosecution', as he was referred to later, was and remains a stiff-necked idealist who believed in the righteous justice of the Empire. He was the kind of self-important borderline idiot that only the British public school system could produce. I am sure you know the type, clueless as to how the world actually works, while remaining absolutely convinced of his own superiority over the lower orders. Those being defined as anyone not born in the Home Counties, and Johnny-come-lately foreigners. He was boorish, pig-headed, priggish, loud and invariably overconfident. All rugby, cold showers, chasing the fillies and 'what-oh'. The only thing stiffer than his neck was his upper lip…

I'd, in fairness, quite liked him up to this point in our acquaintance. Not least because he also lacked the imagination to cheat at cards, or indeed to spot anyone else doing so. Something that had ingratiated him to my pocket on more than one occasion. I liked him in the way you do when you happen upon an actual honest man. If only for the novelty value of such an event.

So there I was lost in my thoughts while trying to stomach ill-cooked food. Thoughts, which though it may reflect badly on me, included how much simpler everything would have been if I'd sent Maythorpe the way of Gunnery Sergeant Hardacre. This may have proved a wiser course, rather than my attempt to bribe him into silence. The attempt to do so proved to be a mistake. It's remarkable how quickly you can go off an honest man I discovered…

Lost in these thoughts, I didn't hear the door to the cell block open again or the footsteps of the man who entered. I was therefore mildly surprised to hear a voice interrupt my contemplation, a soft, refined, gentlemanly voice, which had the ring of a civil servant about it. The softness you only got from mixing a home county's accent with several years in Oxbridge. It was the sort of voice that was used to being listened to without ever having to be raised. The sort of voice that knew that what it was telling you to do, was something you were then going to go do, as you not doing so was frankly unthinkable. A voice that spoke the calm assurance. The voice of a man who could sign a death warrant or blackball you from the club with equal disregard if you didn't listen to it. British officers and civil servants never shout. They never have to. That is after all what they have sergeants for.

"Good morning, Mr Smyth. How are you finding the accommodation the Bailey has to offer?" the aforementioned voice inquired softly.

Surprised, and in truth lacking the clarity to formulate a truly witty retort, I uttered, rather weakly, "It's a bit damp."

"No great surprise there, Mr Smyth. London itself has an unfortunate tendency to be a 'bit damp' as you put it. I believe there are moves in parliament to relocate the city to the Riviera, but the French are being somewhat obstinate on the subject, as I recall. Still, that's the French for you," came a deadpan and vaguely arid reply.

I laughed despite myself as I looked up to see the speaker. Expecting to see some humour in his eyes.

I was slightly perturbed when I saw nothing of the sort.

CHAPTER 2

The Humourless Mr M

On taking close regard of my visitor, he didn't seem a very humorous fellow at all.

What he looked like was every inch to be one of those dour civil servants that so infest the British Empire. A short cadaverous man, in a stiff-collared dark suit, tailed coat and wearing the obligatory top hat. He was indeed indistinguishable from any other Whitehall drone. That mildly comical stereotype so often lampooned in the political cartoons that feature in the likes of Punch and the daily rags of Fleet Street.

There are workers and doers in this world, and then there are also those who do the paperwork. Which is exactly what the man before me looked to be. A pen-pushing civil servant to his hind teeth. The kind I had long ago learned to both loathe and suck up to in equal measure. I can't pretend not to have some prejudices when it came to his type. Parasitic little shits to a man, in my opinion, and this one looked more the parasite than most. There was something unpleasant about him. Like that itch on your scrotum that you can't scratch in public, he gave you an uncomfortable feeling that made it hard for you to be at your ease. It was something about the blank stare that lacked any human warmth behind his bespectacled eyes.

Observing his arid expression, my bitter half-laugh ran dry in my throat. I realised, much to my irk, that I wasn't entirely sure he was making a joke after all. Indeed his offhand comment had been made in complete seriousness. I could almost imagine a gaggle of civil servants of his ilk discussing the idea in dusty meeting rooms. The idiocy of the idea of no concern, they merely put forward an advisory committee, after all, it was up to other men to actually do things. Move London to the Riviera indeed… It was a slightly disconcerting idea if truth be told, but it would hardly be the most ridiculous idea ever to have come out of Whitehall.

After this, a rather odd silence fell between us, and I found myself feeling more than a little unnerved by him. I was not, as I am sure you have surmised, in the happiest frame of mind to start with, but there was something about the man's demeanour that made me feel downright itchy.

This went on for a lingering moment, while he showed no inclination to expand on why he had chosen to visit me in my death cell. He just continued to peer at me through those thick round spectacles of his. As if I was some kind of exhibit to be observed, or perhaps scrutinised is a closer word. I felt like the subject of a voyeur and wondered to myself if he was a man who just enjoyed the sight of a doomed man's final hours.

As I said, he made me feel downright itchy.

Unnerved, to fill the developing silence, I cleared my throat. In the process, I realised just how dry it now felt. So I ventured a request, with little hope. "I don't suppose you're here to offer me a drink?"

The civil servant, uncharacteristically for him I suspected, smiled at me. It was though a smile that held no more than a smidgeon of arid humour. "I am afraid that is not the case. Though I am reliably assured, they serve breakfast to the condemned at some time in the morning."

"They already have," I replied, turning my gaze to the grim remains of the tray in front of me. "If you can call this slop breakfast, but for some reason, they were decidedly lax in serving a drink with it," I added, trying to keep an air of civility to my tone. I was in all honesty, however, starting to feel a little irritable. Which was doubtless betrayed in my voice when I uttered my next words. "Who the hell are you anyway?"

This outburst caused him to raise an eyebrow of inquiry, accompanied by a little audible tut. The same reaction I'd have expected for being rude at a dinner table. His rebuke, however, was altogether more scathing.

"Oh, my dear Mr Smyth, is incarceration and an impending death sentence all it takes to remove your manners? What hopes for our wondrous Empire if a prized example of its manhood such as yourself can be so easily vexed? Perhaps you are not the man I require after all if that is indeed the case," he said, all uttered in the nauseatingly self-assured and utterly belittling tone only a British civil servant could achieve.

At this point in the conversation, I should have noted the faintest glimmer of hope. Which as a condemned man was more than I had any right to expect. 'The man I require' after all, was a suggestive turn of phrase, words that implied

I might yet hold out hope of avoiding the noose. If that was, I proved that I could be valuable elsewhere.

Indeed, I dare say that had I noted said he 'the man I require', I'd have wisely minded my tone somewhat. I'd have trodden that careful, if precarious path, between humility and toadying we all learn to walk in our lives. Massaging the officious swine's ego a little, as it were, may have proved the wiser course. A saying about gift horses and mouths spring to mind. However, this little gem of insight slipped past me at the time. So instead, I found myself inclined once more to use some choice words in regards to another man's parentage.

That said, with the benefit of hindsight and considering all that has happened since, I'm not sure the noose was such a bad alternative to what was hinted at in that ominous 'the man I require'. It would have spared me a great many indignities all things considered. But I digress, and really shouldn't get ahead of myself.

In any event, I didn't get a chance to try and ingratiate myself with him. No doubt because he could see the anger brewing in my face. With something akin to the dismissive, he raised his hand to cut off any angry reply and spoke on.

"Your pardon, however, as I also failed in my manners, so I must endeavour to rectify the situation. My name, I must regrettably inform you, is a state secret, and as such something I am unable to share with you at this time. You may, however, refer to me by my title. M."

"M? Just M… your title is just the letter M?" I asked, mildly bemused and irritated by his condescending tone.

The man calling himself M smiled ever so slightly, the thin smile of someone offering sufferance to another.

"Indeed, Mr Smyth, just M. Further than that, I cannot, and indeed will not be drawn. I can, however, tell you that I am at present engaged by the crown to deal with matters which, like my name, are designated state secrets. Ones to which I equally can not make you privy at this time. Though given the current position you find yourself in, you are unlikely to become privy to any state secrets anytime soon."

This last was followed by a slight snort, which may have been a laugh at my expense. It was hard to tell.

"Though it is the aforementioned state secrets which have made it necessary for me to seek you out this day. Unfortunately, the necessity of them may make you late for any pressing appointments you happen to have, though one suspects you will not find this too disagreeable in that respect. You only have the one appointment to keep, I believe."

I listened to all this with a degree of disbelief, while trying to swallow my temper. My brain had, you see, caught up with the conversation, and with that 'the man I require' he'd left hanging a moment before. Though his formal approach to conversation was less than conducive to an actual explanation. As a rule, I've found I prefer a little more in the way of plain speaking when I'm resident in a death cell.

It is strange, now I consider it, to realise just how often I've had occasion to find myself inside a death cell. Suffice to say, enough times to have come to the conclusion I prefer not to be flannelled by someone when I am…

In any regard, I did my best to remind myself that I was a gentleman and an officer, despite my incarceration. Or at least that was how I preferred to present myself to the world. I am in actuality, a lying thieving swindler, who just happens to wear a uniform and hold pretensions to civility. Though truth be told I've always considered that to be the definition of an officer and a gentleman. I'll add I have seldom met anyone who has proved that definition false, saving perhaps Maythorpe, unfortunately for me.

Regardless, by this time I was intrigued and the faintest glimmer of hope was starting to vest itself upon me.

Hope to the condemned man is something taken where he can find it in my experience. The mysterious M seemed an unlikely sort to visit a condemned man without a damned good reason. Come to that though he seemed an unlikely fellow all round, what with his talk of state secrets and that odd single initial name.

'M for Mountbatten perhaps?' I pondered. Everyone was aware after all that Lord Mountbatten had some strange ideas. Ideas that due to his rank and position were probably considered to be state secrets. But that seemed unlikely, whomever M was, he didn't look like a man who reportedly spent his weekdays in charge of the Queen's purse and his weekends holding the purses of infamous transvestites.

That particular 'state secret' was a scandal that was being carefully kept out of the periodicals. It did, however, travel through the whispered conversations in the gentlemen's clubs of Soho. Which, in fairness, made it a very widely known state secret.

I remember shaking my head as I dismissed this idea. Whoever this M was, he didn't have the insipid half-dead look of royalty.

"I see, Mr M, if I may call you that?" I said at last. Though I didn't see at all, not really.

"Just M will suffice, Mr Smyth. There is no need for title here," he replied primly.

"Then you should call me Hannibal, as we're being informal," I said, falling back into old habits. When in doubt I have always found it wise to make the effort to sound like a gentleman, while holding a slight measure of indignation in my voice. It was an affectation I'd carefully acquired over the years. If you wished to be treated like a gentleman, you had to make sure you both sounded and behaved like one. Which is to say with that certain sense of entitlement to your mannerisms. The ones that declared you were lowering yourself just to be holding this conversation. That was unless of course your credentials were impeccable, in which case you could act however you wished.

I was all too aware my own credentials were shaky at the best of times. Thus I'd carefully schooled myself over the years to sound like the gentleman I wished people to perceive. Even in such reduced circumstances as I found myself in right then, it was my natural default.

"Oh Mr Smyth, we are most definitely not being informal here," M told me with a snide tone. "And indeed, if we're being informal, I would venture I would be calling you Harry."

I've no doubt that my face showed my surprise. It was all very well to try and hold myself aloof, but Harry was a name from my past. His use of it caught me completely off guard.

To the world, I was assuredly Hannibal Smyth, Gunnery Ensign in Her Majesty's Royal Air Navy. An officer, a gentleman, and that special kind of straight bat playing Englishman that had made the Empire what it was today. At least, that is who I had been until my arrest and several unfortunate discoveries by the police afterwards. But despite that misfortune, to the world, I was still Hannibal Smyth Esquire. I was no longer plain old Harry Smith.

Harry Smith, you have to understand, was a ghost from the past. A long-forgotten dirty faced orphan, so far down the social ladder he'd not even seen the bottom rung. Harry Smith aspired to the gutter, which is a long way off from the vantage point of the sewer. Or he would've if the Harry Smiths of this world aspired to anything beyond their next meal and somewhere dry to sleep.

In short, Harry was a name I'd long buried. So long buried I barely remembered him myself. Hearing it now threw me somewhat out of my stride. Even the court hadn't used that name when it condemned me to the noose. I said as much when I replied.

"You have the benefit of me, sir. That is a name I thought consigned to history," I said, an edge of tartness in my voice. Blame my circumstances if you will, but I was struggling for the best of humours. This resurrection of old ghosts was doing nothing to help my mindset.

"Mr Smyth, you will find there is little consigned to history, and next to nothing is ever forgotten within certain quarters of Her Majesty's government. We are nothing if we are not fastidious in this regard. Which is good news for you 'Harry', for if it were not so, we would not be having this conversation. For were you not 'Harry' you would not be of use to the crown." That same snide undertone was there when he pronounced my birth-given name. He used it like a nasty little knife to jab at me.

Beneath his cold Whitehall aloofness, there lurked a malicious bastard, I realised. The kind of man given to tormenting his underlings. Something I clearly was considered to be. And he would do so for no better reason than because he could. A type of man I had come across all too often in my life.

Regardless of this I determined to ignore his little jibes. He held all the cards, after all, and sometimes not rising to the bait is all you can do.

"And what quarters of government would that be Mr M?" I inquired, enjoying the flicker of irritation that crossed his face.

Whoever he was, the 'Mr' rankled him, perhaps because he hid a Lordship or a sir somewhere before his actual name. It wouldn't have surprised me if that were so. I'd little doubt the more common form of address niggled him. It was petty of me, I know, but I made a mental note of that irritation all the same. Small victories and all that.

"I represent a Ministry of the crown, one not given to the use of further title. We deal with things the other Ministries do not. Indeed we arrange matters so other Ministries do not need to," he replied with a degree of aloofness.

"So, it's M from The Ministry?" I pushed.

"Quite so, Mr Smyth. Quite so…"

"Just The Ministry?" I pushed a little more. Mainly if I'm honest because I could see that the note of inquiry in my voice irritated him. He was not a man used to answering questions, which only encouraged me to ask more because I found him quite objectionable, what with all his detached pretension. That and the very obvious way he let me know that I was insignificant to him.

It niggled me all the more, no doubt, as I was a man condemned. In such circumstances, you don't need anyone to remind you that you're of little note and I've never been fond of being looked down upon at any time, though of all my character flaws that is one I share with most I suspect. That fact that M looked down on me was self-evident. I was at best a tool he planned to use for his own devices, nothing more, and no one likes to be used.

That said, it had occurred to me that it was better to be a tool in someone else's game than a corpse feeding worms. So I was fighting my worst impulses at this point and trying to swallow my over prickly pride. I just wasn't being overly successful in that fight.

"Just 'The Ministry'. Yes, it has a fuller name but one I have no reason to divulge to you at this time, Mr Smyth. It is of course another one of those state secrets you are not in a position to be privy to. I am sure you understand our position," he said with a sniff, which suggested whether I understood my position or not was of little consequence to him. Which I am almost certain was true.

In any regard, I believed him about the name. The idea of any branch of government not having a full and embroidered title was all but laughable. Civil servants like their titles as much as the military. The smaller and less important The Ministry, the longer the title was always the rule in my experience. Noting that should have told me something about one known only as The Ministry if I had been paying attention to such details at the time. I was, however, a little preoccupied for such reflection.

"So, am I to take it you have come to offer me my freedom in exchange for a service to the crown?" I asked, with more bravado than hope.

Remarkably at this, his serious veneer vanished for a moment. The vaguest whiff of an amused smile crossed his lips.

"Your freedom?" He almost chortled. "My dear Mr Smyth, whatever freedoms are afforded the subjects of Her Imperial Majesty, may God save her, are no longer within your grasp. You are a convicted murderer and traitor. Your freedom was left behind in the courtroom. You are sentenced to death, and that sentence will be carried out have no fear that. So no, I am not here to offer you your freedom. I can assure you of this much, you will die at Her Majesty's pleasure… so you have been sentenced, so it shall be."

To be fair, his reply came as little surprise. All the same, hope suddenly leaving the building was disappointing, and I found the anger I'd been suppressing up to that point running in to fill the void left in hope's wake.

"Then I am not sure why you're wasting what little time I have left with this conversation, Mr M. I find you're not to be the most entertaining of fellows, and I have better ways to spend my few remaining hours than listening to you. Such as sleeping, or perhaps a little self-abuse. I might even bang my head against the bars for a while and see if I can knock myself senseless for the hell of it. It would be still more worthwhile than listening to your odious nasal whine."

It was a catty response, I know, and far from wise. But I was annoyed and past caring. I even went as far as to rattle my chains at him, ragging at my own wrists in the process. All of which made me feel a little better about myself for a moment at least. Besides, my bravado prickled him a little, judging by how his moustache bristled at me, and as I said, small victories.

"Oh, I believe you will wish to hear what I have to say, Mr Smyth. You are, it is true, sentenced to die at Her Imperial Majesty's pleasure. I am, however, here to offer you a chance to extend that pleasure for a while. Indeed, a chance to be of some service to your Queen and country one more time. Perhaps you may even gain some little redemption into the bargain, as well as extending your worthless life a while longer."

Now what I wanted to say at this point was something along the lines of 'Her Majesty can go pleasure herself, the decrepit old hag'.

Or perhaps some insightful social commentary along the lines of 'Last time Queen Victoria ever showed a moment's pleasure was before Prince bloody Albert died a hundred and god knows how many years ago'.

Not, so you understand, that I'm some kind of anti-royalist like those idiot anarchists in the East End. I'm as loyal to good Queen Vic as the next man. Well, if the next man is an average Brit anyway. Her long life is a gift for the stability of the Empire, at least, that is what we are always told. So, like any other loyal subject of 'Old Iron Knickers', I'd defend her clockwork heart with every fibre of my being.

Well, just so long as I didn't have to take too many risks with my own.

That said, even a lifelong royalist like myself struggles to care greatly about the pleasure of 'She Who Is Seldom Amused' when they are awaiting the noose. It is something that can make a man a little tetchy. But when you're being offered a lifeline, it's impolite to throw insults back at the man offering it. So what I actually said was…

"What is it you want me to do?"

Feeble of me, I am aware. But when someone is offering a choice between death today or death tomorrow, I'll take tomorrow every time.

Besides, my mind was already working overtime. I was considering all the possibilities that could be present themselves to a man no longer confined to a death cell. London is, after all, a big place with plenty of dark alleys to disappear down. Much the same could be said about the Empire as a whole. No matter what use M might have for me, if I didn't like it, I could always find an opportune moment to make a sharp exit.

I'd more than a few contacts on the darker side of London. People who could be, if not entirely trusted, certainly bought. Not that I had anything to pay them with, but that was a problem easily solved by a man such as myself. A little larceny goes a long way, after all.

So, whatever plans M had for me, I assured myself I would soon have plans of my own.

Go ahead, call me naïve.

"All in good time, Mr Smyth. All in good time. Am I to take it I can be assured of your co-operation in our enterprise?" M asked, leaning on a walking cane I'd not even noticed before. It had a long ebony shaft tipped in silver at both ends, with a handle that was a curious facsimile of the Queen's head. So it looked for a moment as if she was peeking out from between his thin fingers. There was a touch of leer in his tone that should've warned me to tread carefully. But as I said, the lifebelt that is hope to a drowning man, is something always grabbed for.

I straightened up, well, as much as the chains allowed. Feeling, for some reason, it was expected of me to attempt to give off an air of military bearing and I managed some bluster.

"Sir, you have my word as an officer and a gentleman."

He laughed again, that same irritating snivelling sneer of a laugh.

"Mr Smyth, you are no longer the former and were never the latter."

I was about to further bluster a response to that that would've been both witty and cutting, but he bullied on regardless.

"However, be that as it may, even if we of The Ministry were fool enough to take you at your word, we would not be fool enough to do so without assuring ourselves of your acquiescence with some small form of guarantee. I am sure you can see our position here," he said, and if a voice could bare its teeth at you, his did right then.

He tapped his cane on the floor two times, and the doors to the main cell block opened. Two men entered. At least, I say men. As in regards to their general appearance that is what they were. I could not, however, claim to know if they were men in any true sense. They wore heavy coats buttoned to the neck with huge brass buttons. Coats which were either heavy on the padding, or the men beneath them had the build of the average gorilla.

Their faces were hidden behind heavy gas masks with trailing pipes that went to brass boxes strapped or, for all I knew, bolted to their chests. Dark eyepieces, that somehow failed to reflect any light, made it impossible to discern the eyes of whoever wore the masks. Their heads were crowned with short top hats, as black as the rest of their sinister garb. Each had mounted on their left arms a heavy brass and glass instrument that resembled an oversized syringe, the needle of which extended out like a stiletto dagger beyond their gloved hands. On the sleeves and lapels of their heavy coats they wore an insignia. A pair of crossed syringes below a crown. A symbol that was seldom published but everyone in the Empire would recognise all the same. Not that I even needed the symbol to know what the hulking figures before me were.

Sleep Men.

A child's nightmare made flesh, enforcers of Imperial will. You can run from the police, you can dodge the courts, you can avoid the army, and you could even avoid Her Majesty's tax men. But if the Sleep Men came for you... At least, so it is said.

A tingling shiver of pure unadulterated dread ran through me and as I watched them draw near, a strange misty cloud seemed to be flowing out around them. It came rolling from beneath their coats and rising slowly as they walked towards where M stood in the doorway of my cell.

As the vapours began to reach me, vomit formed in my throat. There was a strange smell of almonds in the air, and as I looked, I realised M was now holding a small breathing mask over his mouth. Passively watching me, utterly unperturbed as I started to struggle for breath. An edge of panic struck me.

As they approached, I backed up towards the rear of the cell, as far as my chains would allow. As they passed through the open door, I found I was trying to get down into the corner and huddled tightly in a ball, fear washing over me as the sickly sweet smell of almond got stronger, the clouds of mist billowing around me.

I was aware of someone screaming. It took a moment to realise it was me.

I was fully gripped with utter panic. A fear that seemed to gnaw at the very core of me. I've many faults, but abject cowardice is not normally one of them. I've faced fear more than once and stood tall before it. I've even faced it bravely when called to do so. So when I say that this fear paralysed me, you must understand that it was not a normal reaction. It was far from normal.

By the time they reached out for me, those cold black eyepieces had come to resemble nothing so much as the eyes of giant insects. The trailing pipes of their masks were mandibles and the figures as a whole, some form of evil demonic creatures intent on devouring me.

I have the vaguest of recollections of pain as a needle pierced my arm.

Then nothing more but darkness.

An all-encompassing engulfing darkness into which I was falling.

CHAPTER 3

A Spider In the Eye

I was falling or rather was I watching Hardacre fall.

I was in both places at once.

The observed and observer.

The bomb bay doors opened out before me, as I watched him fall.

As I fell myself.

Gravity pulling me down towards oblivion.

Or was I floating, still and unmoving, as the airship rose up away from me?

I was falling through the clouds, it felt almost peaceful, tranquil. I wanted to stay there forever. In that endless plunge through the whiteness.

It was dreamlike, a dream that had become so often a nightmare of late. A dream I knew was a dream and yet, a welcome retreat from the hard realities of the world. An escape from the squalor of my cell, an

escape from the impending doom before me. An escape from the world
and all its horror, manifest in the hangman's noose that awaited me.

Better to fall through the clouds, to feel this weightless nothingness
that was true freedom…

Of course, that could not last. In reality, or this dream of reality, I
was still plunging to my doom, but even knowing that, it was a peace,
a freedom, a moment of blissful joy. Falling through the clouds and
watching myself as I fell…

I was suddenly, shockingly, cold and wet.

Very wet.

The brightest of lights erupted before me. Burning into my eyes, making it hard to focus. Pain erupted on my left side just below the rib cage. Even in my dazed state I recognised that kind of pain but the sting from salty water running down my face stopped me from focusing on it. My vision swam and the lights seemed brighter still. From beyond those lights, hidden behind impenetrable darkness, a voice spoke out, a voice harsh with authority, and it said…

"Again."

I'd gained enough of my faculties at this point to focus a little and saw the bucket enter the pool of light. Propelled forward by thick arms in long black coat sleeves. Time enough to see the torrent of water hurtle towards me. On reflex alone, I tried to avoid it. Attempting to duck my head and move to the side.

It was, therefore, at this juncture the realisation came to me that I couldn't. For I was heavily restrained in a chair of some description, and very tightly restrained at that. I could no more avoid an icy cold wall of water that hit me, than I could avoid the second punch to my side that followed it and the kind of pain that held the suggestion of something rupturing inside me.

I should perhaps admit, I'm not one unused to the concept of restraints. Although generally in more salubrious and recreational settings than these. To wit a small but discreet gentleman's establishment in Soho. Had I the time or inclination at that particular moment I may have even reflected on just how very professionally I'd been restrained. Indeed, as something of a connoisseur of such arrangements I would probably have been impressed.

Instead, I had a panic attack and not a mild one. There is a difference between recreational restraint and the ones I found myself in. You see, I suspected a safe word, even if I'd known one, was not going to facilitate my release.

In any event, I couldn't, as it turned out, duck the water. Not even slightly. Not only were my legs and arms very firmly strapped to the chair, but my torso and throat were too. Even my forehead was strapped back against a hard wooden board of some kind, making it impossible to even turn my head from the torrent.

To say then that I was restrained, was in truth, putting it mildly. That I was trussed up like a Soho harlot at the Rear Admiral's Ball would be a better description.

The water hit me hard in the face in the way that only water can be hard. It was also as I mentioned cold and salty. No more than a few degrees above freezing. The rushing shock of it burned away that last vestige of my grogginess, I was suddenly and fully, awake.

That shock gave way to a relentless cold drip of moisture as the water ran down my bare chest. I tried to look down but thanks to the restraints I could only see my knees. I was, at least, relieved to find I was still wearing trousers. Though it was a relief so small as to barely register beyond the shock and naked terror I felt at that precise moment.

I became vaguely aware of a warm patch in the soaking wetness of my trousers, and shame hit me. A shame I last felt as a schoolboy in my first term at Rudgley. Waking to a wet bed and abusive laughter from my dorm mates. It felt no less shameful to me at that moment sat in that pool of light. Fear returns us to the small child in all of us.

"Good morning again, Mr Smyth. Glad you're back with us. I was afraid you were going to sleep through the whole day, and that would not do at all. I am interminably busy with affairs of state after all. The crown is always moving, Mr Smyth. Always moving, if only to stand still."

I recognised the voice as that belonged to the insidious M. But then who else but that horrible little rodent of a man?

I couldn't see him, however. He must have stood ahead of me, beyond the light.

I tried to venture a reply; perhaps I even tried to put out some brave defiance to make myself feel better if nothing else. But the straps holding my head still were also clamping my jaw tight shut. Making it impossible for me to express my joy at making his acquaintance again. Or more likely comparing him to a rutting man of ill determined parentage.

Another wave of panic hit me. I thrashed at the restraints, achieving nothing but aching muscles fighting against the hold upon them. I still felt nauseous, and a little on the groggy side. Whatever the Sleep Men had pumped into my arm was still in my system. My coherence would've been minimal at best even if I could talk. But whatever mumbled noise I made, the architect of my restraint took it upon himself to interpret my replies.

"Yes, yes, I am sure you are quite angry to find yourself tied up by the business of the crown, and I am sure you wish to complain loudly about it, at great length. Unfortunately for you I do not have the time to spare, so I am afraid I must deny myself the pleasure of your insights," he said with a dismissive tone. Then laughed to himself. Had I been more with it, I'd perhaps have appreciated whatever subtle joke amused him. Though I suspect it was less humour and more the special kind of vindictive sadism that the public school system beats into its pupils.

"Mmmehuh."

"Yes my dear fellow, quite right, indeed we should get on. Time waits for no one, and the sun may never set upon the Empire, but it moves past the yardarm. I would offer you a gin and tonic but we must restrain ourselves while business is at hand, must we not?" he said, laughing that nasty snivel of a laugh once more.

"MMmehhshhh," I replied with feeling. The more coherent my thoughts became, the angrier I was. I raged against my own jaw, until it was aching from the pointless effort to speak, which says something of my state of mind.

I saw M's hand appear in the pool of light just long enough to wave someone from the side. More panic ensued as I noticed a figure in my peripheral vision. One of the Sleep Men, I was sure, moving with slow malevolence to my left. I wished I could turn my head to see what the figure was doing. Then I considered that it might be a blessing I couldn't. There is some benefit at times to not knowing.

No one quite knows who, or for that matter what, the Sleep Men are. Well, no one I've ever spoken to anyway, but everyone knows a dozen or more rumours, each one worse than the last. I guessed M could have told me, had he been willing, or I in a position to ask. But I was far from sure I wanted to know. The rumours always claimed they belonged to some ministry or other, and worked only on ministry business. No one ever said which ministry. I guess now I knew the answer to that particular riddle. What was I just saying about the benefits of not knowing…

The revelation that this mysterious ministry spoken of in hushed tones, that employed Sleep Men to further its aims, was the one M hailed from did nothing to settle my disquiet. A shadowy ministry, they said, one that didn't have official documents published in the press or report to the house. A ministry that did things that the others could not and reported only to the palace. The kind of rumours spoken of in the back rooms of the pub by men with skittish eyes and one too many pints in their bellies.

Personally, until now I'd always put it down as so much hogwash. Like most conspiracy theories. As close to the truth of things as that crazy story about Old Queen Vic visiting a hush-hush pool in darkest Africa every few years and coming back younger than she left. Or that the French had a surreptitious craft that sailed under water and committed acts of piracy with impunity. Or any of the other crazy stories that people told with one too many in them.

If I'd time to reflect, I'd have probably been hoping right then that most of the rumours I'd heard about The Ministry were overblown codswallop. Later, much later, I came to think of them as the tip of a very dark iceberg. But I get ahead of myself again, so I'll say no more on the subject for now.

In short, then, I'd found myself restrained, and was still in somewhat of a panic about it when M finally stepped forward into the pool of light. His face was emotionless and cold, even with the vague smile on his lips. He peered at me, as one might peer at an insect pinned to a display in the Natural History Museum, if you are inclined to entomology. I was quite certain at the time that this was exactly how he perceived me to be.

"Now Mr Smyth, I am going to present you with an opportunity, one which if we are honest with each other you do not deserve at all. But the empire has found itself to have a need for you, and you are a man of some talent, even if those talents are mostly for fraudulent activities and criminal acts. You do, it seems, have an uncanny ability to lie with a certain convincing quality to everyone, including yourself.

The Empire always has a use or two for good liars and thieves even if we do not choose to admit such publicly. Luckily we seldom find ourselves to have a shortage of them."

"Mmmemmhh," I replied with bitter anger.

"Come now, a man should admit his talents, even when they lean to the petty and larcenous."

"Mehhh."

"Quite, Mr Smyth, quite. Nevertheless you also have at least one quality which is unique in your case. One which is of certain use to the crown in a delicate endeavour. So I have found myself empowered to offer you an opportunity to avoid the noose and redeem yourself."

He leant closer to me. Close enough that I could smell the small man's cologne, a hint of cigar and a good single malt. I wanted to turn away. I didn't understand what M was getting at. Don't mistake me, I've a gift for manipulation, of people, of situations, of truths. But that hardly made me unique. In my experience, everyone lies a little about who they are. Both to others and to themselves. I'd no idea what unique quality I possessed which could make me of use to this man. Who for all his protestations showed little inclination to get to the point.

M pulled back from my field of vision for a few moments, before returning, holding an intricate little wooden box. Cedar or some other hardwood inlaid with brass etching. It reminded me of nothing other than an overlarge snuff box. Something I'd never evolved a taste for myself, even when they started adding cocaine to the mix. Mainly in truth, this was because it remains a preserve of the rich due to the prices of the best mixes. I have never quite been in a position to afford my own supply. Give me a pipe of good tobacco or a cigar any day.

Besides which, it always seems a waste of good cocaine to mix it with the rest of the stuff they put in snuff.

Despite my aversion to the snuffing up of copious amounts of the noxious powder that was such a fad these days, I could recognise quality workmanship in such boxes. A by-product of having a certain avarice for small portable things that are easy to pass off to less honest pawnbrokers. M's snuff box, for example, would have caught my eye if left on a saloon bar table unattended. It was of particularly fine quality. Though at that moment I was more concerned with the brass etching on the top of the box than thoughts of avarice. It bore the same crossed syringe crest as that which was emblazoned on the Sleep Men's sleeves.

"Now Mr Smyth, personally I feel we should be able to trust you. You are I am sure a loyal subject of her Britannic Majesty after all."

"Meheehhhh," I replied, which in truth was an attempt to affirm. Mainly because I felt it was required of me and that now wasn't the time to remonstrate. There was something particularly threatening about that otherwise unassuming little box and what it might hold within it.

Maybe it was residual effects of whatever they had gassed me with, maybe not, but that box seemed the most terrifying thing in the room. Given the circumstances I found myself in, that says rather a lot.

"Yes… Yes… Of course. You're as loyal as the next Englishman, I am sure. But as I am sure you are aware, these are dark days, Mr Smyth, dark days indeed. Dark days for Britain, for the Empire, why for the Queen herself. Don't you agree…?"

"Mehhhehhh."

"Yes, of course you do, and I am sure as a loyal subject of the Queen you can no doubt understand the need for a little caution on my part, a little insurance as it were. We, by which I mean Her Imperial Majesty's government, are about to send you on a delicate and important mission. In such circumstances, it would be remiss of us not to hold to some guarantee of your loyalty. Beyond that is, your 'honest' word. Dark days Mr Smyth. Dark days, when an Englishman's word is not enough, I know. All the same, one is obligated to live in the modern age. Victoria's reign is as strong as it ever was but the word of Englishmen has proved somewhat weaker of late than we would care to admit. It is in the here and now of it that we must dwell, not the forgone days when a man's word was all that was ever required. I am sure you understand."

"Mehhhhhh," I replied, with an edge of panic once more, though it was panic on top of panic it should be said. Also a measure of exasperation. M, however, seemed to warm to a captive audience, and I was very much that.

"Allow me then to introduce you to a little friend of the crown, a wonderful little device designed by a Mr Gates to whom we had the great pleasure to offer asylum. An American, you understand, a tad eccentric and colonial for my tastes, but a dashed clever chap all the same. Unlucky for him, he was born in the former United States. But one man's excrement is another man's manure, and he is working wonders for us, a real boffin you might say, as long as we keep him away from the windows. He has proved himself to be a boon to the Empire with his clever little devices. Like this one…"

As he spoke, M pushed open the lid of the box and held it up for me to see. Inside there seemed to be nothing but a tiny spider. I almost wanted to laugh.

'Was this it?' I wondered. Some elaborate overdone version of an age-old schoolboy prank. A spider in a box. Did they think I was an acrophobe or something? It struck me as so ridiculous, for a moment, just the slightest of moments, I felt the grip of panic releasing me.

For a fleeting few seconds I even thought that the spider was dead. Just a curled up dead spider in a box. I could've laughed. If I wasn't tied to a chair and gagged, that is…

That was until it started to move slowly around in its little cell. It was only then, when the light struck it, I realised it wasn't truly a spider at all, but a thing made of some strange metal. With that realisation, relief was replaced once more with fear.

I wasn't unused to the oddities of technology. I was an airship man, after all. But this oddity seemed wrong in some way, uncanny even. A child's toy made into a fearful apparition, as its tiny mechanical legs snapped around. It could move with frightening swiftness.

"This is what Mr Gates calls an Arachno-Oculus. Dash clever name, wouldn't you say? From the Latin. Arachno for spider and Oculus for the eye. It really is a very clever bit of machinery as well. It is powered by body heat, though dashed if I know how, leave that kind of thing to the boffins. But clever, is it not? Indeed, it's the vicinity of our bodies which has woken our little friend up just now."

"Mmmehhhh."

"What's that? You wish to see it up close? Why of course, dear chap. Here let me bring it up to your eye so you can see it clearly," the vile M said.

The last thing I wanted was to see it close up, but M raised the box all the same. I became more aware of M's pet Sleep Men to either side of me as their hands clamped down on my shoulders. Holding me firmly down, as if the restraints that rendered me immobile weren't enough. I can attest from my struggles that they were.

The closer the spider came, the more I wanted desperately to escape. The more in turn the Sleep Men tightened their grip, as if they could sense the building fear in me.

The box was raised until it filled my field of vision, and I watched, unable to do anything else, as the first of the spider's legs came over the brim. The body, tiny though it was, followed.

For a moment it seemed to sit on the lip of the box, staring at me with tiny multifaceted eyes. The repulsion I felt was palatable. Panic consumed me. It remained there, staring, its foremost legs moving like feelers as it rocked back and forth slightly.

Then suddenly it leapt forward. Straight towards my left eye.

The world turned white. A blinding painful white that was accompanied with a pain the like of which I'd never experienced before and never wished to again. It seemed to consume my world, till everything within it was pain. Pain which seemed to last an eternity.

Slowly, so very slowly, the pain faded until I was aware only of an itching scratching sensation on the surface of my eye which made me desperate to rub at it. Colours looked wrong somehow out of my left. A little darker, yet sharper at the same time. The focus was all wrong. It was like being drunk in just one eye. Everything was slightly clouded for a moment, then it would become clear, then clouded again. As if a lens I was looking through was moving independently of my eyeball.

Which of course is exactly what was happening.

I felt a surge of vomit in my throat and thrashed against the restraints. Desperate, not so much to escape, but to get the spider thing out of my eye. I lost all control of myself but had no time for schoolboy shame now. Instead, I was consumed with a revulsion that was overwhelming me.

"Time to sleep again, Mr Smyth," the voice of M said, barely penetrating the pain. Then I felt needles jabbing into my exposed forearms, and the world spun and plunged into darkness once more.

CHAPTER 4

Vibrations In The Air

I woke to the comforting sensations of an air-ship in flight. Airmen like myself are much like sailors on water-bound ships; we are adjusted to the pitch, yaw and updraft of our craft. They have sea legs, we have air legs, for want of a better phrase. Modern airship compensators make for smoother flying, but we can still feel the craft moving in the air through the deck plates. Likewise, we can feel the vibrations of the engines and hear the subtle subsonic pitch of the propellers. Once you've spent enough time aboard airships, you get a feel for all this. It seeps into your blood like salt in the veins of a sailor, so much so that you barely register any of it. Yet in its absence, you feel uncomfortable for a while when you first return to solid ground.

So when I woke to feel all those little signs, I was granted a few moments of comfort, of feeling everything was right in the world, that I was safe, that I was where I should be.

First Ensign Hannibal Smyth of Her Majesty's Royal Air Navy. A trusted and loyal gunnery officer with one eye on promotion and the other on a profitable sideline in the black market munitions trade. An officer and a gentleman who, for all the world knew, was beyond reproach. True, there was the occasional bit of fencing of stolen goods to the Empire's more remote outposts for some of the most nefarious criminals in old London town. But as long as that greedy bastard Hardacre kept up his side of the bargain while I cheerfully turned a blind eye for half the profits, where was the harm in that...?

Yes, life was good, for that fleeting moment of ignorance when I woke...

Then of course, as it always does, reality flooded back. Hardacre was dead by my hands after the debacle at the Heathrow masts. I'd been tried, convicted, stripped of rank and honour, and condemned to die by the noose. Then I remembered one more thing... a cadaverous civil servant from a shadowy ministry who had placed a mechanical spider in my eye...

An eye which suddenly itched like an air-man's crotch after a night's ground-leave in Amsterdam.

A wave of vertigo hit me, which had nothing to do with heights. A trembling started in my hands that spread to my arms, and I lay my head back down on the hard pillow, closing my eyes, waiting for it to fade. I tried to focus on my breathing and nothing else, fighting back the urge to panic, until I felt myself starting to calm a little and the shaking stopped. My eye still itched like hell, but at least I was fighting the urge to scratch it.

"Okay, Hannibal old boy, let's just take stock for a moment shall we?" I whispered to myself. Then became aware I was talking aloud. 'Get a grip on yourself, Harry,' I thought, angry with myself as no one else was about to be angry at. It's an old habit that, I may be Hannibal to the outside world, but to myself, I was still just plain Harry, the orphan. The lost little boy, seeking his way in a big bad world and terrified of it.

We can change what the world sees in us, but it's a whole lot harder to change what you see in yourself.

'Get a grip on yourself, Harry,' I thought to myself once more, taking a breath, trying to take stock of where I was. 'Okay, you're on an airship in flight, and the last thing you remember is being strapped to a chair and having this thing put in your eye, so they must have put you on the airship. Okay, that's a good start, nice and logical, you're on an airship, and you were put here by The Ministry. Makes sense, doesn't it? And because airships go to places, they must be sending you somewhere, and you have a spider in your eye. No need to panic now, is there…? Airships are fine, we are good with airships. So let's see what else? Okay, you have just been out for a few hours or so if they got you to an airfield. Well okay, probably more than a few hours or so. But no more than a day anyway. So you're on an airship, been sent somewhere for the government. Fine, nothing to worry about here, everything is just fine, and there's a spider in your eye.'

I was starting to relax a little by now. Calm, even. Letting the gentle buffeting of the airframe seep through me. That all so familiar gentle sway as the air sack moved in the wind. The occasional slight, almost indiscernible change in pitch and yaw caused by turbulence, soothing in its familiarity. I let myself listen to the distant familiar whispered groan of the engines. Keeping calm, telling myself, 'I'm aboard an airship, nothing could be more reassuring to an airman like me.' And this worked for a little while, I was starting to feel calm, relaxed…

'There's a spider in your eye.'

I sat up sharply as the pain of a dozen tiny needles seemed to clamp around my eyeball all at once. Whether that was my imagination or the thing in my eye letting its presence be known, I wasn't sure. Though why anything thought I could forget M's tiny mechanical monstrosity is anyone's guess. My first instincts were to panic, which I promptly went with.

I clamped a hand over my eye in a misbegotten attempt to stem the pain. If anything, the sensation of pressure increased. Indeed, my eye felt like it was going to pop at any second.

I fell from the small cabin bed onto the hard metal of the floor plates, the jolt of pain from the impact seeming to ease the pain in my eye, or just mask it for a moment, the respite allowing me to get my bearings a little. Small victories and such.

Stumbling to my feet, I lurched across the tiny room, making for the small sink that lay against the far wall. One hand clamped over my eye, I fumbled with the other at the tap until I got the water flowing. Then I tried with panic-driven urgency to wash out my eye. Fear gripping me, the pain feeding my paranoia.

The thought hit me that the implanted spider might be malfunctioning or worse perhaps the mysterious M had decided that I wasn't going to be useful to him after all and had turned his insidious mechanical arachnid against me.

I fought for calm as I feverishly washed at my eye with the water that was slowly starting to steam as it ran too hot. Breathing heavy, laboured breaths, I fought the urge to gouge into my eye to remove the spider, while the water only made my eye sting all the more.

Then there was a pulse of bright burning light from inside my left eye that was over in an instant. It left in its wake an after-image seared on my retina. The kind of reddish blur you get when you stare too long at an electric light or up at the sun. The pain of the light caused me to close my eye, which just made the after image more visible. I realised to my horror it wasn't random at all. It was fuzzy and indistinct, but it was readable all the same. A clear, definite letter B.

I just had time to recover my wits before my eye exploded with light twice more, a few seconds in between each burst. O... O.

Then suddenly the pain was gone, as though the spider had released its grip. Almost as if someone had thrown off a switch. Later, looking back, I came to the conclusion that this was exactly what had happened. Somewhere M or one of his agents wanted to get my attention. To drive home a message perhaps that I was now their toy, their plaything. The pain and the light had been a reminder. Just in case I thought for even a fleeting moment that I was free of them.

As for the 'BOO', well it was clear to me whoever was controlling my little friend was the kind of person who thinks that jumping out on unsuspecting people while dressed in a sheet is the high point of sophisticated humour...

I remained there, holding the sink for support and stared into the greasy mirror. I let my breathing slow, with forced deep controlled breaths until I once more felt calm enough and relaxed enough to let go of the cold porcelain of the sink.

Once I was back in control of myself, I ran wet fingers through my hair in a forlorn effort to straighten it out. All the while I was staring at the mirror, my point of focus my own left eye. The iris was wrong, fully black with no hint of blue. A dark window into my soul, which something else was choosing to call home. It still hurt, with the ghosting after-pain of the light, but it was at least starting to ease off a little.

Then, while I stared, I swore I saw movement across the iris. A shadow's passing. I shuddered. The alien presence in my own eye disturbed me more than I could tell. I fought the urge to panic once more. Forcing myself to remain calm, I found myself wondering what the spider really was.

Could they see what I saw through its gemstone eyes? Was that how they sought to control me, their insurance as M called it? That and the burning light it produced. For all I knew it could even have a small explosive charge. It wouldn't need be much, enough to punch a hole in my skull. It was perfectly placed to do that, after all. To be honest, it didn't matter if it did or not. It wasn't like I'd be prepared to take the risk.

It was all too strange. The whole concept would've seemed fanciful to me. Something manmade, so small it could fit in your eye, see what you saw. Communicate with you after a fashion. Inflict pain, even kill you. Insane, ridiculous, unthinkable, leastways were I not the one with the spider in my eye. But I was the one with the spider. So instead of being simply fanciful, it was instead terrifying.

The memory of the painful light that had so recently abated was still fresh with me. I'd no doubt they could turn it back on whenever they wished. Even if by some miracle I found some way to remove the spider, how could I do so without them knowing? And if they were capable of such devices in the first place, would it even matter if I did?

That thought sank in. I realised now I was nothing more than The Ministry's puppet, or perhaps more correctly The Ministry's slave. For a passing moment, the noose seemed like it might have been the better after all…

'But,' I reasoned, 'the thing about being alive is, well, it's always preferable to the alternative.'

I closed my eyes and let myself relax some more. Dwelling on the spider was getting me nowhere. I needed to switch focus. I needed to do something to take my mind off the damn thing, anything in all honesty.

Taking a heavy breath, I took a moment to examine the tiny cabin that I'd found myself in properly, and get some bearings on where I was. I didn't recognise the layout. For a start, it was too luxurious. Not that it was a five-star cabin on a transcontinental liner, but it was far removed from the low-rank officer quarters I used to share in the navy. Instead of double bunks with heavy course military grade blankets to be shared in rotation by watch officers, there was a single reasonable size bed with white, if slightly faded, linen, trimmed with parallel blue lines. The small porthole over the bed had the same blue-trimmed linen curtains. The walls were painted in an off cream that may have once been bright white a few years earlier. It was an improvement on the standard navy grey paint I was used to coating every flat surface. The whole cabin had an aged quality to it. Right down to the discoloured taps on the sink, which had once, no doubt, gleamed in chrome. It was neat and well maintained all the same. Some old ship, a passenger liner of some kind, I suspected. Not that this nugget of information brought me any closer to knowing where I was, beyond aboard a moving airship in the sky somewhere.

In the hopes of gaining some answers, I opened the small closet and found a uniform hanging within. Not one of the dark blues of Her Royal unamused Royal Air Navy. Instead, it was a somewhat faded red with gold braid trim. Colours I recognised, and groaned inwardly, as those of the East India Company. To be more exact the colours of EICAN, as the badge on the arm proclaimed.

The implication of the uniform was obvious to me. I was clearly en route to India and for god only knows what reason The Ministry wanted me ensconced within the EIC's air naval arm. You can imagine just how well that sat with a RAN man like myself.

For all my faults and despite my recent disgrace, I considered myself still to be a member of the finest service in the Empire. Which I was technically, even if that technicality was that they never bothered to actually dismiss me.

The Royal Air Navy has a tradition going back over a hundred years. While the Army has won its honours on the field, and the senior service its honours at sea, it's the RAN that really maintained the power of the Empire. Which was a matter of some pride amongst my brother airmen. To become an officer in the RAN is a goal for many a young man, and perhaps we who are, tend towards arrogance. Certainly, it leads to the odd scuffle in bars with officers of the other services, the occasional friendly argument or two. But at least our rivalry with the other services is a rivalry among near equals. Whereas officers in the East India Company, on the other hand… well everyone knew that was where you went if you couldn't afford a commission in the real services. The Company was a place for adventurers, ne'er do wells, and washed up failures, not true officers and gentlemen. Every service agreed on that point.

It may seem petty all things considered, but even in disgrace, I counted myself better than EICAN. Even if, as I tried to remind myself, playing the part of a Company officer was a step up from being a corpse dancing the Tyburn jig.

'You're still alive, Harry, remember that…' I consoled myself.

This period of reflection upon my lot passed and I determined I should go and explore the ship The Ministry had seen fit to plant me on. And if I was going to explore the ship, it made sense to get dressed properly first.

'And while you're at it, Harry old boy, may as well make some effort at looking a tad more respectable…' I thought. 'Even if it means wearing a bloody East India Company uniform. It beats stalking the corridors in nothing but long johns.' Which, I considered, may raise a few too many eyebrows.

The possibility that I may have been installed as an officer on that very ship struck me. But I dismissed it. No captain worth his salt would take a new crewman aboard without them being vetted by him first. Particularly in the case of an officer. It may not always be their choice, politics of the fleet and all that, but to have an officer foisted upon you by the Admiralty was considered a slight in the service and the same was no doubt true of any civilian liner. To have said officer not report to you on his arrival would be considered just plain insolence. So it seemed far more likely I was merely a passenger for once, which was a slightly odd idea for an air-man such as myself. I still wanted to know more about the craft I was flying aboard.

Resolved to find out exactly what ship I was on and where it was taking me, I started to dress. I was at least pleasantly surprised that the uniform was cut to the right size, though it has to be said it was a little loose around the britches and stomach. I suspected though that was down to the weight I'd lost while incarcerated. It was, however, neither of the quality nor the cut I was used to. As every other officer in Her Royal Shortness's armed forces does, I bought my uniforms on Savile Row. Appearances are important after all. It doesn't do to merely be an officer. One has to look like one. But it struck me that standards in the Company were doubtless more lax in this regard.

Probably because when you're a second class navy, you got used to making do with second class everything. I found it vexing all the same. Did I mention vanity was one of my flaws?

That said, once dressed, I examined myself in the mirror, and I cut a reasonable dash, I must say. True, I looked somewhat haggard and drawn thanks to my recent existence on prison rations. I was also in need of a shave, my hair was a tragedy, and I'd have cheerfully killed for some moustache wax. All things considered though, I could have looked a lot worse.

A short search of the closet revealed a gentleman's vanity kit, much to my delight. Devoid of moustache wax, unfortunately, but with everything else I required to make myself presentable. Resolved by this, I divested myself of my jacket once more, rolled up my sleeves and filled the sink. I then set about lathering my face for the first decent shave in weeks. Admittedly I'd have rather have visited a decent Turkish barber, but small victories and all that.

I'd just happily raised the cutthroat to the place it was named for, when I heard the key turning in the door and the creak of the handle.

I spun round alarmed, razor in hand, thick foam dripping from my chin, which speaks perhaps of the nervousness that resided at my core right then. I was, however, ready to defend myself as best I could, all the indignity of the last few days boiling up inside of me at once and if someone was going to assail me, then this once I was ready for them.

The door swung open, and there followed an ear-splitting scream. Surprisingly it was not my own.

"I'm so sorry, sir," said a mousey-haired cabin maid, furtively collecting both her wits and the clean set of towels she'd dropped to the floor on entering my cabin. She seemed somewhat shaken, but in fairness finding herself facing a snarling man, covered in shaving foam, holding a razor aggressively, probably came as a shock, and she looked a timid sort.

Luckily her reaction and the time it took to recover the towels covered my own embarrassment long enough for me to collect my shredded wits. 'Steady yer'self Harry...' I remember chiding myself. 'Thrown out of sorts, by a chambermaid of all people, that's a story not to tell...'

Yes I am aware of the irony, but I am being honest here, and it speaks of my state of mind at the time.

"It's perfectly fine," I told her snappily. I was a little irritated, though mostly with myself. I'd all but roared at the girl as she entered. I was living on my nerves, but that was a poor excuse. Regardless, I was being short-tempered, and she bore the brunt of it. I should've been slightly ashamed of myself, though in light of later events, not so much.

"I was told all the passengers were dining at noon, sir, or I'd have knocked," she explained. Her accent held a hint of the East End, which she was trying to disguise as best she could. No doubt to seem a better class of scullion, I would posit. Most people, in fairness to her, wouldn't have noticed, but I'd the benefit of having hidden my own Southward accent for years. I could recognise the odd dropped vowel for what they were hiding.

"I'm afraid I slept late. Just drop the towels on the bed, lass. I shall sort them out after I've shaved," I replied in a half-hearted effort to mollify her. She looked caught between trying to smile and trying not to look flustered. Failing on both counts, she dropped the towels again while trying to get them to the bed.

'Must be new,' I mused, due to her apparent ineptitude at so simple a task.

Partly out of a desire not to embarrass the poor girl further, and conscious of the shaving foam dripping from my chin, I turned back to the sink and commenced shaving my cheek, doing my best to see clearly in the steamy mirror.

I blame that steamy mirror for what happened next. If the room had had a bit more ventilation, she wouldn't have got the drop on me.

As it was, I almost sliced my cheek open with the razor when I felt the snub of her pistol in the small of my back.

CHAPTER 5

The Washbowl Interrogation

"Don't turn around, Mr Smyth," she said, the cold steel of her pistol nestling in my lower back.

That pistol was enough of a reason not to move. I'd no delusions about that. She didn't have to be a great shot, or even vaguely competent, to kill me from that range. Indeed, I rather hoped she was an expert as that lessened the chance of the gun going off by mistake. On the whole, I'd far rather I be killed on purpose than by mistake any day. It's true enough that dead is dead, when all is said and done, but at least if she meant to kill me, I'd be dead for a good reason. Though not being shot at all was still my preferred option.

"I wouldn't dream of it," I replied, trying to sound unshaken by this turn of events. There may have been a quiver to my voice as I spoke, but stiff upper lip be damned. Frankly, I was rather sick of finding myself at the wrong end of one situation or another. It was starting to grate on my nerves a little.

"Continue with your shave, by all means. I am sure a man of your reputation for villainous endeavour is used to keeping a cool head under pressure," she goaded.

I can't say I agreed with her assessment. My hand felt anything but steady as I scraped the edge of the blade down my cheek. Though shaving gave me something to focus on that was not the gun in my back.

I bit back the desire to make a wit-laden reply, having no real yearning to antagonise the woman, whoever she was. Call it a symptom of my long incarceration, waking up not knowing where I was, and having a mechanical spider in my eye, but I was feeling cautious.

"That's it, smooth steady strokes... Now, so we understand each other, Mr Smyth, you're not to turn around. I'm sure that the 'Ministry' will have fitted you with one of Mr Gates' little toys. Do keep your eyes on your reflection. I have no doubt you're rather proud of it, you seem the type..." she said.

I narrowly avoided nicking myself when she mentioned the 'little toy'. Yet I found myself less than surprised she knew of it. She knew my name, after all. That should have been surprise enough.

There was something else, I realised as I cleaned lather off the razor, her accent had changed dramatically. No longer did she seem to be hiding East End vowels. Instead, it had been replaced with an American drawl, though I couldn't distinguish which part of America. Not that it made a great deal of difference which petty dictatorship she was working for. None of them had much reason to be fond of the British; we'd done nothing to help prevent the fall of the union after all. Indeed there were rumours the opposite was true, but well, there are always rumours I guess...

"What do you want of me... Miss?" I asked, leaving the question hanging in the air. Though I was less than hopeful she would be forthcoming with either her name or the name of whomever she was working for. But having no idea who she represented wasn't helping my paranoia at all. I didn't like the idea of having enemies I was unaware of, though I was starting to think that might be a longer list than I suspected.

"Of you, nothing. What I want to know the details of your mission, Mr Smyth. What is The Ministry sending you to India for? Why are they so interested in Wells?"

I wasn't sure what to say. Indeed, she seemed to know more than I did about what The Ministry was up to, although, given I knew nothing, that wasn't much of a challenge. Unfortunately, I suspected she would be unhappy if I told her so. Given that she held the gun, I wasn't sure I wished to disillusion her. As such, I was caught between a rock and a hard 'gun barrel' placed in my back. I chose to stall, not that I could think of many other options.

"I don't know what you're talking about, Miss..."

Judging by the way she pressed the barrel harder into my back I'm all but positive she didn't believe me.

"I suggest you would do well not to disappoint me, Mr Smyth. I know who you are and who you are working for, and I have my own orders. So let's not play foolish games. Where is Wells and what do the British want with him?" she asked, an urgency to her tone which suggested she didn't want to hang around. She made no bones about prodding me hard in the back with the gun to punctuate her question, just to reaffirm the seriousness with which she was taking all this. Not that I'd any doubt about that.

I collected my wits, as best I could, and determined my best bet was to keep stalling. She was unlikely to shoot me, if only because she needed the information I didn't have. I'll admit this was somewhat woolly logic on my part. It was just as possible that getting me out of the way permanently was an option for her. If, that was, her masters wanted to put a spur into the British boot. But I preferred to focus on the former option.

"You seem to have the advantage of me, Madam," I said stressing the 'Madam', which was probably slightly spiteful of me, not to mention a tad foolish with a gun at my back. In my experience, few young ladies like to be called 'Madam'. As such it has a tendency to rile them, which was less than wise in this case, but small victories and all that.

In truth, I was more than a little afraid she might just put an end to me. Bravado is often the first resort of the coward. So I determined to at least appear confident and so I continued to shave carefully, trying my best to keep my voice even and finding an odd comfort in the truth, bitter though it was.

"You seem to know more about my business than I do. They've told me nothing of it. Last I remember I was in a London cell, not bound for India and I've never heard of any Wells. Though I suspect you're not talking about Tunbridge. I can't see them going to all this trouble for that sinkhole."

She laughed, not I should inform you, a delightful laugh. As laughs go, it was about as delightful as the laughter of a bunch of schoolboys when you're the one they're victimising in the showers after rugger. A laugh I would far rather be on the other side of and, while we are being honest, I generally would've been in the past. I vastly prefer to run with the pack than to be the prey.

The punch in the back was hard and caused me to drop the razor in the sink, which was at least preferable to taking a slice out of my throat, where my razor had been poised.

I'm not sure why but I suspected my lame joke about Kent's own little spar town hadn't gone down well with her. But then everyone's a critic at times like these.

If you have never felt a pistol barrel slammed into your lower spine with some venom, then trust me on this, you're better for not knowing how it feels. It left me clutching the porcelain for support.

"You expect me to believe The Ministry sent you away without a briefing?" she snarled at me.

"Frankly no," I replied in utter honesty. "But unfortunately for me, it's the truth. Perhaps if you come back in a day or so, they'll have made contact, and I can tell you whatever you wish to know. Over a nice cup of tea and a scone perhaps."

She laughed again, a somewhat gentler laugh all told, but I can't lay claim to my finding it overly reassuring in the circumstances.

"Really, do you think I'm a fool, Mr Smyth? Am I supposed to believe you would just betray your country in so casual a manner?"

It was my turn to laugh. 'If she only knew,' I thought to myself as I did so, then told her with utter candour, "Right at this moment I'd betray it for a bag of Shillings, and a head start."

I carefully picked the razor back up, partly to resume my shave, but mainly because it felt better to have a weapon in my hand, although I had little hope of turning the tables on this American woman in our current positions. All the same, the feel of the ivory handle was still some small reassurance. While doing so I collected myself a little more, feeling, at last, I was gaining a modicum of ground on the world in general. Then I asked her a question of my own.

"Madam, are you aware of the term pressganged?"

"Of course," she replied, a modicum of curiosity suddenly in her voice.

"Well, I have been most assuredly pressganged into my current service. It's not a situation which inspires one greatly to loyalty. Indeed, if the price were right I would happily sell you all the information you need."

You may be thinking the best of me here. That this was nothing more than an obvious ploy designed to buy me time. That, however, would imply you have been paying less than full attention to me up to this point. I'd have happily sold the American anything I could if it bought me passage out of this mess. For all I cared, frankly the sun could set on the good old British Empire if in doing so it saved my life. It had had a good run after all.

My American friend, I suspect, considered this no more than bravado, although I'm not entirely sure what she thought, beyond being less than enamoured of me. Which she certainly was to judge by her response.

It was a rather sharp response that consisted of me being struck across the back of the head with the butt of her pistol. Oh but Americans do love to do things with their guns.

It all, as it were, went black at that point.

CHAPTER 6

Old *'Friends'* In Unexpected Places

I was, I'm sure you will find it all too easy to believe, rather sick of the lights going out. Over the past few days, as I chose to call the short periods of consciousness I could recall, I'd not had the opportunity to just lay down on a bed and drop off to sleep. Instead, people seemed insistent on putting me to sleep in violent ways. I'd been gassed, drugged and now bludgeoned unconscious with a pistol butt.

It was all becoming rather irritating. As such, I wasn't in the best of moods when I finally regained consciousness.

Matters weren't helped by the fact that I returned to consciousness on cold steel deck plates, with half my face still covered in shaving foam. Foam which had a definite red tinge to it, and had crusted over, like the top of a lemon meringue with raspberry sauce dribbled over it.

I struggled to my feet, looked in the mirror and noticed a shallow cut on my throat where I had caught myself with the razor when I'd been struck. It had scabbed over at least. But while it mightn't have been the most serious in the world, it had certainly bled enough. If it had been deeper, it would have bled a whole lot more and while nothing ruins a clean-shaven chin like a fresh scab, bleeding out ruins it a damn sight more. Yet, somehow despite this near miss, I wasn't in the mood to count my blessings right at that moment.

My cabin, predictably, had been ransacked. My feminine friend obviously hadn't had much faith in my word. The upturned mattress, the clothes flung about the place and the ripped open drawers strewn upon the floor, spoke of the place being tossed in a hurry. Perhaps she'd feared that my sudden lack of consciousness wouldn't last, or perhaps that it wouldn't go unnoticed. She had, you'll recall, made sure I was looking in the mirror throughout our conversation. She had also taken pains to keep her face out of view while I faced it. It occurred to me then that it suggested she knew more of the device in my eye than I did. Which was as near damn all as made no difference, I'll admit. Perhaps she thought eyes other than mine might be watching; it was a chilling thought.

What irritated me the most, other than the banging headache I woke to, was that I'd no idea if she'd found anything. I hadn't searched the place myself before her intrusion. For all I knew she'd actually have found all the information she needed. If that was so, I'd little doubt she would have taken it with her, leaving me devoid of instructions. Which, I was sure, wouldn't go down well with my new masters.

I'll admit I didn't give a flying fruitcake what went down well with my new masters, but I did care about keeping them from blowing my head off my shoulders.

In the circumstances, I was feeling a little put out, which is an understatement as you would know if you had ever taken a pistol butt to the back of the head. As there was however little I could do about it, I ran some hot water and recommenced my ablutions while trying to recall exactly what the American woman had looked like, because chances were I'd bump into her again and I decided I'd rather not be surprised next time.

Oh what bitter vanity that proved to be, but let's not get ahead of ourselves…

Unfortunately, as I'd been taken in by her clumsy maid disguise, I'd not paid her a great deal of attention when she had entered the cabin. At least until she demanded my attention at the end of a gun. So the most I could recall was her mousy hair, which could've been a wig for all I knew and her general stature. It was less than nothing to go on. I realised then she could walk right by me, and I'd never know. Which was a worrying thought.

Once I'd shaved, I dressed and felt at least a tad more presentable. As I tidied around the sink, I had a thought and slipped the cutthroat into my trouser pockets. Considering all that had happened to me of late, I didn't want to be without a weapon of some kind. My uniform had a pistol holster, but it had proven to be sadly but unsurprising empty. I was, I suspected, aboard that old tub as a passenger. Any weapons that came with my uniform would no doubt be locked in the hold. Given I had already been assaulted by a woman with a pistol, did not inspire my sense of safety.

I did, however, find a wallet on the bed among the other detritus little Miss not-a-maid had thrown about. To my surprise, it even had some money in it. Not, it has to be said, a great deal of money. I suspected my good friend M had no desire to supply me with enough funds to make a break for it, little arachnids insurance implanted in my eye or not. But it was something none the less.

Among the notes in the wallet I found a couple of ticket stubs for the master at arms, which at least meant I could recover my weapons when the ship got wherever it was going. Which was something more. Not that it helped me much right at that moment.

I did at least have the cutthroat in my trouser pocket. The reassuring weight of it assuring me I had at least one weapon at my disposal should I need one. Which I had the uncomfortable feeling I might before too long.

As I sorted myself out and dressed once more, I pondered the questions little Miss not-a-a maid had asked me. India and Wells, Harry, what do The Ministry want with Wells? Who or what was Wells? A person seemed the more likely of the two, though she could have been talking about holes in the ground for all I knew. Though it has to be said, I suspected The Ministry wasn't much given to caring about irrigation projects in the Punjab.

I wasn't, as I may have mentioned, full of joy at the prospect of India. Jewel in her nibs' crown the sub-continent may be, but it was also a boiling pot of insurrection. Peaceful protests against British rule had been a thing of the past since they'd sent that beatnik Gandhi packing to South Africa. News from India was always a story of troubles and the Company's attempts to keep a lid on that pot. Bomb one village of insurrectionists and three others sprang up. Violence begetting violence and the locals not learning their lessons. The press always seemed outraged that stamping down hard on insurgents created more insurgents. Clearly this was the fault of troublemakers and religious zealots stirring things up. The only answer was of course was to call for more bombings…

I have long suspected the British press, much like the British government and whoever was the incumbent Viceroy at the time, didn't care a fig about villages in the Indian interior. Not as long as the East India Company kept the profits rolling in. Turning a blind eye to the Company's excesses had for time immemorial been government policy, and the press followed the government's lead as it ever did. Besides which, bombing insurgents was always a popular move with the masses, according to the press at any rate…

Privately I always suspected not bombing a few villages for a while might go a long way towards resolving the problems, but don't quote me on that. Such opinions have never proved popular.

Thinking of the Company reminded me that I was now, it appeared, an officer within its ranks. I found this a depressing thought. As I said before, Company officers didn't sit in the highest of esteem. Merchant adventurers to a man, and a short step up from the pirates and robber barons of another age. I may be a rogue, a liar and a thief, but I like to think I've some standards.

Heaving a heavy sigh, I straightened up my cabin as best as I could be bothered before deciding the misbegotten gas bag I was aboard probably had some real maids on its crew. Ones who wouldn't stick guns in my back, but who'd tidy up the rest of the mess while I was elsewhere with luck. So I decided to go in search of the ship's bar. Frankly, I needed a drink. Answers, I reasoned, could wait a while if a good bottle of gin could be found.

There was a key by the wallet, which fitted neatly in the door so I locked the room behind me. Not that there was anything left in it worth worrying about. So after a final check of my reflection in the mirror, I set off wandering down the corridor on a dimly lit passenger deck looking for the stairs.

I'd not gone far when I found a sign that informed me I was on level B2 of The Empress of India, with a small cutaway plan of the craft which allowed me to get some bearings. Judging by the plans, The Empress was an old boat. A long-liner with a single air sack, unlike the modern two or three bag liners which flew most of the major routes. The main decks were on the lower floor, designed that way so you could look down through observation windows at the world below. It was a popular design among older craft, built back before terrorists started to take such a delight in rocket launchers, and armoured plates became the fashionable thing to have on your keel.

I've always had an appreciation for older ships. One's crafted in a time before sheer speed was the overwhelming imperative. The Empress was an elegant craft. Its carpets and drapes were maybe a little on the faded and threadbare side, but the brass work was polished to within an inch of its life. You could see your face in it. And that brass was everywhere. Brass piping, brass fittings, brass signs. That and leaded glass coloured in somewhat garish fashion. Ornate light fittings, speaking tubes and god only knew what else. It all had the haunting sense of faded beauty. The kind of beauty that was lost in the heavyset functionality of more modern craft.

I found the stairs and headed down to the main lounge, in the hope of finding a bar still open, as I wasn't overly sure of the time of day. The sun had still been at the porthole in my cabin, but I was woefully short of a watch and my sense of time, as I'm sure you can appreciate, had taken a bit of a battering over the last few days. In truth, I'd still no idea how much time had passed, or what day of the week it was.

The way to the lounge turned out to be down a spiral staircase wide enough for three to walk abreast, with a handrail of oak on brass spindles, inlaid with mother of pearl. The lounge itself occupied the full width of the gondola and was more like walking into a palace than an airship deck.

An art deco clock hung above the centre of the room, showing four o'clock. This, at least, gave me a point of reference, even if it meant I'd missed lunch. My stomach obligingly growled a little as I realised how hungry I was. The last meal I could remember was my 'last' breakfast at the Bailey. My throat felt the bite of thirst too, and in truth, I'd more desire for a drink than food, no matter what my stomach told me.

Normally, you should understand, I'm not one to drown myself in drink. Oh, I enjoy a single malt as much as the next man. But growing up in the east end of old London town I'd seen more than my share of those who took to mother's ruin. I'd seen where that road lay, the wasted lives of London's poor, kept compliant with cheap spirits. Until the cheap spirits took their livers, their minds, or both. I told myself long ago never to slip down that particular path. But, all things considered, I felt I'd earned a drink in light of recent events.

I paused at the head of the stairs and took in the room. In part, if I am honest, out of a sense of trepidation. At least one person I knew of aboard this boat intended me harm. Judging by the way my luck was going, the chances 'Not-a-real-maid' being the only one seemed slim.

Those passengers taking their ease in the lounge were a mixed lot. Indians and British mingling as they ever have. Whatever tensions there were between the heart of the Empire and its jewel were ever hidden behind good manners and considered smiles. I was sure old grudges would lay behind those smiles, but there was ever little dissension between the chattering classes. The Mountbatten concessions had kept a lid on the more rebellious malcontents among those wealthy enough to afford air travel, since the last mutiny back in the forties. Besides which, if you could afford air travel even on a stately old liner like this, you were probably doing alright for yourself out of the status quo.

So saris mixed with European fashions among the ladies present, while turbans and dhoti were matched by men in European business suits and officers' day uniforms of several services. Silks, satins, tweeds and flannelette, all were present in a mildly dazzling array of colours, and a dash of ostentatious wealth.

My lazy scan of the room was edged with mild paranoia, I shall admit. I was also looking for one person in particular, but, unsurprisingly, I couldn't pick out my attacker. In truth, I doubt I would have recognised her if she had stood in front of me. The maid disguise had thrown me completely as I said earlier. It seemed likely she wouldn't still be playing the maid either. She could just be hiding in plain view. I hoped that at the very least the fact I was still breathing meant her intention hadn't been to kill me. It seemed at the time a slim mercy, what with my head still ringing from the dent her pistol butt had put in it. But then had I known what was to come, it may not have seemed a mercy at all. But I'll not get ahead of myself.

As I reached the foot of the stairs, my search of the room threw up someone else of interest. A woman, one who couldn't have been my mystery assailant, drew my eye. She was an Indian girl judging by the sari and her complexion, but unusually tall and proud in her deportment. She stood with her back to me, staring out of a viewing window into the blue sky. She had a fascinating elegance to her, and a tinge of arrogant pride in how she held herself. She drew my attention in a way no one else did in the room. I'm not too proud to admit I felt strongly attracted to her from that first moment.

With hindsight, that was probably why I missed what should have first caught my attention. However, I doubt I am the first or the last to be distracted by a good-looking woman.

She was stood next to a man who seemed overdressed for the occasion. The lounge was warm, heated by hot air vented down from the boilers, I've no doubt. Yet he wore a heavy full-length coat of black wool. He must have been thick set even without his coat because, within it, he looked a solid block of a man. He was very tall too, though the top hat in the same mortuary black may have had added to that impression of looming height. He was facing the same way as the woman when I first looked, but as I strode away from the foot of the steps, he turned momentarily in my direction and a lump caught in my throat. It was the breathing mask with its dark lens which put the shivers in me.

'A Sleep Man, here of all places,' I remember thinking in horror.

The memory of being held down by his compatriots while M brought the spider up to my eye flashed across my mind. That and the creeping unease they had inspired in me from the first moment I had clapped eyes on them in the Bailey. I suddenly had far less desire to make the acquaintance of the young lady who kept such company.

He, it, whatever they are, held my gaze for a moment, although with the dark lens it was impossible to know if he was looking at me or someone else. I must have been frozen to the spot; I dare say I looked a damn fool just standing there, rooted to the spot at the foot of the stairs. I was lucky no one else was coming down them behind me, or they would have bumped straight into me. In what was probably no more than a few seconds but seemed to last an ice age as I stood there, I became uncomfortably aware I was holding my breath.

Then, the Sleep Man turned his gaze back to the window.

I breathed out, feeling my whole body relax. The urge for a drink was all the stronger, and feeling I'd just dodged a bullet, I strode to the bar.

So in my defence, between the beautiful woman and the Sleep Man, I was still a tad distracted when I walked over. It may not be the best of excuses, but I suspect I haven't given you the impression that I'm a man who is always aware of his surroundings. Which is a fair comment, given the events I've recently eluded to. What with being taken roughly from behind, in a strictly smacked to the back of the head kind of way by the 'maid' a few hours ago. Regardless, let me tell you now, I am normally a man who takes pains to be aware of his surroundings.

In utter defiance of this awareness, as I stood at the bar ordering a single malt, I felt the annoyingly familiar feel of a pistol barrel being pushed into my back.

Blame frustration. Blame waking up one too many times with a sore head that was nothing to do with a good time being had the night before. Blame a short temper brought on with feeling much abused of late. Blame all that, but I snapped a little.

"For the love of god, woman, I can tell you nothing," I said rather loudly, and started turning on my heel, and planning to snatch the gun from her hand. After all, it wasn't like she'd shot me last time. I was sick of idle threats. I was sick of being treated like a walk over. I was damn sick of people threatening me. As it turned out, however, in my assumption of who was doing so, I was much mistaken.

"Smyth, you bastard, I don't know who you were expecting, but if you move another inch I will fill your head with lead, you traitorous swine…"

My latest assailant hadn't given me a chance to unarm him. He'd taken a step back out of reach and held the gun high, pointing at my noggin. But it was not the gun that gave me a sinking feeling. It was the voice.

I knew the voice, and as the cigar smoke cleared from my eyes, I recognised the man the voice belonged to.

The sinking feeling in the pit of my stomach got worse. Of all the men to stumble across, standing before me in full uniform was the last man I'd have expected or damn well wished to clap eyes on.

"Maythorpe!" I swore.

CHAPTER 7

A Bad Day For Captain Singh

The captain of the Empress of India was a man feeling much put upon. Which I could tell quite clearly from the look on his face.

He'd the look of a man who had woken up that morning expecting his day to require nothing more taxing than a little light shouting at subordinates. If winds were fair and the ship ran true, then a dull evening hosting passengers at the captain's table would doubtless have awaited him. At worst there would be a little light conversation between courses with boring, self-important men and perhaps, if he was lucky, the odd attractive young woman impressed by a well-tailored uniform with gold tassels and a peaked hat.

What Captain Singh didn't expect, I've no doubt, was that his day would involve dealing with an incandescent lieutenant Maythorpe, of Her Imperial Majesty's Royal Air

Navy waving his service revolver around and shouting the odds in the Empress' wheelhouse, while two of the ship's stewards restrained a man in an EICAN uniform. Which was of course me.

I doubt it was helping the Captain's mood that Maythorpe was insisting I'd been hanged for murder several days before. Especially as this was somewhat in defiance of me standing in the Empress' wheelhouse, looking red-faced and just as angry as Maythorpe, but otherwise in rude health for a dead man.

In other circumstances, I'd have felt sorry for that Captain Singh. Well, maybe not sorry exactly, but one had no axe to grind with the man. I was, however, far more concerned with my own troubles. Selfish of me perhaps, but the way Maythorpe was swinging his service revolver around in my direction while ranting was causing me some trepidation. I was a tad nervous that his gun may go off at any moment resolving the issue of my continued existence, but not in a way that I would overly welcome.

Two other stewards, one of which was no doubt the man at arms, stood with hands on pistols behind Maythorpe. I suspected that they were there as much to make sure he didn't start swinging his pistol in the captain's direction as to make sure I behaved, but it did little to make me feel better about the situation regardless. My own attention was firmly upon Maythorpe's revolver. To the extent that I was paying little attention to what anyone was saying and I almost missed Captain Singh's calm if slightly ruffled voice, saying with ill-disguised disbelief.

"To be clear here, Mr Maythorpe, what you're telling me is that this man was hung in the Old Bailey for murder four days ago?"

It was probably that 'Mr' that cut through Maythorpe's raging. A ship's officer to the core, he instinctively deferred to a captain's authority, even the captain of a commercial liner. He made a show of collecting himself, stiffly, and even lowered his pistol a little, which took a modicum of tension out of the room at least, and certainly did wonders for my own piece of mind.

"Yes, Captain," Maythorpe replied, indignance and anger still in his voice, but with a gentleman's control to it now. "Or he should have been. It was reported in The Times."

"Really, what is the world coming to when you can't believe what you read in The Times…" I said, trying to inject a little levity into proceedings.

Ill-judged on my part, I suspected, but let's be honest here, The Times of London has been going downhill for years. Ever since they turned it into a tabloid and started putting pictures of girls showing rather too much ankle to be considered decent on the third page. It has, in short, long since become a cheap scandal rag compared to the broadsheets.

Personally, I am rather fond of it.

"We can do without any of your witticisms, Smyth," Maythorpe snapped, the anger back in his voice. He raised his gun in the general direction of my face once more.

"Please, Mr Smyth, if you could kindly confine your comments to answering questions while we get this all sorted out," Captain Singh said calmly, reaching out to take a firm hold on Maythorpe's pistol barrel and guide it downwards while adding, "And as Mr Smyth is restrained, I will thank you for putting your gun away, Mr Maythorpe."

To give Captain Singh all due respect, he was doing his best to calm the situation. I suspect he also had half an eye on reducing the possibility of bullet holes in his airship. Such things always put a crimp in a captain's day, I have found.

I had to admire the man's self-control. Frankly, in the Captain's position, I would've been tempted to have my men restrain Maythorpe as well and have us both thrown in the brig till we got to wherever his old gasbag was going.

The aforementioned RAN officer seemed to remember himself, bristled slightly and holstered his pistol once more. Taking a step back, presumably to distance himself from me in case treachery was infectious. Maythorpe was far from happy, which I must admit was something we had in common at that point. He may not have been pointing a gun at me anymore, but he still had one, more's the pity, and I was still being restrained by two rather burly stewards. Things were far from even between us.

I'd have dearly loved to have a pistol of my own. Sadly, however, while members of her Royal Air Navy are allowed to bear arms on a commercial craft, as it increased security on board, members of the East India Company's private navy were not. Hence rather than a pistol I had a ticket stub for the arms locker from the master at arms.

Some parliamentary weak chinned idiot or other championed this law after the 9/10 incident. Blowhard reactionary as most parliamentarians may be, and no doubt wishing to be seen to be taking steps against terrorists on airships in the light of that little palaver with the world's fair. The government never really trusted Company men, however, so while allowing the Queen's forces to bear arms at all times may be a vote winner, but EIC troops was another matter entirely.

As I may have mentioned before, EIC troops were scallions out to make a fast buck, adventurers that were one step up from pirates, or men just not good enough to serve in the real navy and that was the extent of them. No one would countenance Company men carrying arms on commercial craft. They would be a liability at best.

It was an opinion I shared, to be fair. Disreputable though I may be, I was still a RAN man at my core. I may be a convicted murder and a thief, but I was still, in my own eyes at least, a cut above those in hock to the Company Shilling. I wouldn't want those types to be walking around an airship I was a passenger on carrying live weapons either and would have happily told you so a week before, even while I resided in my cell at the Bailey.

Which is all the more ironic considering the situation I'd found myself in.

Maythorpe nodded acquiescence to the Captain, stowing his pistol and buttoning down his holster. He even went so far as to take a step backwards, putting a little distance between us. For which I was grateful at least. His vitriol was bad enough, but I really didn't appreciate dealing with his spittle in there as well…

"Thank you, Mr Maythorpe. Now let's try and make some sense of all this, shall we?" Captain Singh said and put his hands behind his back, adopting the pose of ship captains everywhere talking to subordinates, which said as plainly as any words 'I'm at my ease, so you would be wise to give me no reason not to be at my ease, because if you do it will not go easy on you.'

"My apologies, Captain. But I really must insist that this man is placed in the brig under my authority," Maythorpe said, the newly calm veneer to his voice fooling no one, I suspected.

"You don't have any authority here, old boy." I risked a jab at the prig, mainly to see him bristle once more, but also banking on the assumption that the more unreasonable he sounded, the better it would go for me.

"Mr Smyth…" the Captain raised his voice slightly, the warning clear.

I nodded my head in acquiescence, not wishing to rile the Captain.

"I insist…" flustered the prig, causing, much to my mirth, the Captain to bang his hand down hard on a control panel, which beeped alarmingly for a moment. The violent interjection stopped Maythorpe mid-sentence, and the Captain took a moment to stare down the RAN officer, before, with surprising calm, he made his position clear.

"You would do well to remember you're a guest aboard my ship, Mr Maythorpe. This is not a Naval vessel, but you are a naval officer. I'm quite sure you are aware aboard any ship all authority stems from its captain. This is true here as it is upon any of your fine gunships, and I will assure you of this, I will not be dictated to in my own bridge by anyone. So you will supply me with a reason why this man should be incarcerated and why you feel the need to wave a gun about in my ship's public lounge. Or you will find yourself enjoying the comforts of my brig for the rest of your journey and the Admiralty will have my letter of complaint upon its desk before you see the Arch once more."

Frankly, I could have kissed the man for that. Just for the distraught look on Maythorpe's face. The threat of letters to the Admiralty put the fear of God in him, as letters to the Admiralty are want to do with young naval officers.

If I've a fault, it's that one revels in these small victories, as I'm sure you have gathered by now. It's not becoming, I know, but in my position, you would've also found yourself smiling right then.

"This man is a convicted murder and traitor to boot. He was the arsonist who set fire to Her Majesty's dockyards at Slough. He was to be hung. Indeed it has been reported as such. How he comes to be here aboard your craft, I have no idea, but as an Englishman and a subject of Her Imperial Highness, it behoves me to see he is arrested and placed in chattel. If you place him in my custody in Cairo, I shall see he is taken to the rightful authorities and subject to the full weight of the law," Maythorpe said. I would say he said it with an eerie calmness about him, but that would be a lie.

He was more like a boil aching to pus at any moment and reddening under the strain.

"I see," said the Captain, bristling slightly. I suspected Maythorpe's high-handed tone and the way he said 'Englishman' had something to do with it. Singh was a subject of the Empire, and no doubt he disliked the inflexion of English superiority in the prig's words. Colonials in positions of authority, I have found, are less than fond of being reminded they are considered the lesser partners by their Imperial masters. Maythorpe was doing his case no favours by speaking so, which, needless to say, pleased me no end.

"And you, Mr Smyth, what have you to say to these charges?" Singh asked, turning to me.

"I'm not sure I can tell you, Captain, I am afraid. There is an act of parliament prevents me from telling you everything," I replied, borrowing a trick from my 'friend' M. "I can, at least, confirm that I am indeed Hannibal Smyth, formerly of the RAN and now of the East India Company. But beyond that, I'm not sure how much I'm allowed to impart." I was bluffing, of course, and for all I was worth. As much to buy me some time to come up with a more effective lie.

"Hannibal, like the man with the elephants?" one of the random thugs, come, stewards, behind me said, which earned the man a belittling glare from his Captain who didn't appreciate the contribution.

"An act of parliament, you say?" the Captain asked, looking me in the eye once more and holding my gaze. I've no doubt he was trying to weigh up the lies I was telling.

'Well good luck to him,' I thought. I knew I'd lied to better judges of human nature than Singh in the past and gotten away with it.

"Yes, Captain," I said, still stalling. I'd had plenty of time in the holding cells of the Bailey to come up with plausible lies. Sadly, none of which were of much use while I was in the cell, but right now it was just a case of deciding which one to go with.

"Well, Mr Smyth, you will need to tell me something, or I am afraid I shall have to place you in the brig and let Mr Maythorpe deal with the proper authorities in Cairo when we put in tomorrow evening."

I smiled falsely, suppressing an inward groan, as Maythorpe's eyes brightened. You might think that I might leap at the chance. Certainly, if you know anything of Cairo, a city with a thousand alleyways, each of which has a man holding a rusty knife in the shadows. It was the kind of city that anyone could get lost in, whether they wished it so or not. If I could escape Maythorpe's clutches and avoid getting my own throat cut, I could easily disappear into the bowels of Africa's greatest city.

'If,' I told myself swiftly, 'you didn't have The Ministry's damn spider in your eye, Harry.'

Thinking of The Ministry, I realised they wanted me in India as far as I knew. Getting myself banged up in a Cairo jail, I suspected, was something they would consider counter to their wishes. If I am honest, I wouldn't give a grain of sand from the Sahara for their wishes, but if I defaulted on our deal, I suspected my life would be worth less than that grain of sand.

I thought fast and remembered something my old mum used to tell me when I was a lad. "If you're going to lie, Harry, my son, then lie big…"

Of course, mother was generally off her trolley on gin most of the time, but in essence, it was still sound advice. People are always more likely to believe a big lie than a small one. If only because they are used to believing large lies. It's the basic principle on which all politics is constructed.

Human nature can be a wonderful thing. With this in mind, I went for it.

"Okay Captain, if you insist. However, I must caution you this is to go no further than this room. I assume you can vouch for everyone present?" Maythorpe all but rolled his eyes and looked poised to speak, but a look from the Captain silenced him. Instead, he just narrowed his eyes at me. I suspect he was hoping I'd just give myself enough rope, as it were, and not entirely figuratively.

"I can vouch for my men of course," the Captain replied, sounding at least partially intrigued. People, I have observed in the past, like secrets, and offering them one is always a good way to bring them over to your side. Then with a delightfully obtuse look on his face, he added, "Mr Maythorpe however?"

I could have kissed him for that one. I don't mind admitting. However, I replied, "Maythorpe is as loyal to the crown and honest as they come, I have no fear on that score." In all honesty, more's the pity. I wouldn't have been in this mess but for the priggish buffoon after all.

"Whereas Smyth here is a liar and murderer," the prig scowled.

"Mr Maythorpe, for the last time be silent. I will hear this man speak," the Captain snapped, shutting him down before he could rant once more.

I nodded my thanks while Maythorpe glowered.

"Okay, if I may…" I said in what I felt was a dramatic and conspiratorial tone. "For propriety's sake, I'll have to keep to broad strokes rather than details, you understand. Matters are delicate and of great import, but I'll explain what I can."

"While I was serving in Her Majesties Royal Air Navy, I became aware of a group of criminals within the service. A simple smuggling operation, or so I thought at the time, but when I reported it to the rightful authorities, they engaged me to operate in the shadows for them. They wished me to infiltrate the group, you see, and play the disgruntled naval officer. They recognised that while my loyalty to the service and indeed the crown was absolute, matters of my… station, shall we say… were such that I could pass for one of more flexible loyalties. I am, you see, one who began my career as a member of the working class which has unfortunately caused some little friction with those of higher birth, regrettable as that may be. As such while I'm nothing if not loyal to the core, there are always those willing to question my position, earned as it was on merit not privilege."

Captain Singh nodded knowingly at this. It always pays to know your audience, and if anyone knew about earning a position through merit and still being looked down upon by those who owe their own positions to a privileged birth, it's an airship captain of an Imperial liner of Indian descent. Buoyed by this, I continued in much the same vein.

"I was asked to discover the extent of this smugglers' ring. Why authorities believed I would have a talent for such work? I couldn't say, but when I discovered I did, well, I was as shocked as anyone. Nevertheless I saw it as my duty to take on this mission, Queen and country demanded it, and who was I to refuse? What can you do but your all when your country calls after all? A man must take a stand for what he believes. It does not become him to ask what it may cost him. Duty is all, I am sure you would agree, Captain Singh."

I was warming to my subject, pacing back and forth, having been released by the heavy-handed stewards. Hands clasped behind me, straight-backed, and full of vim. I could see the men nodding at my vitriol, and, dare I say it, feeling privileged to hear me speak of such things.

"I joined the smuggling ring as a mole, reporting all that I found, what profits came my way I donated to charity, a children's hospice in Croydon I know only too well. If good came of my deceptions, it was there I hope the most good came. I regret only that I never had chance to visit in that time and see what little joy those gains ill got may have brought to the children's cherubic faces."

Yes, I know what you're thinking, but as I say if you're going to lie then lie big and lay it on with a trowel. Lay it on I did, to appreciative smiles from one or two of the stewards. Thugs though they were to a man, even thugs love a tale of smiling children. I continued...

"Over a year of my life was spent infiltrating this group. In that time, it became clear the ring was larger than we had ever imagined. Worse, its plans extended far beyond smuggling. They had infiltrated into every facet of the Imperial services. I was afraid for my life, for the Empire, for the crown itself. There were nights I couldn't sleep for fear of discovery. I don't mind admitting the stress my double life was causing me to suffer. The further I infiltrated the organisation. The more names I collected, the more dangerous it became. But through it all, I kept my upper stiff as any of us here would do, I am sure."

I was playing to my audience, I must admit. But it was a performance and a half. Hand gestures, righteous indignation, thinly disguised anger at the villains of the piece. I have often thought that I should tread the boards one day. Though the thought of having to spend every day with a bunch of Lovies puts me off, I must admit.

"Finally, my luck ran out. An airman called Hardacre, who was in deep with the ring discovered my true loyalties by ill chance and sought to gain favour with his sinister masters by killing me. I have little doubt the black heart would have blamed my death on an accident. There had been other accidents, after all. I would not have been the first, for the perfidiousness went far beyond mere avarice. I would just be another body to dispose of. By chance I saw him coming and we fought, crashing around the bomb deck, till luck being with me I managed to scupper his plans to kill me. Sadly, to my shame I was forced to kill the man to save my own life. I wish I could have merely overpowered him, but at the last he tripped and fell out of the ship through the same hatch he would have thrown me through had fate not spared my life. That is my one regret in all this, the necessity of killing him. I consider it to be a failure on my part that he didn't live to stand trial for his crime. That he could not have been made to reveal all he knew of the conspiracy that rots at the core of the Empire. But fall he did, and it was then by ill fate that Maythorpe came upon us, just as the blackheart fell."

"He's lying. I saw him murder Hardacre with my own eyes," Maythorpe cut in, though the look on his face was unsure all of a sudden. My performance had unsteadied his own belief in the events he had witnessed. I almost broke out in a grin at that point, but I did my best to remain earnest in my portrayal of the wronged hero.

"Yes, yes you did," I replied, my voice laced with phoney regret. "And I can't blame you for drawing the conclusions you did from what you saw, and would that the agency for which I worked could have stepped forward and illuminated you as to the truth of events. But there was a problem, the sinister ring of conspirators was still intact, and should they discover I was, in fact, a spy in their ranks they would have time to hide their tracks. To slip back into the darkness and plot further against us all. The agency needed time to uncover more. They had other agents in place, and they needed to be protected, until they can bring down the whole job lot of them. So my trial was arranged, as was my execution staged and a commission arranged in the East

India Company to keep me out of sight. It's a cruel trick of fate that Maythorpe is on the same ship and recognised me, as I am supposed to be travelling incognito. Captain Singh, you have my sincere apologies that I've brought this trouble to your ship. I would ask you forgive poor Maythorpe as well. He acts only according to events as the agency would have people perceive. But with all I have told you now in mind, I trust I can rely on your discretion."

You have to admit, it isn't a bad story. To say I made up most of it as I was going along, I was quite proud of it. Sowing the seeds of doubt around Maythorpe's chain of events. Massaging the egos of all present. I could see in his eye that even Maythorpe half doubted himself now. It helped I'm sure that Hardacre had been a less than exemplary airman to start with. He wanted to believe me, I think. I could see it in his eyes.

I realised at that moment that Maythorpe was the kind of romantic fool who believed in honour. The kind that believed those who wore the same uniform as he did, his fellow officers, were all men of duty and courage. Indeed, that was probably why he had come to hate me so much, for in his eyes I had let down that uniform, and in doing so let down them all.

Yes, I was certain that he wanted to believe me. That he was indeed, fully taken in by my performance. He opened his mouth to speak, and I knew what he would say. He would make apologies to me there and then for doubting my honour and commitment to the crown. No doubt, he would offer to stand me a scotch, call me a hero and a damnable brave one at that for all I had sacrificed.

Sadly neither Maythorpe nor Captain Singh had read the script.

"What a load of tosh," Maythorpe said.

"I agree. Boys, throw him in the brig," Singh put in, adding, "And don't be too gentle about it."

Which was about the point something heavy which may have been a steward's blackjack hit me from behind and the world turned what to me was becoming an increasingly familiar shade of black.

CHAPTER 8

Whispers
Louder Than Sin

My head, which had been sorely abused of late as I am sure you recall, hurt like something which had been beaten repeatedly over several days when I next awoke.

To be fair, that would seem to be an accurate enough description of my last few days. The loud pounding noise that seemed to be rattling my skull made it all the worse.

Thump, thump, thump.

Constant, and as steady as a drum beat. It echoed through me.

Things were all the worse because I was in the dark. Literally, as it happens. Wherever they had put me, there was no light to be had. No portholes letting in starlight. There was not even a slim slither of light seeping under a doorway. Even the cells underneath the Old Bailey had had more light than this.

It was warm too. Well, hot would be a better word, uncomfortably so and cramped with it. I was sitting down because when I tried to stand, I realised I had no room to stand in. The bang on the head from my encounter with the ceiling did little to help my headache. While the thumping, I now realised was probably the engines, continued unabated.

Thump, thump, thump.

Wherever they had put me, I realised it must be somewhere in the bowels of the ship. Close to the engine room. From the smell of coal dust and the confined space, what passed for the brig on this ship was actually a spare coal bunker.

My wrists were tied with loose cord but otherwise I was unrestrained, though being in a room too small to stand, in pitch blackness, served to keep me very much contained. There are, I am told, rules about these things. The conditions you're allowed to restrain people in, and conditions you're not allowed to do so. Apparently, the latter did not apply on Captain Singh's ship.

I could feel an approaching migraine from the thump of the engines, or perhaps it was the repeated blows to the head. That, and all else I had endured of late, was possibly the source of the pain I suddenly felt around my eye. Though I suspect it was caused by something more sinister. Which it proved to be as the darkness was suddenly flooded with explosive bursts of light, with that now familiar afterglow.

As a method of communication, it had some painful drawbacks as I may have mentioned.

"W.. W..I..L..L.. C..O..N..T..A..C..T."

Was the message all but burnt into my iris. As I remember, at the time, in between a bitter outburst of swearing that would have shocked even my old dear mum.

I was angry that they repeated that first 'W'. Bad enough someone was doing their best to blind me, but you would think they could type their messages correctly at the very least...

The pain in my eye eased off, and I ceased to vocalise impassioned outbursts of anger. The thudding in my head grew worse all the same thanks to that ever-present thump, thump, thump, of the engines. I was, it's fair to say, a tad on the miserable side and doubting the efficiency of The Ministry's devices. Something which would have cheered me up in other circumstances.

Typical of the civil service, informing you that you're going to be contacted, just after you get incarnated in the darkest pit that someone could find.

Thump, thump, thump.

The engines continued unabated, and I started to recognise a slight whine in their pitch every few seconds, caused by a loose bearing probably. So to add to my woes, I was not even incarcerated on a well-maintained craft. I started to sulk at that point.

I've read, as I am sure well-read people like your good selves have also, that it is at moments like this when people take stock of their lives. You know the kind of thing. Consider all they have done. What brought them to these straights and what not. Then having considered all this they come to some great conclusions about their lives. What had gone wrong, what they should have done. How, indeed, they could be better people. How they could make their world and everyone else's, come to that, a better place.

Thump, thump, thump.

The longer you're confined in such a small dark place, cramped up and sweating profusely from the heat, the more time you have to dwell on such things. I expected they would frogmarch me off the boat when it arrived in Cairo. Clapped, no doubt, in irons. Until then I wasn't going anywhere and had nothing but time. I was not even sure how much of that I had, how long it would take to get to Cairo, or how much time had passed since I took yet another trip to the land of the unconscious. But I suspected it would both not be long and would seem like some time just short of an ice age. A very hot, humid, dark ice age…

Regardless, I found myself dwelling on the recent past, and I did come to one very firm conclusion about what I could have done differently. Indeed I identified my only real mistake. To wit, not throwing Maythorpe out of the bomb bay doors right behind Hardacre when I'd the chance. Something I felt determined to rectify should I get the opportunity.

So then, so much for a prisoner's self-reflection.

Some more time passed…

Mostly as I tried to ignore the ache of my head, and the groan of my stomach that was trying to remind me I still had not eaten since that breakfast in the Bailey. And while I tried to ignore these twin pains I dwelt not so much on my mistakes, but upon the various ways I could kill Maythorpe. Which became a string of happy delusions. As were the various looks that I imagined on his ratty little face when I finally did him in.

There are small victories, and there are really small victories, but sometimes the really small victories are all you have to get you through the dark hours.

I think my favourite involved throwing him into a giant piston shaft made of glass so I could watch the crank turning the piston head down on him with constant thudding repetition. That I will concede was probably inspired by the noise of the engine I was having to endure.

Thump, thump, thump.

It was driving me a little towards the edge of what you may laughingly call my sanity, I don't mind admitting, that constant, unrelenting noise.

Finally, after what could have been aeons, there was an eruption of bright light which flooded my cell. In an instant, I went from slowly being deafened to utterly and painfully blind. As such, it took me a few moments to gather my shredded wits enough to realise what was happening as someone started dragging me out of there. I was struggling as well, in a quite ungentlemanly fashion as I tried to break the Queensbury rules by the placement of my foot in the groin of one of the stewards doing the pulling. I was rewarded with a cry of pain, which, at least, meant I'd brought tears to someone else's eyes for once.

I can say in my defence at this point Lord Queensbury did not envision a man being tied at the wrists and spending several hours confined in a coal bunker when he drew up the rules of gentlemanly conflict.

Frankly, I was in a mood to do some more kicking when my wits finally cleared enough that I could make sense of what Captain Singh was saying.

"Mr Smyth, I really am most terribly sorry." He sounded flustered. He'd also repeated this sentence, at least, three times before I heard it properly. At which point I didn't cease to kick immediately but got at least one more good one in before I stopped struggling.

It was after all not a sentence I'd been expecting to hear anyone say, so it caught me off guard a moment.

"What?" I managed, eyes still adjusting to the light, and my wits with them.

"I said that I really am terribly sorry. I must ask you forgive your confinement. It is utterly regrettable, I trust you'll make no mention of this unfortunate misunderstanding in any report to your superiors," the Captain said, repeating himself once more.

There was a somewhat toadying edge to his voice. A wringing of hands you could almost hear in his tone. Like a politician caught with his trousers round his ankles and a King's Cross rent boy's lips on his… well, you get the gist. He was obviously uncomfortable. No man, least of all the captain of his own ship, likes to discover they have been batting for the wrong eleven. And I suspect an Indian captain of a passenger airship is not a man who wants his ship's owners to hear about entanglements with Imperial government officials. However, and I blame my hours of confinement for this, I was still struggling to catch up, so all I managed was…

"What?"

"Miss Wells has explained everything. We were unaware you were part of her… her party. She confirmed you're working for…" He almost choked the next words out. "The Ministry… Again, please, I must say how terribly sorry I am that I mistakenly was taken in by that fool Maythorpe's story and did not pay rightful credence to your own, as I should undoubtedly have done. I am sure you understand, under the circumstances, it was a simple error of judgement on my part. I did not make it with malice towards your good self or… The Ministry…"

"Sorry, just to check I'm understanding you correctly, you're saying Miss Wells confirmed my story?" I asked, confused. The vague memory of something the Not-in-any-way-a-maid, come skull cracker, had said came to mind. Something she asked me, in fact, almost the first thing she asked me. 'Wells… Why are they interested in Wells?"

I acquired a sinking feeling, as you can possibly imagine. This particular sinking feeling was regarding that same American, who-was-certainly-not-a-maid, who had somehow come to my rescue. The words getting out of the frying pan only to be dropped into the heart of a roaring fire sprang to mind. I was still fighting to get up to speed here, but I wasn't sure I liked that possible destination.

"Yes, yes, Miss Wells. She and her… associate… showed me their credentials. She is waiting for you in my office," he said still flustered. Thankfully, too flustered to realise I had no idea who he was talking about. Though there was something in the way he struggled with the words 'associate', a dread in his voice that sent a shiver down my spine. Whoever the 'associate' was, was what really scared the Captain, and if it scared him, it was putting the willies up me, that was for sure.

Though if he thought I looked worried and confused at all, he probably put it down to my confinement. If anything he was probably relieved I was not shouting the odds right then and threatening his command. To be fair, he would have been right about the confusion, my eye still stung from the light, and my back was killing me from being cramped up in the coal bunker.

"Your office?" I inquired, out of the vague hope that some answers to the growing list of questions would ease my state of mind.

A hope as vain as it was vague of course, but all the same listening to apologies was getting me nowhere, and unless the apologies came with a single malt, a cigar and a three-course meal, I tired of hearing them.

"Yes, yes, I shall take you there now," the Captain told me, then shouted something in Hindi at the steward still rolling on the floor clutching his unmentionables. I've no idea what he said, but I got the general gist as he kicked the steward in a none too gentle way as he walked past. Flustered the Captain might be, but he wasn't above issuing out abuse to a subordinate to vent his frustrations.

He led me down through the bowels of the ship from the air-sack engine room, the steward limping along behind us. These older crates, built before terrorists and rocket launchers became such a fad, were built upside down. At least, if you compared them to the older still ocean-going vessels on which they were based. The engines were built up into the air sack, the ballrooms and lounges on the bottom deck furthest from the engine, staterooms above them, and second class then the cargo holds and third class cattle pens in the air-sack holds themselves.

As we moved down through the ship, we passed from coal dust and axle grease to plush carpeting and polished brass once more. The Captain, apart from the occasional swear words in Hindi, kept his own council. No doubt not wanting to muddy the waters further. I played along with the silence as my head was still clearing, and I was trying to make sense of everything.

Not least of which was the message I had received earlier. 'W WILL CONTACT.'

'W' for Wells perhaps, it seemed as likely as anything else. If this 'Miss Wells' was my ministry contact, then it seemed unlikely she was the American girl. On the other hand, if it was Not-a-maid-no-really-she-wasn't, she was playing some game of her own. It didn't need much in the way of paranoia to consider that if it was her, she might be using my detainment as leverage. After all, if the Captain handed me over to her what was I going to do, ask to be locked up once more?

I was sorely in need of time to think and get a handle on all this.

I didn't get long.

Captain Singh led me to his private cabin, at the back end of second class. Surprisingly not far from my own tiny cabin. I guess the owners of this gasbag line didn't see any point in wasting too much paying passenger space on their Captain's comforts. No matter how highly regarded he may be, he was Indian after all, and privileges of rank were a lesser concern than if he had been an Englishman. It was probably why they employed a native in the first place.

By the time we arrived, I felt boxed in by circumstance. So as he opened the door and ushered me through, my paranoia was running rampant. I'd pretty much convinced myself I was about to come face to face with Not-a-maid-but-a-gun-wielding-harpy and her roughshod American drawl, once more. A reunion I was not entirely sure I wanted. Instead, however, I was greeted by a delicate Home Counties tea party tones…

"Hannibal, at last, dearest, Oh but you have been in the wars, haven't you? Now tell me have you ever visited the pyramids?"

The voice was that of the young Indian woman I had so admired in the lounge. She was sitting behind the Captain's desk, and had been reading what appeared to be a cheap romance novel of some description to pass the time. She seemed perfectly comfortable taking her leisure there, despite the obvious breach in etiquette. Or perhaps because of it. By sitting there, she was leaving no doubt where authority lay in that room.

It was no surprise the Captain seemed uncomfortable with the turn of events, though that may have been something to do with the other occupant of his office. The one, the Captain, had referred to nervously as 'her associate'. On seeing him, I can't say I blamed Captain Singh for that.

Miss Wells's companion was one in the same as had been stood with her in the main lounge. Dressed as they always seemed to be in a heavy military style coat and wearing one of those ever-present breathing masks. He, or 'it' as I preferred to think of them, stood stock still. The sound of its rasping respirator somehow filling any silence, an odd plume of smoke whispering forth from its mask each breath. A damned Sleep Man, looming behind the relaxed woman at the desk. Intimidating all present but her by its presence alone.

"I'm sorry, what?" I managed.

In my defence, I was probably still a little out of it. But her question, which seemed a little absurd in the circumstances, had caught me off guard.

In truth, I was also a little enamoured of the woman. There was something in the way she held herself, a pride and assurance that I could not help but feel attracted to. I have always had a fondness for a woman with a certain strength of character. Though I must admit, it didn't harm at all that she was also even lovelier close up than she had been in the lounge.

Her long dark hair framed a face that spoke of eastern mystery. Her skin was fair for an Indian, a light tan that suggested she was unaccustomed to being out in the sun all day. I suspected also she had mixed blood, but who didn't in Indian society these days. She was undeniably a beauty, but there was a strength to her as well. This was no fragile blossom waiting to be picked, if you'll pardon the phrase.

I think it was her eyes that did it for me. They were unusual in a woman of her heritage in that they were green. Like the brightest jade. They were impossible to ignore. That and the warm smile she was presenting me with. Things, it seemed, were finally looking up.

Yes, okay, I know I seem to be laying it on thick. Let's just say I found her both striking and alluring in equal measure, and I'm not a man easily befuddled by a good looking woman.

There was something about her voice as well. It had an odd tint to it, an accent that was neither Indian nor British, for all it held a little of the Home Counties. Regardless, I felt my heart beat a little faster and became a little flushed. Perhaps it was because I found her so attractive, or just the relief that she wasn't my 'friend' the Not-Actually-A-Maid-At-All American. But even with the company she was keeping, I was quite genuinely pleased to make her acquaintance.

If you were to ask me, there and then, and I had been an honest man, I would probably have told you I fell a little in love with her right at that moment.

In hindsight, I blame the repeated blows to the head.

"The pyramids, Hannibal," Miss Wells said, "I thought we should have a cream tea beneath the Sphinx…"

CHAPTER 9

Cream Tea
Beneath The Sphinx

The Empress of India made dock in Cairo a couple of hours later. The sun was setting behind the pyramids as we docked, which is still one of the most stunning sunsets in the world. Even in these latter days when the industrial quarters of the city have long since enveloped the ancient tombs, there was still something about the sight that would stir the hearts of even the most jaded romantic.

With red sky over the sands of the Sahara, the great red orb that the pyramid builders thought was the god Ra sinking behind those sandstone monuments, well, it is enough to put your life, nay the whole gloriously torrid British Empire, into a degree of perspective. A sight to take away your breath and make you think in terms of aeons. How fleeting is all that we have built compared to this the last of the seven wonders of the ancient world…

 It probably says something about me that I missed this stirring sight completely because I was in the shower at the time.

Possibly, you may think it says I am a shallow, vain man, with little regard for the world beyond himself. I can't really argue against you on that score. Though in my defence, if you spend hours locked in a hot dirty coal bunker, with the constant thud of an airship's engines your only companion in the darkness, I suspect you would also choose the long hot shower over spectacle any day of the week.

Despite the hot shower that washed away the coal dust and eased some of the aches in my limbs, I remained in the dark in all other respects. The delightful, charming Miss Wells hadn't been overly forthcoming with any actual enlightenment. Which is to say she didn't tell me anything. Other than making Captain Singh apologise for the misunderstanding repeatedly, which had as much to do with her looming associate as anything else. She left the Captain's cabin after 'suggesting' to me that we meet by the Sphinx at eleven the next morning.

She hinted, in somewhat conspiratorial tones, that it would be safer to pursue our intrigues then, as many passengers would be taking their leisure in the city.

The 'Empress', it seemed, would be laid up for the day at the masts at the edge of the city. Cairo was always the scheduled stopover on the long haul to India. There or New Alexandria.

I suspect she added the tidbit about intrigues for the benefit of the Captain, whom she seemed to take a measure of delight in terrifying. I have seldom met a man in his position who wanted to know less. Though I can't blame him overly much in the circumstances. He clearly wanted nothing to do with The Ministry. I suspect he would be pleased just to have us off his ship for a while. Indeed if we got delayed in the old city and missed our flight, he would have been delighted. The last thing he wanted was to know more. The looming presence of Miss Wells's Sleep Man was enough to convince him of that. All he really seemed to care about was that there would be no official report of any kind.

I was not entirely looking forward to the morning, for all Cairo itself was as ever the Empire's Middle-Eastern jewel. Seas may be the lesser highway in these latter days of air-power, but the canal at Suez remained vital to many an ambition. The mystique of the old city still drew tourists and historians aplenty. I'd never been there myself but had been informed in equal measure that it was a wonder all of its own and stank to high heaven of camel dung.

If I am honest, the pleasures of visiting ancient ruins have always escaped me. The sights I prefer to see in exotic cities were the three b's, bars, brothels and bordellos. So the prospect of drinking tea beneath crumbling sandstone blocks, even in such lovely company as Miss Wells was minimal. It didn't help that I suspected I would be doing so with the Sleep Man in attendance. The Captain was not the only one it put the willies up.

Only Miss Wells herself seemed immune to the threat of its presence. Indeed she managed to seem utterly indifferent to the hulk. Which gave me the impression it was her bodyguard. Its sinister presence was to her merely a part of the furniture of her life. Oddly it made her seem all the more attractive somehow. I'm not sure what that says about me...

In short order, Singh, still hand-wringing no doubt at the threat of The Ministry hanging over him, had a steward escort me to my room, as much to get the gathered company out of his cabin, I suspected, as any desire to placate yours-truly. Though he did have the ship's cooks send a freshly cooked meal up to my cabin. When it arrived, my stomach growled with anticipation, even though I half expected that the food had been spat on. The steward who brought it to my cabin, you see, was the one my frustrations had left walking awkwardly.

Hunger won out over paranoia, so I tucked in regardless. I couldn't remember the last time I'd eaten by this point. It must have been a while because even the usually inedible airship food actually tasted good.

After that, I'd hit the shower, then hit the bed. Glorious sunset, the exotic delights of the souk, even the tantalising possibilities of belly dancing beauties in the shady bar in the old quarter, could all go hang compared with the joy of a good twelve hours or so in the sack. Not least, because it was a rare opportunity to drift into unconsciousness by choice.

I'd, however, double locked the door and wedged the handle with a bar from the wardrobe before taking to my bed. Given how the last few days had gone for me, I was taking as few chances as possible. Besides which, in the back of my mind was the thought that Maythorpe might do something stupid. After all, it was Maythorpe, and him doing something stupid was almost to be expected. The thought of waking to him leading a troop of guardsmen knocking down my door to take me into custody and 'damn the Captain's eyes' held little appeal. But I can't say I would have been overly shocked had it happened.

All things being equal, it came as a pleasant surprise to sleep through the night unmolested, and equally pleasant to discover on waking that no one was banging on my door shouting the odds.

I kept the door firmly locked, however, as I took the opportunity to shave, trim my moustache and make myself as presentable as possible. The little scabbed over cut on my throat was all the reminder I needed of the last time I tried to shave in that room.

'Best foot forward, Harry old lad,' I thought to myself, feeling something akin to cheerful for the first time in months. No matter what else this day held in store for me, I'd a rendezvous with a beautiful woman to attend. That, if nothing else, was a pleasant thought with which to start the day. Even if the woman in question had a Sleep Man in her shadow every time I laid eyes upon her.

When I unhooked the door handle and sprung the lock, I paused for a moment before opening it. Call it anticipation or if we are more honest about it, fear, but I was suddenly wary of what lay beyond the door.

'One must pad up when you're going out to bat, Harry lad, one must pad up,' I thought to myself, remembering the only really valuable lesson they taught me at Rudgley.

I was all too aware that the last time I'd walked through that door, I'd landed myself in a cell by being less than wary. Mental 'padding' is as important as anything else. I consciously checked I'd put the cutthroat back in my pocket after shaving. Being mentally armed is a fine thing, actually being armed is better still, even if it's only with a razor.

'Pad up and face them down,' I thought once more. That Rudgleyism had served me well on more than one occasion. It was the unofficial school motto of Rudgley School for The Children of Empire. The school that made me the man I am today, which was the kind of proud boast you're supposed to make about the old school…

As the man I am today was a murdering smuggler, arsonist and petty thief, drummed out of the service for his crimes and supposedly hung by the neck, I suspected the school might not consider me there finest alumni.

Okay, scratch that, not a petty thief, one has some pride after all. Let's call me a criminal mastermind, at least I was before my unfortunate arrest. I'll admit getting myself arrested takes a little of the gloss off my self-image.

Rudgley, or 'Rudgers' as other old boys I am acquainted with have been known to call it with the misplaced affection of those who have forgotten the ice-cold showers. They also always seem to have forgotten the inedible food, dorm room beatings, fagging, bullying and flying chalkboard erasers aimed by former grenadier's sergeant majors who approach classroom discipline as they would boot camp. I'd been told 'Your school days are the best days of your life.' My abiding thought when I left was 'If those were the best days of my life then life sucks and not in the way a girl in a reasonably price Soho brothel does…'

I had some very straightforward ways of thinking when I was still a fresh-faced cadet.

The masters of my old school held firm to the belief that the Empire had been forged on the playing fields of England. As such almost everything the school taught was around the sports field, or edged with sporting wisdom like 'Pad up and face them down'. I may have hated the place, but some of my old school lessons stuck with me. As things do when they are beaten into you hard enough.

Despite my fears, the corridor proved to be empty of Scots guards, or Welsh, come to that. The same was true as I made my way through the ship, which was all but empty. Most of the passengers were off enjoying the layover in the Egyptian capital, I surmised. I did pass a couple of crewmen, who at least directed me to the boarding ramps, so I found my way, with a certain ease, onto the gantry.

The main Cairo gantry tower is a triumph of Imperial symbolism over good taste. Now don't get me wrong, I can appreciate the need for grandiose statements. From the lions in Trafalgar Square, to the glorious statue of Britannia astride the channel bridge, welcoming travellers from across the continent into Britain between her ample bronze thighs. The Empire erects these monuments to itself and its rule everywhere. A visual reminder of who was in charge, to keep the locals in check. 'Here's John Bull, look how mighty is he.' As the old song goes. Complete with the none too subtle undertones that Mr J Bull could stamp on you from a great height if he so desired. After all, what is the point of being the greatest Empire in the history of mankind, if you don't make sure everyone is reminded of it as often as possible.

Generally, I have no issues with the monuments of triumphalism that so grace Imperial architecture. Yet somehow, building a two hundred foot high statue of Old Iron Knickers herself, with arms outstretched to form airship moorings, within a mile of the Giza pyramids, struck me as a tad overdone.

British rule in Egypt had been going on for almost a century and a half. Keeping the peace between the native factions with typical Imperial diplomacy whenever possible and by force whenever necessary. Its official status was that of a protectorate, and as such, the ancient kingdom had thrived. Not that some of the locals appreciated it over much. Occasionally left-wing agitators, and religious factions would kick up a fuss, or flare up little insurrections. But I have never met a wealthy Egyptian that complained about their nation's protectorate status, while the poor would be poor anyway. I doubt they cared who they called master.

I took the lift down to the ground, where I walked out into the desert sun and a wave of heavy dry heat I hadn't expected. The breeze on the walkways had masked the heat of the morning. Down on the ground, the air as dead as dreams of independence. As old Ra beat down on my head, I wished that I'd a hat with me at the very least. What's the old saying about mad dogs and the midday sun? Well, it's a good saying. The sweat was soon running from my brow, and it was only mid-morning, a fact I found mildly distressing. I'd served most of my career on short hauls and patrols around northern Europa and the Baltic States. I wasn't used to the heat of tropical climes. Experiencing the desert heat made me even less eager to spend time in India. Of course, I was unaware of how cold it gets in the lost valleys of the Himalayas at the time, but I am getting way ahead of myself there.

I flagged down a steam camel, or whatever they called the weird contraptions that pass for taxis. What I wouldn't have given for a Hanson cab, though in truth I'd have given more to be catching one up to Piccadilly and a few of my old haunts.

The contraption jerked and rocked, like a real camel as it fumbled its way along. Whoever thought it was a good idea to raise a boiler engine up on four stilts then attach unsprung wheels was, I decided, an idiot. An inventive idiot with a certain measure of genius, but an idiot all the same. A real camel would have been far more suited to the sandy road that led up to the pyramids.

As I rode the damnable thing, I remembered hearing at some point in the past that some people have been known to get seasick on the back of a camel. It's one of the reasons they get called 'the ship of the desert' in the first place. As an idea, it had always sounded a little absurd to me, until I sat on the back of that infernal contraption. Shared misery does wonders for empathy, I find.

The ride, if the pitching and yawing about like a dingy in a force nine gale could be called such, took about ten minutes. The driver twittered on for the whole drive, in between furiously lashing at the device with a small whip. As a method of driving the machine, it made no sense to me. All I could think was the driver was hitting it with a stick because that's how you got a real camel to do anything. I tried to ask the driver about this, but his English was so broken and accented he might as well have been speaking his own language for all I followed what he was saying. About the most I managed to gather between a flurry of Arabic insults he hurled at the machine was 'Designed, be like real camel, but three times faster.' Given as to how I was being tossed about more than a fat girl on a waterbed, I'm not sure it was worth the speed.

At the foot of the ancient majestic monuments to the time of the pharaohs, there were a bunch of tourist centres. All flying the flag as it were, the old Union Jack that is. It struck me, as such places always did, a symptom of the British abroad, to always seek to recreate the old country. Visiting the pyramids was like visiting Lake Windermere at the height of the season, or some old castle in Cornwall. Little gift shops, café's and cake stalls lined the road. Of course, there were local stalls pitted about as well, to add some authenticity to it all. Selling cheap Bakelite models of the great pyramid, with a little union flag sticking out of the top. But other than that it could be any attraction in England. Well, if it weren't for the dust and heat. The odd pile of camel dung. The locals, shouting in Arabic. And of course, the tents pitched between tea shops selling carpets and steam bongs. In effect, it was all the bits of Britain I missed the least. All cream teas, tat and polite little finger sandwiches.

I wandered amongst the shops looking for some place called The Victoria Tea Parlour where I was supposed to be meeting Miss Wells. It was an exercise in dodging beggars and hawkers alike. I'd no doubt there would be pickpockets too, but I relied on the uniform and my demeanour to dissuade anyone from taking a dip. Any good pickpocket knows a bad mark when they see one, and even a bad dipper knows better than to dip a uniform.

The day was getting hotter, and my temper was getting the better of me when I had to shove away another Arab trying to sell me a 'genuine' statuette of Ra from Tutankhamun's tomb. Judging by how many of them I was being offered old Tut must have had a tomb larger than the great pyramid itself. Ancient Egypt's lower kingdom must've extended further than Egyptologists believed as well, as one had a 'Made in Stoke on Trent' sticker on its base. Still, it was good to see the potteries could still find a market for their tat, if nothing else.

Finally, after an argument with a man selling sweetmeats about my lack of desire to taste his candied goat parts, I spotted a little tea parlour, nestled between the front paws of the Sphinx. Which was both my intended destination and the worst example of Imperial encroachment I'd seen so far in Giza.

Luckily, I also spotted Maythorpe along with a couple of thugs in uniform I took to be the local police. They both wore fezzes with goggles attached on spring drops, as well as copper epaulettes that must've been like strapping hot-plates to your shoulders in this heat. I was, however, more concerned about the side arms in their white leatherette holsters. It was obvious that Maythorpe hadn't yet given up on the idea of feeling my collar. I'd have called him an idiot, but the words I actually muttered under my breath were somewhat more choice.

I ducked between two stalls and tried to be inconspicuous. As I was wearing my Company uniform, that was not as easy as it might have been. Red really is not the colour to wear if one is trying to sneak around. Despite this impediment, I did my best to remain hidden from view and watched the ever-earnest Maythorpe direct the police about their business. Wondering to myself what Maythorpe was doing when the theory of ambushes was explained at Sandhurst. Why he thought standing around in the middle of the road in uniform with two policemen at his side was a good plan, I can't imagine.

Regardless, with Maythorpe being so conspicuous I was tempted to chalk the whole expedition off as a bad idea. I was about to turn round and return to the ship, when a fight broke out between two local stall holders. They started yelling at each other in Arabic, that most aggressive of languages to my British ears. For all I knew they could've been lovers quarrelling, or two old friends happy to see each other, and sharing a boisterous joke. Though judging by the reaction of the two local policemen with Maythorpe, it was more serious than that. The local fuzz, or should that be fez, ran in to stop the argument escalating to violence as one of the stall holders pulled a knife from under his robes, all of which added further to the general ruckus.

Maythorpe didn't help matters, running after the fez shouting the odds. He was greatly irritated by the sound of him. From my hidden vantage point I found it hard not to laugh at the fool, so laugh I did, as he gesticulated wildly at the officers. He was clearly of the school of thought which dictated that when you spoke to the natives, you did so loudly and with much arm waving to negate the language barrier. The two fez equally clearly didn't give a damn about what he had to say right then. They had their hands full with the man with the knife and a crowd enthusiastically egging him on. It was the kind of street theatre that was the same the world over.

It was petty of me to laugh, I am sure, but I am a petty man at times, and seeing Maythorpe's ill-conceived plans go to ruin pleased me no end.

Small victories and what not.

I was still laughing to myself when someone came up behind me. I caught a whiff of perfume, which considering the overwhelming smell of the market, camel and scones are an odd mix, came as a pleasant new assault on my senses.

Not least, because I recognised the scent from the Captain's cabin the previous day.

"The thing about arranging a distraction, my dear Mr Smyth, is once those you're distracting are, not to put too fine a point on it, distracted, one needs to make the most of it," the wearer of the perfume said, while nudging me forward gently but with a certain firm insistence.

"Of course, Miss Wells, of course," I said, still in good humour and, taking the hint, I walked towards the tea room, skirting the edge of the baying rabble. Maythorpe had now progressed from gesticulation to outright arguing with the local fez, loudly too, just to add to the general uproar.

It was a measure of my buoyant mood that as I fell into step with the delightful Miss Wells, I wasn't even fazed by her looming, ever present, companion. She did hurry us along, however, no doubt as aware as I was that the distraction would only last so long and the irritating Maythorpe would undoubtedly be a problem once more when order was restored. Though as a local fez steam wagon turned into the street, air horns blaring I came to the conclusion it might be a while before everything calmed down.

I risked a look over my shoulder as we ducked through the curtain draped over the doorway. In time to see the knife wielder throw his blade aside and shrug at all the fuss, while Maythorpe was surrounded by half a dozen fez now. All of whom seemed more interested in arguing with the English officer than arresting anyone. Maythorpe seemed incandescent with rage, though it might just have been sunburn.

Inside the café, we were greeted by an Arab woman who was dressed for a Dorsett country fair. She even had a hint of a West Country accent mixed in with her local patois. This made for a strange mix of language.

"Take a seat my loves, and the prophet watch over you," she said as she showed us to a private sitting room in the back of the tea shop. It had a fine red leather settee with odd brass handles on the arms, nestled into the corner, but no other seats, or even a table beside it. Which struck me as a little peculiar.

While it was, of course, improper of me to join Miss Wells on the settee, she indicated that I should sit beside her, so who was I to argue? Besides, such gentlemanly manners as I might possess were not going to get in the way of sitting beside her if she wanted me to.

"You may want to hold on, my loves, Allah be merciful," the Dorsettian Arab said from behind her veil, as she wiped her hands on her daisy print cotton pinny. Before this had a chance to register as an odd thing to say, there was a loud clunking sound. The settee heaved, and as the floor began to rise around us, I realised that she meant the handles and not to each other.

To be more exact, the floor was not actually rising, as was my first befuddled impression. Instead, the settee had started to descend down through the floor, or rather the section of flooring it was stood upon did.

"What the hell?" I managed to say, aghast.

"I did say we should have tea beneath the Sphinx," Miss Wells replied, sitting primly, with one hand nestled on the brass handle at her side, and an utter lack of concern on her face. Her self-confidence managed to make my own surprise seem all the more foolish.

At the corner of the settee, there was a small mechanical music box. A wax cylinder within it started to turn as we descended and a slightly irritating tune began to play. Crackling badly and partially drowned out by the sound of heavy cogwheels grinding at the side of the settee, it was nonetheless recognisable as the one about the girl from that beach resort in Brazil, going for a stroll.

'DoBee, DoBee, Do Do, DoooBi,

DoBee, DoBee, Do Do, DoooBi….'

This was, I decided, quite the most irritating thing to happen to me all morning.

CHAPTER 10

Below The Sands

"Mr Smyth. It's so good to see you in more auspicious circumstances. You're acquainted with Miss Wells as well, I see. How positively delightful. Do please come through."

The man speaking wasn't one I ever remembered meeting. He was also, how can I put this, 'odd' is perhaps the best word, though it doesn't really convey very much. Odd is such a bland word at times. Uncanny perhaps would be closer to the mark. There was definitely something uncanny about him. Unsettling too come to that.

It was, I concluded, the spectacles that did it, definitely the spectacles. The lenses were just too thick; they magnified his eyes in such a way that when you looked straight at him, it was like looking at them through a pair of goldfish bowls. It was that and the way his hair was permanently greased down flat like limp seaweed out of the water. He also seemed to be always smiling too hard, as if he was making himself do so because smiling was a human thing to do and he wished to appear human. Which as that's what he was, was all the more odd, when you think about it. There was this forced quality about him, a desperation to be liked, but in trying so hard to be likeable, he failed utterly in that goal. To be honest just looking at him made my skin crawl.

I'll admit a little hindsight may be creeping into my description here, but even with the merest of first impressions, I could tell he was an oddball, in a way that made even the oddest of people seem normal in comparison.

"Hannibal and I are barely acquainted, Mr Gates," Miss Wells replied, somewhat stiffly before I could say anything myself. I got a distinct impression from her tone that she didn't much like the man who'd been waiting to greet us when the sofa reached the bottom of the shaft.

For his part, he didn't seem to notice.

"Oh I am sure you will be in due time. You are after all both working towards the same goal and doing so under protest. Such things draw people together, or so they tell me," he said, still smiling.

I wasn't sure I followed what he was saying. I wasn't entirely sure he knew much about people either. He did, however, seem to be implying that Miss Wells was working for The Ministry under duress, not unlike myself. I filed that little snippet away for future reference.

"I'm surprised they let you out of the lab, Mr Gates," Miss Wells said, a touch of venom in her voice.

"Mr Gates…" I muttered, with vague civility, while holding out my hand for a shake. His name rang bells in the back of my mind, though right at that moment I couldn't tell you why.

He looked at my hand as if for all the world he'd no idea what to do with it. Then looked back up at me with that same false smile. Miss Wells shook her head at me to signal I was wasting my time, so I shrugged and put my hand back down. A tad more disconcerted than before, if that was possible.

"Erm, yes, well... M wishes to discuss things with you both in the meeting tomb," Gates said, then turned and began to lead us away through the complex.

I tried not to think about the word 'tomb', assuming, quite wrongly it turned out, that it was a slip of the tongue.

"Is he entirely all there?" I whispered to Miss Wells as we walked a few paces behind him.

The lady, however, declined to comment, taking a sharp breath instead and just shaking her head at me as we followed Gates around the corner. Which was where we walked past the first of the Sleep Men.

It was standing stock still in an alcove, so still indeed that he could've just been a manikin. Though I've yet to see a day when fashion's ever whimsical nature dictates a Harrods dummy be dressed in a heavy black woollen coat, top hat, and gas mask. It gave me a shiver to see him, despite the heat which was as prevalent down there as it was above ground. That they could dress so in such heat just made them seem even less human, if that was possible.

That Miss Wells's own guardian was a few steps behind us, keeping steady pace as his iron-shod boots hit the stone floor with an eerie rhythm did nothing to help my unease. I had expected the one she had in tow. He had been there every other time I had seen her after all. I had, however, hoped to avoid any more of them. A hope in which it would seem I was going to be very disappointed. The one in the corridor was only the first down there. We passed several more as we moved through the complex of dusty hallways and rusting iron doors.

The stones looked old. The doors, for all their rust, actually looked new in comparison. Installed by craftsmen who clearly had cared more about the practical than the aesthetic. Steel bolts had been driven into the sandstone walls, and frames hammered into place.

There were paintings on the walls. Ancient things, the like of which you would expect to see in a museum. Egyptian of course. Those odd little pictograms, and figures in odd hats. The paintings were all flecked and worn but still impressive for all that. As we walked, I realised the whole complex stretched out under the sphinx and must have dated back millennia. For all, I knew the pyramids themselves were constructed over those same ancient tunnels. Hidden away under the desert sands, lost and forgotten, until the British Empire decided to co-opt them for its own nefarious needs. Raking scratches into walls and pictograms as they hung doors and bulkheads alike with little thought for posterity. Rigging up lights down forgotten corridors, by stringing up cables with galvanised hooks, with the same lack of regard for the history within those walls. An Egyptologist would have a fit were they to see the damage the Empire had done here.

I passed at least one painting of a pharaoh with a hook nailed into his eye in order to run a rubber-coated electrical cable. If I was of a philosophical turn of mind that would have made for a wonderful metaphor for the Empire's occupation of Egypt no doubt. For my sins, I found it more amused me than anything else. Though I suspect Miss Wells didn't appreciate the mirth it caused me, considering the sharp look she gave me.

After we had trekked what seemed like a mile or more underground, we came to another of those rusted iron doors, this one with two Sleep Men standing as silent guardians. Their heads turned in unison to watch us walk towards them. Causing me to miss their ridged brethren we had pasted earlier.

Gates fumbled for a while with a large bunch of keys, all fidgety and nervous. This was either his normal state, or we disturbed him as much as he disturbed me. I got the feeling once more that he was a man unused to dealing with people, but then I got the feeling he wasn't quite able to understand what people were. This, in hindsight, would explain much about William Gates.

Eventually, he got the door open, which was all to the good as far as I was concerned. The ominous, brooding presence of the men in heavy coats was playing with my own nerves, and I was sick of dim-lit corridors. If truth be told, I was sick of being in the dark in general. If nothing else, beyond those door there may be some answers at least.

Ignorance is not, I find, bliss. Not knowing what is going on is bloody dangerous in fact. Like a footman walking in on Old Iron Knickers helping her old flame to fit a new ring. It could get you in a world of trouble.

"In here then, both of you, come on now," Gates said, still fidgeting strangely as he ushered us through the door. He pulled on a large contactor switch as he did so, bringing the lights on in the room beyond.

The room was large. A couple of dozen yards or so square, with four columns forming a square in the centre of the room where there was what at first looked to be a stone desk set up. Between the far two columns, some scaffolding had been installed, built with the same lack of care as the doors and lighting in the passageways. Large disc shaped things were bolted to it. Dozens of them. The discs were like brass lined portholes and of all different sizes. In them were all kinds of images, a different view in each.

The images themselves were clouded. Occasionally static would interfere with them, making them drop in and out of focus. It was like looking out upon a hundred different places at once through goldfish bowls. I remember wondering in an amused way if this was how Gates saw the world through his own jam jar thick glasses. It's strange what thoughts will cross your mind at times like that.

Gates ushered us towards the stone desk. It was only as I got closer I recognised it for what it actually was. A relic as old as this complex itself, which had been put to a new use. As this dawned on me, I wondered if the corpse it once contained was still inside the sarcophagus, wrapped up tight in its bandages, its inner organs still in jars elsewhere in this strange complex. I couldn't decide what would have offended me most, if it had been removed from its resting place, or if it still lay within while its tomb was being used as a reading desk.

I pondered on which ancient king may lay within it. Waiting to start his journey to the afterlife. 'Poor sod,' I thought to myself. 'You die, they pull your brains out through your nose, stick your heart in a jar, then some bastard comes along a few thousand years later and doesn't even use a coaster when he puts his coffee mug on your tomb.'

After this moment of strange reflection, I found myself drawn to stare at the different pictures on the porthole devices. I was fascinated by the way they moved, the way the images seemed to each be from the perspective of an individual. Most were hard to place, they could've been almost anywhere, but in others, I saw images that sparked recognition.

A view of a street in London, one just off King's Cross, I was sure, because I recognised a public house that swung into view. A tatty little place but one that did boast a decent hand pumped ale.

Another was of Venice, if I am any judge, the Grand Canal, I suspected, though the steam-powered gondola floating past was a bit of a clue in its case.

Yet another I recognised as somewhere in America from the flag of the confederates hanging tattered and bullet-ridden from some white stone mansion or other.

There were plenty of others that sparked no recognition in me. But they were often inside buildings or looking out across a table at someone or other. A couple were just black and featureless, yet the little lights on the side that flashed would suggest they too were working.

Then I saw one that made me pause, in the corner of the array. The view from which was of the array itself. It took me a moment to realise it was a view from close to the spot on which I stood. I thought the camera must be on the back of the column to my right, but as I started to turn to look, I realised to my horror the image was panning with me.

"What are these?" I asked Gates, already a little certain of what the answer would be. The view was disturbing. I walked towards the porthole, and once I got close enough my own reflection stared back ghosting on the glass, then ghosting again inside it. A double vision of my own reflection, one inside the other, then as I got closer still I saw those reflections going further back, into infinity. A view of my reflection from my own eye in the screen.

"It's just something I am tinkering with. I've not got it working perfectly yet, the reception varies sometimes, and the delay factor needs some work," Gates replied with the enthusiasm of a boffin for his creation.

I looked sharply at him. The bells that his name rang earlier suddenly chiming loudly.

"The spider," I said. It wasn't a question, though Gates didn't seem to realise that.

"Arachno-Oculus," he corrected, and in doing so he almost sounded like he was chiding me.

"Spider, Mr Gates, it's a god damned spider!" I snapped back in return.

Miss Wells looked as uncomfortable with the conversation as I was with the thought of the thing in my eye. This was the man responsible for its creation. I can't pretend I wasn't tempted to do some bloody violence upon him at that moment. The fact that there was a lady present didn't do much to dissuade me a great deal either, truth be told. Ungentlemanly it might be, but as I've mentioned, I'm not so much the gentleman as I pretend to be.

Besides which, I suspected Miss Wells wasn't the kind of wallflower to be offended by acts of violence. The way she'd been looking at Gates since we arrived made me suspect she might well hold the desire to thrash the snivelling little swine herself.

"I will admit some similarities in the design, Mr Smyth. Indeed it was how we came up with the name. Latin, you know. Spider eye. Clever, isn't it. I suppose if the Arachno-Oculus is a spider as you say then this is its web. Well, this and the host array in London. With it we can monitor The Ministry's 'ahem' web of agents throughout the wide world, if you'll pardon the pun." He chortled at his own joke.

No one else did.

"I really don't see why that upsets you so much. There is no need to be antagonistic. Indeed it would please me greatly if you could temper your language. I am you see, unused to profanity," Gates said, suddenly looking a little flustered.

I growled at him, but in a moment he was somewhere else, lost in a well of thought that had little to do with the rest of the conversation. Ignoring me completely now he muttered something under his breath. As if he was trying to grasp an idea that had just come to him. "Web World Wide... hum... yes, that sounds, no, it's not quite right, yet somehow... perhaps... you see it is an iatrical web of connections... of course, yes, there are connections, but it's a web, a web, an iatrical web or a net maybe... damn it why are names so difficult to get right?"

Whatever he was trying to figure out, it clearly had nothing much to do with reality. A place William Gates seemed to pass through only on the way to somewhere else most of the time. He was lost in his own erratic mind, which was getting us nowhere. An observation that Miss Wells seemed to share, as she coughed loudly before she started to berate the greasy haired pipsqueak.

"I think, William, that Mr Smyth's antagonism towards you stems from having one of your creepy little devices inserted within his eye against his will," she snarled, which had the desired effect of pulling him back to the conversation. Her voice contained a level of spite to it that almost shocked me. Not that I'm unused to women of a forceful nature. Indeed, I'm rather fond of them if truth be told. I grew up surrounded by strong-willed women in the East End, and I'll admit to having an affection for a certain forthrightness about a lady, in some quarters at any rate. I just didn't expect such a tone from Miss Wells here. I was however gratified to realise she was doing so in my defence; it gave me a little hope for some further mutual understanding down the way.

Gates was clearly unused to strong women, or possibly women in any regard. So became flustered once more.

"Well," he stammered, "I, I, I can't be held responsible for, for that, and while I apologise if that is the case, Mr Smyth, it really is not my fault. I just design the devices. I have no control over what your masters do with them. As such, I feel I really must protest..."

As far as I was concerned he could protest all he liked, it wasn't going to dissuading me from giving him a good lamping if I had half a chance. Oh, I know it may seem petty of me. What he was saying was perfectly true. I couldn't hold him to task for the actions of The Ministry. Any more than it would make sense for some half rotten plague victim to beat up the inventor of the virus bombs after they were used on Washington at the end of the second American civil war. But I'd be the last person to hold it against anyone who survived that holocaust wanting to plant one on the eminent bastard who did. Just like I wouldn't have lost a lick of sleep if I had given William Gates a black eye right then.

Even small victories are victories after all.

Indeed, I was in the process of pulling back my fist to give him a good old East End hello when there was a crackle of static from over near the sarcophagus, followed by a voice I'd never wanted to hear again. Speaking out of the ether.

"Mr Smyth. We would take it as a kindness if you did not strike the good professor Gates. I would have to censor you, and I deplore the need for violence over something so trivial."

To be more precise the voice came out of a radio speaker. But crackly though it was, I could still detect the self-same nasal smugness about it. It grated on me somewhat, as I am sure you can appreciate. I was still more than tempted to ignore its utterings, after all, it might have been the only chance I ever got to pummel Gates, and I sorely wanted to. But regardless I relaxed my arm, collected myself and turned towards the direction of the voice. Memories of the pain Gates's little pet in my eye could inflict were enough to keep me in line, as I had no doubt our friend on the other end of the speaker would have no compunction against using it on me if I didn't relent.

Some victories are, after all, too small.

"Mr M, so pleased to hear from you, old boy. I can't tell you how much I've missed our conversations," I said to the air as I turned. Then was unsurprised to see the voice's owner's visage filling the largest of the porthole screens. He winced ever so slightly at the 'Mr M' as if it had left an ill taste in his mouth.

Which did much to improve my mood.

"Front and centre, Mr Smyth, if you would be so kind, and you as well, Miss Wells. Gates, go play with some of your equipment elsewhere if you please. Let's keep you out of Smyth's reach for a while, shall we?" M said through the speaker.

It was hard to tell from the image where he was, beyond he was sat behind a desk in an office somewhere. In London, I assumed, given in the background there hung a picture of dear old sticky Vicky herself, but for all I knew he could be in the next room along.

"I should really monitor the reception to make sure the delay across the iatrical-web doesn't become too distorted…" Gates uttered, making no effort to move, other than to fiddle with some equipment on the sarcophagus.

"The what?" M asked, looking irritated.

"The iatrical-web, it's what we are calling this now," Gates replied. Clearly pleased with his new found word.

"No!" M replied sternly. "I do not think we are."

"But…"

"No, Professor Gates, now off with you."

"But. The reception…"

"No, Gates, I am sure we will be fine, so off you go now," M said, pleasantness returning to his tone, but pleasantness which did nothing to disguise the dismissal.

"Well if you're sure…"

"Quite sure, thank you," M said and ushered him off with a wave of his hand.

Gates wandered off, sloped is perhaps another word, and in a couple of moments had left the room.

Silently I watched him go and regretted the lost opportunity to rearrange his nose.

"Irritating little man," muttered M after Gates had gone, in what was the most human display I'd seen from him. A definite chink in his civil service armour. I almost smiled at this realisation.

"I don't suppose you could tell me what all this is about, 'Mr' M?" I asked after a moment, which was redundant I suspected. It was far and away the most likely reason I and my delightful companion had been dragged below the sands, but it gave me a sense of self-determination to ask.

"You don't know?" Miss Wells said, having the decency to sound surprised.

"Unfortunately," M replied for me with an unexpected amount of regret showing in his voice. "We required Mr Smyth be on his way rather urgently and we did not have the liberty nor the time to give him a full briefing. Other actors are on the stage and time has become an imperative."

The other actors part of that statement worried at me. I suspected I'd met one of them already in the form of a particularly vicious little Not-in-any-conceivable-way-actually-a-maid. With that in mind, other actors meant… "The Americans…"

I uttered that thinking I did so under my breath, but apparently the microphones in there could pick up almost everything.

"Among others, yes. Affairs move swiftly, as they are want to do these days. There are the Russians as well of course, but most regretfully there are also certain ill-informed sections of the British government that have taken upon themselves to instigate some actions also," M told us.

The latter came as a surprise to me, but with hindsight, it shouldn't have done, Whitehall was ever full of different factions pulling against each other. I'd thought, mistakenly, The Ministry would be above all that. I should've known better. In my time in the Royal Air Navy we'd a saying, The Ministry of Defence has to be prepared to fight three enemies, foreign governments, insurgents and the bloody home office, and it's the latter which were our biggest enemy.

When M paused, letting this revelation sink in, I came to a realisation, but being a tad slow, I came to it a moment after Miss Wells.

"Maythorpe…" she said, without making any effort to hide her distaste. I suspected she'd had a run-in with him just before I had been released from the coal box.

"So it would appear, yes. It's no coincidence he is aboard the same airship as Smyth and yourself, Miss Wells. Our friends in the MOD are getting chummy with the Foreign Office and getting creative into the bargain, it would seem. They have chosen to meddle in things far beyond them. It appears they got word that our friend Mr Smyth here was being sent to India. I suspect they do not know why and just wish to make trouble for their betters. It is regretful that in doing so, we had to reveal your own involvement in our plans, Miss Wells."

The way M said the word 'regrettable' implied it was 'regrettable' for them, not for The Ministry. Whitehall power brokers, it appeared, may be about to have a bad time of it all told. In other circumstances, I would've been delighted to hear this. If I wasn't tangled up in The Ministry's machinations myself. Or at least if I could see a way to detangle myself from them…

"Still," M continued, "if needs must, we can always have that pawn removed from the equation."

The callous lack of concern with which M said this caused me to choke slightly. Maythorpe may be a right royal pain in my rear, and I'd be lying if I were to say I wouldn't be delighted to give him a good kicking should the opportunity arise. But I'd no particular wish to see him killed off out of hand, utter twerp though he may be. He was doubtless blissfully unaware that he was being used by Whitehall mandarins. A prawn, for want of M's actual word, in a game he couldn't even envisage, fishy swine though he was. But the implications of M's rather cold statement were all too obvious.

"It needn't come to that. Maythorpe's a buffoon at best. I doubt he even realises why he was put on the flight," I said quickly, though for all my distaste of the subject under discussion, I wasn't entirely sure why I was defending him.

'Twerp wouldn't even be grateful if he knew you were defending him, Harry…' I thought to myself, but if it saved the idiot's life, I'd enjoy telling him that if I ever was in a position to do so. If only to take the wind out of his ever pompous sails.

"I do not require your advice on the matter, Mr Smyth. If it becomes necessary to remove him from the equation, we will do so. As of this moment, however, his actions have revealed the hands of his masters are at play, so steps will be taken in that quarter. Regardless of these trivial distractions, we must turn to matters at hand."

"Would be about time…" I muttered, which raised an eyebrow from M but no comment.

"I will beg your forgiveness, Miss Wells, for repeating things you already know, but we have to bring Smyth up to speed so if you will bear with me, my dear," M said and received the smallest of nods from Miss Wells before he continued. For all the polite nature of this interchange, the look on Miss Wells face spoke volumes; it was the same look of distaste she had earlier reserved for Mr Gates.

"Now Smyth, tell me, have you ever heard of Muldarin?" M asked, and for a moment I thought he might even be joking. Not that the trout faced swine had the sense of humour for anything so elaborate.

"Of course," I replied, "but wasn't he killed some years ago in the Madras uprising? I am sure the East India Company made quite a show of their victory over him. Didn't they parade his body through the streets of Delhi or something?"

"Doubtless they did, but the name had been used before and will probably be used again. Muldarin is a rallying cry, Smyth, for India's disaffected. Due to the bungling of the East India Company, the disaffected would seem to be the larger proportion of the subcontinent's population."

That was true enough. The Company were far from the kindest of landlords. From what I knew, Muldarin was a kind of folk hero in India. He or, at least, men bearing his name, had been fighting their little insurrections against the Raj for the last fifty years or so. Think of him as an Indian Robin Hood. At least, if Robin Hood robbed from the rich, then cut their throats, slaughtered their children, crucified their servants and raised bloody wars of insurrection, in between giving a few loose rupees to the poor.

"There is always unrest in India," I said, which is a bit like saying there's always tea in China, or Americans are always fond of guns. But despite myself, I was curious now.

"Indeed there is, Smyth, and most useful it is too," M replied.

I had to check to make sure I'd heard the last correctly.
"Useful?"

"Divide and conquer, Mr Smyth. Hindu, Sikh, Muslims, and the dozens of other little sects that hold the religious hearts of the continent all have one thing and only one thing in common. Hatred of the British and the hold we have upon it. The Buddhists are none too fond of us either. Each would happily raise arms against us and evict us from our rightful dominion. But what they all hate far more is the thought of one of the others being in charge. The British presence keeps India from going the way of the dis-United States and crumbling into an array of despotic fiefdoms, and theological totalitarianisms. Something we have long averted by the preservation of the status quo. To whit our dominance and rule. The occasional insurrection puts the fear of god into the locals that they will fall under the sway of one of the other factions. Nothing binds India to the British more than the occasional mutiny of a mad Mullah, or Hindu fanatics. On occasion, we have started insurrections ourselves when the locals have not been obliging."

I would claim to be shocked by this last revelation, but I wasn't. Neither was Miss Wells.

"A sad indictment of my people," she said, the melancholy in her voice lending honesty to her words. "Sadly one that is probably correct."

"Indeed, and one that has been the undoing of Muldarin more than once. His last incarnation was as a Hindu, we believe, and it was the Sikhs who gave away his plans in Madras and brought about his downfall. That and a flight of Her Majesty's finest airships, of course," M said, and I felt a tad uncomfortable with the conversation while stood alongside Miss Wells.

I know all about the firebombing of Madras. Everyone did, it was almost legendary for its brutality. Indiscriminate was the word that was usually bandied about if the subject ever came up. The city and most of the countryside around it burned for weeks they said. A hundred airships dumped tar bombs over the whole area. Scorched earth was the least of it. They say the fires could be seen glowing on the horizon from Calcutta, unlikely as that was. What was well-known was that nothing and no one walked out of Madras afterwards. Few airmen I'd ever met spoke proudly of that victory. I'd met none who would ever have admitted being on those ships at the time.

Miss Wells had visibly stiffened at the mention of Madras. I can't say I blamed her.

The British papers originally had the effrontery to call the whole fiasco a 'weak display of our Imperial power' because they had called for virus bombs to be used in retaliation for the atrocities Muldarin had committed. Once pictures of Madras after the bombings started to appear, the newspapers backtracked. Even the editor of The Times took a step back from his more verbose flag waving for a while. Madras was the Empire at its worst, voices in support of self-rule grew stronger on the back of it, and for a while the national collective shame of it all made it seem independence was a possibility.

Twenty years had passed under Tower Bridge since then and the Empire still had its crown jewel. All being said, it was to the good of India, at least to my British eyes. India flourished, or so I was always told. But even so, few Englishmen would be willing to look an Indian in the face and say the word Madras. I certainly wouldn't for one…

I had little time to reflect on all this as M pushed on with the briefing.

"Be that as it may, the name Muldarin is mentioned once more on the lips of rabble rousers on the sub-continent. Which would normally be a worry for our friends in the MOD and the India office. But other matters are delicate right now, and we suspect there is more to this than some Hindu warlord. Indeed, we suspect that the man behind this latest incarnation is not Indian at all but someone else entirely. If it proves to be whom we believe it to be, bigger issues are at stake. Which is why we are sending you, Mr Smyth. We want you to find a way to join him."

"What? Are you serious?" I said with entirely genuine surprise. It sounded a damn fool idea to me.

"Quite serious, my dear boy, quite serious," M replied, holding up an old photograph to the camera. It was an ancient looking sepia thing which must have dated back a hundred years or more. "We believe this man is behind the resurfacing of Muldarin's name in northern India and that his designs are not the foolish idea of India liberty but to bring about the downfall of the Empire itself."

To say I was surprised by this revelation is an understatement. Shocked would be closer to the mark. Stirring up rebellion in the powder keg of India was one thing, but bringing down the Empire... that was unthinkable. The British Empire would outlast the sun, as I'm sure every Englishman would agree. As a concept, it was almost laughable.

I found myself peering at the photograph, oddly fascinated by it. It was the image of an unassuming man in his mid-thirties with a neatly cut moustache, trimmed wavy hair and wire-rimmed spectacles. A man who looked born to be either a civil servant or a country vet. A man to bring down the greatest empire the world had ever known he wasn't. More a mouse of a man, a meek, mild mouse at that. A bank manager's lackey, or a clerk in some minor local government office perhaps. What he didn't look like was a rabble-rousing rebel who could set India alight.

Looks may be deceiving, but they ain't that deceiving...

"Who the hell is he?" I asked, speaking my thoughts aloud as much as asking.

"Herbert George Wells," said Miss Wells, her voice lacking its normal caustic tone. "My great-grandfather."

I looked at her, bemused. This was all swiftly getting more ridiculous. To be her great-grandfather, he would be over a hundred. Though judging by the age of the photograph that would be a liberal estimate. Yet something about the name, beyond his connection to my Miss Wells, rang a bell with me. Though I couldn't say why exactly, at least until M expanded a little on the man in question.

"Indeed, Miss Wells's great-grandfather, and the reason she is also in our employ. A fatuous writer of fictions who once garnered some little fame amongst pseudo-intellectuals and idle dreamers. Before he spent some time serving in Her Majesty's government as an advisor in the late 1800s. Until his philosophies ceased to be in tune with those of the crown," M told me, while the granddaughter in question had a look of quiet fury about her. I found myself wondering why she was working with The Ministry. A suspicion that she might have little choice in the matter began to form in the back of my mind.

"You mean when he decided helping the British Empire grow ever stronger was an error," she said, pleasantly enough. If there was venom to her words, she hid it well.

"Indeed, a mistaken belief on his part, I assure you. The Empire holds the world together. Indeed he helped make it so. As such my predecessors allowed him to retire with grace and disappear. But then we all make mistakes, do we not, Miss Wells?"

She scowled at the image in the porthole screen but declined to rise to whatever bait was being dangled in front of her. M looked pleased with her reaction regardless. Ever one to goad a subordinate when he had the chance. Whatever mistake lay in her past, it was a barb he took delight in throwing her way.

"This is the last picture we have on file, and as you can see, it was taken some time ago. We are, however, currently given to believe he has resurfaced in northern India. Given the nature of his previous services to the crown, we need to know what he is up to. Which is where you come into all this, Mr Smyth."

"Hang on how old is that picture? It looks...?"

"It was taken in 1915 at the Franco-Prussian accord conference in Berlin. He was part of the crown's diplomatic oversight commission," M said blandly as if he was talking about events that happened only recently.

"Then he must be almost as old as Queen Vic?" I said, knowing full well that was improbable.

British science may have kept Iron Knickers young for a couple of hundred years, but no one quite knew how. At least no one who had not signed the official secrets act in the blood of their first born. While I am not a 'Cult of Reginis' nut job like half the Church of England seem to be these days, it's hard to argue with their belief it was a sign of her blessed nature.

Mainly, it's true, because if you did argue with them, they might have you arrested under archaic blasphemy laws and try to stone you to death.

My old mum was a bit of a believer, truth be told, so on the occasions she was sober enough, which weren't very prevalent, she would try to explain to me how 'Blessed Victoria' was a true link between the people of the Empire and God. Hobbs Leviathan made flesh, a head of state that sat truly at the right hand of God. Not that my old mum would know Hobbs if he was selling her gin. But she was fond of the hymn singing, and the idea of redemption, just as long as it didn't impinge on her ability to buy gin.

In one of her more devout phases, she would occasionally drag me along to their coffee mornings which tended towards the fanatical, and the less said about the church fetes, the better. But for all their fervent fanaticism it was easy to believe that they might have a point.

Old Clockwork Knickers's unnaturally long life had indeed held the Empire together. Without her it may have fallen much like the United States did in the thirties. She was the core foundation around which the state was built and while the CofE's fanaticisms left me cold, I would've been the first to agree that it had at least spared us the elevation of the last dozen or so Princes of Wales. Which was a mercy.

Chinless inbreeds the lot of them.

But I digress, and M seemed keen to move the conversation on, regardless of my incredulity.

"Indeed, Smyth, but that is of little note. What is important is that we must discover what he is up to now. He is in a unique position to be a danger to all, so we must discover his plans in order that steps can be taken. You are uniquely placed to gain his confidence, we believe, so that is your task. Find him, find out his plans, and we will take whatever steps are necessary at that juncture, no matter how regrettable they may be."

"Why me?" I asked, which was, as it ever is, a pointless question, but one always asks it in situations like these. Though I will admit, one has seldom found one's self in situations quite like these.

Unsurprisingly M ignored my question.

"The details of your assignment are in the documents before you, Mr Smyth," he instructed. "It goes without saying that we will be watching you and England expects you to do your duty. Miss Wells will help you with the details. She has her own investment in this enterprise. The documents do not leave this room. You can return to your ship once you have digested the details. Now be about your business, I have other matters to attend to, good day."

And with that, the screen went blank.

"This is insane," I said, speaking my thoughts aloud.

Miss Wells just shrugged and stared up at the multiple screens of the array. She seemed to be looking for something.

"Indeed, but then when is anything the British do sane?" she replied after a few moments.

Despite everything, I chafed slightly at that comment. But I could hardly blame her for her bitterness. I let it slide by and started to leaf through the papers.

I found myself once again wondering while I did so what hold The Ministry had over Miss Wells. She obviously had little love for the Empire given all the little digs about it she'd imparted. If this H.G. character was indeed her great-grandfather, that could skew things either way. Relations within a family can be as complex as international affairs, just as illogical and just as damn bloody come to that. Regardless, it struck me strange she would be willingly working for The Ministry.

Against them possibly…

Of all the questions I had buzzing around my head, as I tried to find some kind of logic to the papers before me, that question of Miss Wells's involvement in all this was the one that kept occurring to me.

And yes, I have to admit that had she been less attractive I may have cared far less. I wouldn't claim to be proud of that, but it is the truth. Why I feel the need to burden you, dear reader, with such truths, well sometimes a man just needs to be honest about such things. To himself, if no one else, and in this, you are my conscience. We all have to divest some of our guilt once in a while, but perhaps I say too much for now.

In any regard, I found it hard to focus on the papers before me as the question burned at me, so a few minutes later I just plain asked her why.

She stared back at me for a while. I guess she had no great inclination to trust me with her confidence. Then she turned back to the screens and said nothing for a while. Then she pointed and said, "Look at the screens, Mr Smyth. Tell me, what do you see?"

I put the papers I was failing to read aside, looked up and followed her direction. She was pointing towards the screen relaying the spider's view through my eye. I saw my reflection on the surface of the screen become a double image like before, as was the reflection of Miss Wells. She moved her finger, and I followed it to a second screen next to my own. The image it showed was much the same. Same double image from the reflections on the glass. Same view of the array from where we stood. For a second it struck me as odd. Why would they feed the same image through two screens? Why duplicate the feed from my eye, when all the other screens showed different views?

Yes, I know…

In my defence, it had been a long few days, with intermittent bouts of blackness that had nothing to do with sleep. I was not thinking my clearest.

'Two screens, oh,' I realised somewhat slowly and closed my left eye, watching one of them go dark as I did so, while the other turned to look at me from the side. In itself, that's very strange, to see yourself as others see you.

I opened my left eye once more and turned to look at her, watching with horrified fascination as she placed a finger on her lower eyelid and pulled it down so I could see a glimmer of metal where only her whites should have been.

Her dislike of William Gates all made sense now.

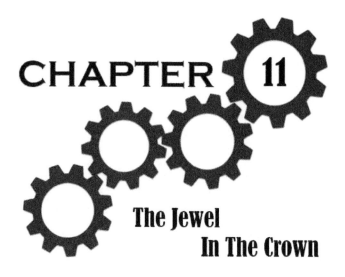

CHAPTER 11

The Jewel
In The Crown

According to the guidebooks, 'Company House in Calcutta is perhaps the greatest symbol of British rule over the subcontinent. A sight that puts pride in the heart of any true Englishman, and the fear of God in all who stand opposed to the Empire.'

'God', as such sentiments are intended to infer, is, of course, an Englishman. Upon seeing the three hundred foot triumphal arch that houses the cogwheels of British rule that is Company House, it is a 'sentiment that you're hard-pressed to counter', as the guidebook put it. I found myself thinking much the same as I rushed towards it on the express line across the river Hooghly.

The arch, covered in bas-reliefs of Imperial pride, Union Jacks, lions and old Britannia herself resplendent, dominates the city, much as the Empire dominates India. The whole gargantuan edifice sits in the centre of Victoria Square, the flagstones of which are laid out to depict a map of the subcontinent itself.

The designers of the Square weren't going for subtlety. But this was after all Imperial India's heart. They no doubt considered that it did no harm to hammer home the message of just who was in charge, not that there could be doubt on that score. The Union Jack flew everywhere in the Indian capital. Rumour had it there were more statues to be found in the city of good old 'far from a virgin' Queen Vic than Vishnu. Though some wags have been known to argue it's hard to tell the difference between them…

On seeing the great arch looming towards me, as the express flew across the viaduct, I was reminded of something Miss Wells had vouched safe to me only the day before when I mentioned my orders were to report to an office within the arch. "It couldn't be more phallic if they shaped it as a damn phallus…" She wasn't far from the mark.

It was amidst one of her more scathing commentaries, one she made while we enjoyed afternoon tea on the flight from Egypt. Delightful though I found Miss Wells's company on the second leg of my journey to India, her opinions on British rule in India were much what one comes to expect from the beneficiaries of Imperial largess. Which is to say, she was of the opinion that India should rule itself, and the British should depart, as it were, in a vulgar fashion. Though her language was never less than ladylike.

For myself, however, I must admit to marvelling at the sight of it as I rode the train in from the airfield. The arch cast against the vista of the city as I passed over. The closer we came to it the more the symbols of India's wealth were there to be seen. If India is, as so often claimed, the jewel in the Empire's crown, then Calcutta is the centre of that jewel, and it sparkles. At its heart, it is a city of mansions built with Company money.

Well, that is once the tenements of the outer city gave way to the white stone villas and marble houses of the Imperial quarter. The slums of the indigenous workforce are no better than the slums of the East End back in seedy old London. Probably worse as the sewers were of the more open kind, and no less rat infested.

What was it that old hack Kipling said of Calcutta? 'A garden of Imperial excess. A garden walled with squalor.' Ever a man who sought to be 'of the people' was old Rudgard.

I will admit, however, I could see what Kipling was getting at. Beautiful though the heart of the city was, it was easy to understand the resentment of the natives. For it was no doubt mostly the British who lived in the city's marble heart while the locals lived in the less glamorous outskirts. Calcutta thrived on the backs of its native population as it ever has.

Don't misunderstand me; I still believed that the Empire was to the good of all its subjects. It struck me the world was a better place for Britannia's rule, of that I had no doubt at all. Yet, as a lad from the East End, I understood what it was to live on the fringes, while others seemed to have it all. I'll admit I find it hard to blame the starving millions for wanting a larger piece of the pie. Particularly as it is a pie that exists because they bake it in the first place. If that sounds like the rantings of that old loon Marx whose writings so inspired the suicidally stupid attempts at Tsaricide last century, well I would never go that far. But let me just say I believe then, as I do now, that everyone deserves a piece of crust once in a while.

It had taken a week to get to Calcutta from Egypt. Much of which, to my pleasure, I had spent getting to know Miss

Wells. Her opinions on British rule aside, she proved to be excellent company.

Sadly, for me, there was no impropriety involved, not, I must say, for want of trying on my part. I'd laid it on with a trowel. She was after all quite the beauty, and I am a man of many weaknesses, as I am sure you've realised by now. An appreciation of a fine turn of the ankle is one of them, if I may use the most polite form. Were I in the RAN mess I would have said something more along the lines of 'She's a fine piece of ass.' Or some other such vulgarity, but then my brother officers were 'gentlemen' all and such is the way such things are discussed after a porter or two. Miss Wells, however, was remarkably and quite regrettably, resistant to my charms in this regard.

Yet, regardless of that frustration, Saffron, as I called her now we had got past surnames, proved to be a delight. Which is to say, her company delighted me, I can't say if I delighted her. She would, however, hang on my arm each evening at dinner.

Sadly, it soon became apparent this was a ploy to ward off unwanted suitors on her part. Nothing more. But one must take small victories where one can. The envious looks I received from other men in the ballroom were frankly quite gratifying. Even if I was only too aware after the first few vain attempts to advance my own cause that there were some other victories that would almost certainly be denied me.

There was another reason for the occasional pained expressions on the face of those who looked in our direction. That of the hulking shadow that hovered behind us at all times. In case you had forgotten that Miss Wells always had a Sleep Man in attendance. I assure you I tried to forget the damn thing myself, but it was easier said than done. Memories of my own encounter with its brothers in the cells of the Bailey were still far too fresh in my mind.

The more attractive of this pairing I came to suspect was taking the measure of me in these sojourns. Miss Wells would slip carefully placed questions into our conversations. Often they were whispered so that an observer would think them trifling flirtations, though they were generally of a serious nature as she rooted at my opinions on many things. Given the nature of our relationship, it was hardly a surprise. Two unwilling agents of the clockwork crown could well share common goals, but she was hardly likely to place much trust in mine.

Wise of her, I'll happily admit, as my only goals were ones of self-preservation, and if at all possible to get her out of her corset and into my bed. Ungallant though the latter may be, I would've forgone that pleasure in a heartbeat for the furtherance of the former in any event. Which I suspect she knew only too well.

I would've liked to report that I remained guarded around her and careful of my confidences. In truth, however, I suspect that after a couple of drinks I would have told Saffron anything on the off chance of impressing her, futile though that undoubtedly was. Even dressed in a fresh uniform, neatly groomed and clean shaven save for my well waxed moustache, I was, I suspect, starting from a low base in her regards, being as I was a soldier of the Imperium she despised, with a murder conviction and a felonious reputation to boot. I suspect she placed all the trust in me I deserved. Which is to say sweet bugger all… If you will forgive my own coarse assessment.

Aside from her skilful inquiries as to my opinions, we spent the evenings making clever witticisms about the other travellers. My own attempts to be droll would gain a polite laugh, an occasional smile or a disapproving look, all depending on her mood. Saffron, on the other hand, could cut a man down to size with the fewest of words, a talent I came to appreciate. Leastways when it wasn't me on the receiving end of her barbed tongue.

When asked to dance to the string quartet's screeching notes, as she almost invariably was by one young man or another each evening, she would refuse with such politeness that most never realised they were being snubbed. But then a cutting remark made with a delicate smile has sent many a suitor away with their tail between their legs. Saffron was most adept at the social crushing of egos. Something which amused me no end.

This was of course until I asked her myself and received the same treatment. Noticeably, it has to be said, without the smile. Instead, she cut me down to size and filleted my ego. It undoubtedly says something about me that this made her all the more alluring. I've no doubt a certain Mr Freud of Vienna would've had a field day with that. I was, however, somewhat smitten, which in the circumstances somewhat tragic, I am sure you'll agree, in time.

There was, however, one major fly in the ointment, a rather large fly at that. Heavy coated, top-hatted, and whose visage was hidden behind a gas mask. The one, as I mentioned, that I did my best to ignore and failed to do so most of the time. Whatever those things had gassed me with, it had left its mark. A residue of fear they had inspired still clung to me, and here one was Miss Wells's constant companion, ever hovering on the edge of my vision.

It hung back like a servile butler, with all the menace of a loaded pistol pointed in my direction. Never more than a few steps behind, it loomed greatly in our meetings. You would have thought, after a couple of days, it would become but a piece of the background, as servants are want to do.

It didn't; it remained as menacing as it had from the first moment I clapped eyes upon it.

It was no servant to Saffron, however, as I discovered when I walked her back to her cabin on the final evening aboard ship. Which I did in hope, one must be honest, of accompanying her back through its threshold.

"I must bid you good night, Mr Smyth," she said as she retrieved the key to her room from her clutch bag.

"No offer of a nightcap?" I asked, with no real expectation there would be, I will admit. But nothing ventured, no dreams crushed...

Saffron looked at me coldly. "I think not," she said and pushed open the door of her stateroom. "Presuming you mean another drink that is and not some strange English knitwear... to which the answer would also be no."

There was an entirely credulous tone to her voice. I was reminded suddenly that while the British and the subjects of the Empire may share a common parlance, they don't always share a common vocabulary, but regardless I thought better of pushing my luck any further.

"Then I guess this is good night, Miss Wells," I said as formally as my semi-drunken state would allow and gave her a polite nod of the head, resolving even as I did so to wander back in the direction of the lounge and another drink. As I straightened up, I became aware that her looming shadow was standing very close behind me, and found myself jostled out of the way as it stepped through the hatchway behind her. Which was something of a tight squeeze for its massive frame. Where the damn thing went at night hadn't occurred to me up until that point. Indeed, in my surprise, I muttered rather disbelievingly. "It sleeps in your room?"

Miss Wells must have heard me as she turned back, her face taking on a serious cast at my inquiry. Somewhat soberly she replied, "Our masters don't afford me the latitude they have given you, Hannibal. They trust me somewhat less, I suspect."

I almost laughed.

The idea that I was trusted was an absurdity. My lack of belief must have shown on my face. She sighed heavily, with a slight shake of her head as she continued.

"I am watched at all times, Mr Smyth, but then I suspect I'm but bait to catch a bigger fish. Whereas you... Well, I'm not at all sure what you are at all."

'You and me both,' I thought, then considered her words for a moment. It was true the Sleep Man was always in her shadow. The only time he hadn't been was when we returned to the airship in Cairo. Gates had sent him back before us with some equipment that was to be shipped out to India. We had shared a camel back a couple of hours later. It had been waiting at the embarkation point for her return, it's true, but she had been unguarded when we travelled from the tomb to the ship.

I pointed this out, god only knows why. I can only claim to being drunk and not thinking it through, and missing the more obvious implications. But even as they occurred to me, I was in the middle of saying, "You were not guarded on the way back." I kept going. When you're up to your neck in it, it's time to stop digging, as my old mum would have told me. Besides, I wondered if she had thought of that imp-plication too.

She had, of course.

"In Cairo, I was being watched by you," she said, with no hint in her voice of the pleasant tone we had conversed with all evening. Which spoke volumes I had no wish to read.

"I..." I started, as eloquent as ever. Then found I had nothing to say. Nothing I could say really all things considered.

She just stared me down and then started to close the door behind her, saying, "Goodnight, Hannibal Smyth, whoever you are. I hope we do not meet again."

And that was that. I heard a lock click into place, which had a certain finality to it.

I stood there for a while, staring at the door in front of me, a little confused, a little drunk and still surprised at what she had said. Not the 'hope we do not meet again' bit, that made perfect sense. But the idea that I was trusted, even in the slightest, was absurd.

For some reason, she thought of me as a trusted agent of The Ministry, a guard dog who had been set to keep her in check? If so, she had applied the same logic to me as I had done with her on our first meeting. It was the blind leading the blind, each believing that the other could see.

Yet somehow that was what Saffron Wells thought of me. A trusted agent, a loyal pawn, when she was held in their thrall as much as I. In short then, she despised me as much as I despised M and his cronies.

It was almost a compliment of sorts. That is that she believed I was a trusted agent of the crown. I almost smiled at the idea. Indeed my younger self would have loved it. To be thought the handsome, dashing hero, risking all for queen and country…

Yet somehow, in the twisted logic of this new life I found myself in, to be a trusted agent of the crown was worse by far than to be a lying sneak thief and a murderer. Though I'm far from sure, she'd have had a higher opinion of me if she knew the truth of me, more's the pity.

Rejecting the delights of the bar, I made my way to my own cabin, trying to make sense of everything. For all it was tempting to just put it down to the mysteries of women, I suspect that even in my most misogynist moments I would have been hard-pressed to sell myself on that idea.

It occurred to me she had missed the most obvious reason I was not guarded. Unlike her, I was disposable, a pawn in a larger game. Whereas, she was guarded at all times. Clearly, she was more important to them. From what little I had gleaned, my job was to flounce about India in the hope that I would be contacted by her great-grandfather, who they suspected, for reasons they chose not to divulge to me, would make a move to do so. God may know why but I sure as hell didn't.

Whereas Saffron Wells was his great-granddaughter, why this H.G. character would try to contact her was clear. She was, as she said, bait, just as I was. She was a better class of bait than I, however. Of course, they kept her close.

Thinking back, it never occurred to me there could be a reason they needed to watch her constantly. A reason they felt the need to have a Sleep Man follow her around. One which went beyond her protection. Indeed, why they might always have one in her proximity for the exact opposite of protecting her, a poised blade at her throat.

She was, after all, a woman.

How could she be all that dangerous?

Yes. I know… Damn you.

But I am not the first man to underestimate the fairer sex. Believe me, I know only too well that it's based on a fallacy. Start thinking of women as anything less than equally capable as any man, and you're on a quick path to a rude awakening. Only utter fools think in such ways… But on occasion, when I was younger, I was foolish, and I underestimated Saffron Wells.

Oh, the naivety of man.

Lost in my thoughts, and wits mildly addled with drink as I worked my way back to my own cabin, I didn't realise I was being followed. All things considered, that was probably a blessing. I have a vague memory of fumbling with my key and seeing someone duck back around the corner behind me as I did so.

I remember peering down the corridor with a moment's suspicion. Then shaking my head, as I entered my cabin, fell onto my bed and resolved to sleep off the booze before we reached Calcutta.

Blissfully unaware I was no less closely watched than Miss Wells, and no less under threat, all be it from other sources.

CHAPTER 12

Assignments
And Assignations

I was to take an assignment as the first mate on an EICAN cutter. One which was due to head north in a couple of days. A tea and crumpets run, up to the spine of the world, flying the Company flag. Slow trawling along the lower reaches of the Himalayas. It sounded like a damn dull billet.

It was a prospect which didn't delight me overly not least because it was to be a three-month routine patrol, which would involve carrying a few supplies for remote stations, showing the Company's presence, and keeping an eye on the hill tribe bandits that were as ever rumbling in the north.

So, mainly dull with a small chance of life-threatening terror, but mostly just dull.

Why in god's name The Ministry thought this would be an ideal way for me to find and get myself within the confidence of H.G. Wells, I'd no idea. The only thing the hill tribes hated more than Englishmen and The East India Company, were each other. Somehow I couldn't see a mild-mannered writer of unsuccessful books, with a few bankrupt political philosophies, hiding out among them. He hardly sounded like the type to become a great leader of rebels, especially not the kind that unites warring factions under a single banner.

I was more than half convinced the whole thing was a wild goose chase. Perhaps a seed born from misinformation. After all The Ministry no doubt had those who worked against them. Other branches of Old Brass Brassiere's government for a start, as my recent run-in with Maythorpe showed.

Now clearly it would be a terrible waste of The Ministry's resources if all this turned out to be a waste of time. Even if it got me off their hook for a while. A few long pointless months flying around northern India may sound boring, but I would take boredom over some other possibilities every time. So, all things considered, I didn't find the idea too distasteful.

One lives in hope. Generally, the hope is not to die in despair, but one lives in hope all the same.

As I waited for my papers to be sorted out, I leafed through a copy of The Times of India. A somewhat more sober rag than its Fleet Street equivalent. Disappointingly it didn't even have a girl showing a scandalous amount of ankle on page three. The editorial was a sombre reflection on some policy or other that the new Viceroy was about to enact, which I can't remember for the life of me. All I recall is raising a surprised eyebrow that the words 'Shocking', 'Disgraceful' and 'Vile' weren't being used at any point. The Times editorials I was used to used such words in every other sentence no matter what the subject matter. It made a change from 'Hanging's too good for them'. Or 'Outrage at Liberal suggestion of votes for the poor'. Nothing it seemed was 'Undermining the fabric of our society'. With 'Weak capitulations to the left' suggesting 'Meritocracies and the end of the old school tie', I found it oddly quaint that an editorial attempted to impart knowledge in a reasonable thought-provoking way.

Though it has to be said it made for an exceedingly dull editorial.

What I did worryingly, however, glean from the paper, before I skipped on to the sports section, was a little alarming. I stumbled across the report of a passenger liner which had been disappeared in north India, the second such occurrence in two months. The paper was blaming this on the new 'Muldarin'. The same one, no doubt, M had spoken about. Of course, the Indian papers always blamed a new 'Muldarin'. The mention of that name sold a lot of news-rags. That was the most important thing to editors. He was the great Indian bogie-man after all. A headline stating that some remote tribal chieftain in the hinterlands had burned a few farms or ambushed a Company patrol was page ten fodder at best. No one cared about such things (unless you were the one being shot of course). But if you started calling them 'The New Muldarin' and threw in a few unsubstantiated gruesome details, then you had yourself headlines for a week or more.

I've long suspected that one of the things the editors of Fleet Street, and by extension their sub-continent stablemates, hate most is when one of these irrelevant little tribal chiefs get caught and summarily shot. Because let's face it…

'Valiant EIC dispatch New Muldarin'

Is a poor headline you can only use once.
Whereas…

'Muldarin Terror Strikes Again'

Is one you can use every time someone steals a regimental goat. Hence, in all honesty, my disparagement of the idea when M first brought up the subject.

But taking down passenger liners. If there was some truth to that. If they had not simply been lost in storms or crashed somewhere in the mountains. If there really was a 'New Muldarin' behind it. Then it required a whole different level of sophistication, something far beyond the usual tribal chief turned bandit.

As to why someone would be hitting passenger ships? I couldn't fathom a guess. Though this writer chap Wells being ultimately behind it still seemed like a bit of a stretch to me. I'd be more inclined to believe there was some international intrigue at play. If I were to take a stab at anyone it would be the Russians. God only knows you can't trust the Tsars. Even if the Romanovs have been intermarrying with the progeny of our good Queen's loins for the last couple of centuries. I certainly wouldn't put it past them. Something was not right about all this, of that I was sure.

The article did, however, manage to add to my trepidation about the three-month patrol in the region. The thought crossed my mind that The Ministry was hoping that my ship was going to be attacked. It made as much sense as anything else I could come up with. It was a far from reassuring thought. Though why they'd think such an occurrence would get me, of all people, close to Wells, I couldn't guess. It sounded like the most likely outcome of such a plan would be a painful, pointless death for yours truly.

As ideas go, that was one I was dead-set against.

Company House proved to be disappointingly bland once you got through the doors. For all its grand edifice, inside it was just a long succession of beige corridors and stuffy offices. Within those offices, people as bland as their surroundings stamped my paperwork. Then they'd tell me to go to another office three floors and a quarter of a mile away to sit and wait for it to be stamped again. This went on tediously for some time. I got the feeling the clerks were playing their own little game of giving Hannibal the runaround. Either that or the bureaucracy of Company House was such that it made the Inland Revenue seem like cheerful amateurs.

Many of the clerks seemed to share surnames, mannerisms, even the same little nervous tics. It was as if a strange experiment in nepotism and inbreeding was underway. Most of the low-level clerks were, in fact, British Indians. We've been in India a long time, so creating white collar jobs for the expatriates' families has long been an industry in its own right. White British Indians had it seemed long ago replaced the native middle class in the caste system, at least in government jobs. And a nation of nearing a billion needs a lot of paperwork I have no doubt, but even so, I got the impression the Company House revelled in creating more, and every one of these tedious little men had their own little rubber stamp to add to my forms.

I was, it is fair to say, hacked off when I finally arrived at the final stamping ground. There I was told that I had to report to the Company airfield the following morning to join up with my berth. When I asked what I was supposed to do until then, I was told, none too politely, "Push off and find a hotel." I was less than impressed.

It was getting towards evening by that time. After four hours walking corridors with a kit bag and collecting stamps, I was tired, hot, and drenched in sweat. So I was feeling more than a little ill-used. The thought of now having to find a hotel, while dragging my kit around, you may be surprised to learn, didn't fill me with a wealth of joy.

My weapons, or at least the ones that had come with the uniform, had been returned to me by the master of arms when I left the Empress. As such, I was walking around armed, and I'd had to fight off the urge to shoot someone. The last of these snivelling clerks who had been wasting my day was top of that list.

The weapons were a standard service revolver in need of gun oil, three pouches of shells, and a well-used airman's sabre. Well-used is being polite about it; it looked as blunt as a butter knife and as well looked after as a rusting pair of garden shears. I'd have given anything for a good blackjack of lead shot, and a switchblade. Thankfully the razor I'd acquired on the Empress made for a reasonable weapon at a pinch and I'd taken to keeping it tucked in my boot.

As I was shipping out the following morning, I'd have no time to find anything more serviceable. So I was going to have to strip down the pistol and get it in good order and lay my hands on a decent whetstone to sharpen the blade.

If I were heading into combat, which this venture had all the hallmarks of, I'd damn well go there with weapons in good order. Sometimes, I knew, running away or surrendering just isn't an option.

That said, running away or holding up my hands were still going to be my two preferred ways of dealing with combat if it looked like it might get dicey. Well, running away, at any rate. Some of the things that happened to those who got captured by hill bandits didn't bear thinking about.

I considered finding a spare office and bedding down for the night in a chair. Just to save me the hassle of finding a hotel. But bunks on a military ship aren't known for comfort, and I was going to be sleeping in one for the next few months. The idea of a real bed won out. So, when I finally found my way out of the maze of beige corridors, I hailed a cab on the pavement.

A cab is probably stretching it a little. What I actually caught was a cross between a steam engine and a tricycle. Powered by an ancient copper boiler that made alarming squealing sounds as it leaked pressure, it proved to be only marginally faster than walking and not entirely as comfortable.

It did have one virtue, a chatty driver that seemed to know where he was going and who had a vague appreciation of the concept of safe driving. I suspect all the same that he went the longest way round and charged me double. So despite the mild worry that the boiler might explode at any moment, and the angry shouts in Hindi the driver directed at other road users, it was much like taking a London black cab ride. In fact, considering the screaming boiler and the likely translation of the names he was calling drivers who got in his way, it was almost exactly like catching a London black cab.

Eventually, I got to the Jewel in the Crown hotel. Which was, despite being apparently owned by the cab driver's 'uncle', halfway reasonable. I managed to get a room, a lukewarm shower, a change of shirt and returned to the bar in short order. Though after all the delays at Company House I had already missed dinner.

There was a piano in the corner of the bar being played by a half-blind tone-deaf man in a monkey suit. Who for a half blind, tone-deaf man who had probably never touched a keyboard before was managing a reasonable rendition of something akin to lounge music. I did my best to tune it out, order a scotch and perched myself at the bar.

I was on my third when I became aware that the seat beside me had just been filled by someone with expensive perfume, who was ordering a gin and tonic in a Home Counties accent. I looked up and made use of the mirror back bar to get a look at the perfume's wearer and got my first pleasant surprise in a while.

She was a diminutive but attractive looking woman, fair skinned, with shortish hair cut in a fashion that had been all the rage in London a summer or two before. So was probably the height of fashion out here on the other side of the Empire. She was also wearing evening wear, of the type that suggests cocktail parties on the veranda, and importantly, from my perspective, seemed very much alone.

Being the gentleman that I'm not, and having a pocket full of rupees that The Ministry had supplied, I offered to pay for the lady's drink. Hotel bars and the oldest of professions being much the same the world over, there was, it seemed to me, a fair chance it would serve as an introduction to a pleasurable evening's commerce. Though such assumptions as I made proved, as usual, to be false.

You would think just once something would break my way, wouldn't you...?

In my defence, I was about to ship out on a three-month tour, which I suspected would be somewhat lacking in female company. No matter what they may say about airmen, in my experience only the usual amount of us are the kind of men who like to grease another airman's piston, and while I have nothing against the chaps who go in for that kind of thing, I prefer to make port when in port with one who isn't a chap, if you catch my drift.

I'd also spent the better part of the previous week in the company of the beautiful, sadly unobtainable, Saffron Wells. A week in which I didn't get so much as a sly peck on the cheek, while spending it with a woman who courted my company when we were together in public, if only to avoid the attentions of others. I would be lying if I was to say that hadn't been the cause of some frustration on my part.

Before that, as I'm sure you remember, I'd spent several months at Her Majesty's less than accommodating pleasure. So, you'll have to forgive me if I was of a mind to make the most of what chances fate provided. I'm not sure any court could convict me on those grounds, and what possible harm could come of it…?

Of course, hindsight is a wonderfully annoying thing, but let's not fly ahead of ourselves.

"My mother told me never to accept a drink off a stranger," the lady in question replied to my offer. There was, however, the slightest of twinkles in her eye as she turned to look at me. Though now I think back, it may have been a squint…

"First officer Hannibal Smyth of the Company Air Navy," I replied, offering her a broad smile and my hand.

"Justine Casey, of the Calcutta Gazette," she vouched safe in return, and with only a moment of hesitation took the proffered hand in a surprisingly firm grip. She shook it twice in a mildly dramatic fashion and returned my grin.

It appeared my luck may finally be on the turn, so I smiled all the wider.

"Well, as we're now no longer strangers, let me buy you that drink," I said, throwing a bundle of rupees onto the counter that were gamefully snapped up by the barman.

Yes, I know it was a hackneyed old line to lay on her, and throwing money about in such a fashion is scarcely better. I'm sure I deserve nothing but your scorn for that, but sometimes you just have to throw a line out there to see if you can hook a fish. Besides, I've a winning smile and as such can pull off such a line. Or at least so I tell myself. On occasion, such a line has been known to at least start a conversation and, you'll note, I never claimed to be particularly original.

"Oh, what the hell, make it a double and I'll let you." She laughed, which to me sounded reasonably promising.

"Justine?" I found myself having to inquire.

"Don't, please, just assume my parents had a sense of humour, okay," she said, and I laughed lightly in return.

Then she added the somewhat expectedly, "Besides... Hannibal?"

"Yes I know, the elephants..." I said, hinting my own parents were to blame for that moniker, which is as you're aware by now something of a lie. My mother called me Harry, and only she knew who my father was... In regards to Hannibal, I am entirely to blame for my misfortune. It sounded grandiose in a good way when I first adopted it.

Four rounds later, with her insisting on buying one of them, we were getting along nicely. She was telling me all the latest Calcutta gossip, which seemed much like London gossip in that it revolved around who was sleeping with their gardener. Who had gone to 'the country' for a few months when the pills had become a problem. As well as which debutants had made their debuts before the season and with whom. All the kind of stuff she could never print of course, scandalous as it undoubtedly would be to Calcutta society. To me, I'll admit, it sounded like the usually bored housewife rag gossip which was probably rooted more in jealousy than truth, but I faked an interest in the who's while laughing at the what's. Which made for an entertaining time of it.

She also talked about the worrying news from the north. Another airship, Russian this time, had disappeared near the Afghan border. It may have been unrelated to the other disappearances of course. The Russians were having the usual problems with the Afghans, which have been going on for a couple of centuries or more.

Every few decades the Russians would leave, and the British would march into 'protect' the Afghans for a few years. Then, in turn, they would march out, and the Russians would take a turn. No one was entirely sure why anyone would want the country, not even the Afghans, I suspect.

Other than it had the misfortune to serve as a buffer between Russia and British India.

Whoever 'owned' Afghanistan at any given time would be fighting a war, until they left again, against tribesmen supplied by the other side. Then when the liberators moved in, those weapons would be turned against them, and the vanquished would take a turn at supplying the tribes with guns and bombs.

It never seemed to occur to anyone that leaving the Afghans to their own devices would probably be the best way to bring peace to the country. The important thing was the British and Russians never shot at each other, only at the unfortunate Afghans. Thus they preserved the peace between the two great empires, and each got a chance to try out their latest weapons against hopelessly out-matched but incredibly resilient tribesmen. Not that those lobbying parliament to liberate Afghanistan from Russian aggression again were motivated by money, perish the thought. I am sure all those arms dealers and manufacturers of airships were solely motivated out of a sense of duty towards the poor Afghan people.

And if you believe that, I have some magic beans for sale...

Anyway, the ongoing debacle of the Afghan wars aside, a Russian ship disappearing over Afghan territory was more than likely just one caught up in that whole torrid mess up there and had been shot down.

Still, that was three ships in a couple of months that had disappeared. Which didn't bode well in my opinion, particularly as I was being sent to that general area. So I was starting to grow a tad concerned if truth be told. Over the years I have found I am rather fond of my airships staying in the air as intended. I am old fashioned like that.

Anyway, to get back to the bar and leave my impending doom aside for a moment... I told several outrageous lies to Justine in between her own stories. Lies which made her laugh, whether she believed them or not. So in this fashion, we entertained each other for a couple of hours and probably annoyed a few of the hotel's more sober guests with our laughter, as we kept drinking.

To cut a long story short, at some point around midnight, I, quite drunkenly and equally happily went to my room with Justine Casey on my arm.

Oh and yes, I know her name sounds made up, I'm not entirely dim. I just assumed that was because it was. Further, if she wanted to use a nom de plume for the evening, that was her business. I certainly had no qualms about that. If by extension she wanted to spend a night with a stranger and no consequences, then I was happy to oblige.

It's all fun and games as long as you're both consenting adults and not looking for more than a one night fling. So if she wanted to be Justine Casey tonight, well good for her. All I cared about was that she was small, blonde, had a cute smile, and a devilish sense of humour, and no hang-ups about going back to a gentleman's room for the oldest of pass times.

All considered, I'm sure we would've had a great night together if, after I opened the door to my room and stepped through ahead of her, she hadn't smashed me across the back of the head with something blunt and heavy.

The lesson here is always hold the door open for a lady and let her walk in first.

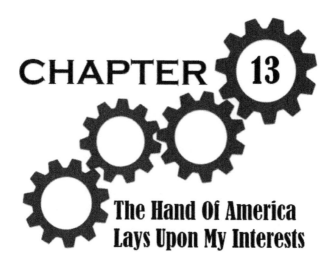

CHAPTER 13

The Hand Of America Lays Upon My Interests

It was the fake-maid from the Empress somewhat unsurprisingly. I recognised her from the way she expertly knocked me out cold. But after all, with my luck who else could it have been?

Okay, that's actually an ever-growing list of suspects, but all the same, she was near the top of that list.

Being taken by surprise and assaulted in some way it appeared was an occupational hazard in my new profession as The Ministry's cat's paw, come pawn, come... Well if truth be told, I wasn't sure what I was at the time. The only thing I knew for sure was an increasing amount of my time seemed to be spent taking blows to the back of the head. I was starting to think some kind of hat might be in order. Specifically, a hat that was steel framed and heavily padded, but I digress.

I awoke this time to discover that I was in the process of having the last of my limbs tied to a bed by an attractive petite blonde woman, further to which I'd been stripped to nothing but my vest, socks, and underpants. Now, admittedly, there have been times in my life when this sort of thing would've counted as entertainment. Indeed, there were establishments that I'd occasionally frequented just off Tottenham Court Road where things like this were exactly what attracted the clientele. Though, in fairness, in such establishments, they seldom brained you with a pistol butt first…

I suspected, if somewhat hazily, that on this occasion this wasn't the prelude to a night of sexual congress for the discerning gentleman. As the lady involved in this odd little encounter, whatever else she might have in mind, didn't look to me like she was acting out of carnal desire.

Sex, in short, was off the agenda. Had I not been somewhere between terrified and confused right at that moment, I might have considered that to be a shame.

As it was, I put up a token defence. Trying as best I was able to free myself and fight off her attempts to tie the last of my limbs down, I didn't even succeed in landing a single kick, however, as she grabbed my only free ankle. I had bugger all leverage because of how tightly my arms and other leg were already tied down, and it was clear she was in no mood for any argument from me.

To add to this indignity, I was also currently gagged. The taste of damp cotton in my mouth attested to that. I was trying to spit whatever she had jammed in there out, with as little success as my attempts to ward her off with a single flailing leg.

In response to what little fight I was putting up, she twisted my foot to the right, hard and with a certain degree of malice, of which she left me no doubt. The resultant burst of pain almost caused me to black out again. She was stronger than she looked, stronger than I'd a right to expect from such a small woman.

I tried to scream through the muffling cotton, as much from the pain as to inform any futile hope of salvation. By the time the pain had subsided enough for me to think clearly, she had secured my leg to the bottom of the bed and I was fully restrained. Added to which, sweat was already dripping down my forehead, stinging my eyes, and the choking feeling from whatever she had stuffed in my mouth keeping me close to panic.

"Now that's all sorted, Mr Smyth, I assume I have your full attention?" she said to me as she walked around the bed to the side and leaned over me slightly. She had an oddly quizzical look on her face. I suspect she was wondering what I'd do. I suspect that is always what people in her position think about when they have you at their mercy. I would not have put it past her to have been making little bets with herself. Would I cough up everything in a bid to save myself? Would I maintain that ever infamous British stiff upper lip in the face of adversity? How much would it take to break me? That kind of thing.

If she knew the real me at all, she would have realised the answers were yes, no and nothing whatsoever. Frankly, I was still feeling ill-used by M and his damnable Ministry. Convincing her of that might be difficult, however. It's hard to spill your guts figurative speaking, if you actually know next to bugger all. This, I couldn't help thinking at the time, was going to be a bit of a problem.

In reply to her question about 'having my attention', I nodded, quite vigorously, as I was still gagged.

How do you say 'I'll tell you everything' with your mouth stuffed full of cotton undergarments? Don't ask me how I knew it was undergarments, I just did, alright.

The Not-A-Maid-No-Really-She-Isn't-I-Think-We-Can-Safely-Say-That-Now's accent was once more American.

The Home Counties were gone the way of the promise of an illicit and enjoyable encounter between consenting adults. If I'm completely honest, at this point that still felt something of a disappointment to me. She was, as you will recall, an attractive woman and one I was still finding attractive even in my predicament. But before you start judging me, let me remind you, in my defence, she'd been arousing me with her feminine wiles all evening at the bar.

Unfortunately, she noticed this was the case too.

"Oh my, Mr Smyth, you appear to be enjoying this…" she murmured, leaning in close until her lips were only a few inches from my ear when she spoke. Then, in a manner that would have made a Soho madam proud, she slapped the palm of her hand down hard on my crotch.

The pain that exploded in my genitals was… well, such an occurrence requires little description, I am sure.

"I hate to dash your hopes, my dear, but I have no interest in this 'little' thing of yours…" she said and then in deference to her words, she clenched her gloved left hand tightly onto the thing in question through my Y-fronts. Her fingers felt like they could keep on squeezing till it popped and I don't mean in the pleasant much sought-after fashion. She'd an unnaturally strong grip, vice-like, and her face showed nothing in the way of effort being involved. It was as if she wasn't even trying. Considering the pain she was inflicting right then, it was the most terrifying expression I could have seen on her face. Fear over-rides any other emotion in such a situation. I'd have quickly withered within that grip, if the blood had somewhere to flow to.

I was left gasping, dragging what breath I could through the cotton in my mouth. I felt light-headed once more, and that sharp blinding pain was utterly intense.

She must have known exactly what she was doing to me. She released the grip just before I blacked out yet again. My heart was pounding, and I continued gasping for air. The relief almost as bad as the pain had been, though the ghost of it still throbbed away.

The target of her abuse quickly withered away now it could. Though there was nothing in the way of relief involved. Meanwhile, my eyes still stung with the salt of my own sweat. They must have been bulging too. It was hard to focus properly even with the pain slipping away.

"Now that little thing is dealt with, Mr Smyth, we can move on to more important matters, I'm sure," the Maid-Who-Was-Not-A-Maid said, and slowly started removing her elbow length gloves, first from her left and then ever so slowly from her right hand. My eyes widened slightly as she did the right, understanding as to the nature of her unnatural strength coming to me as I saw her right arm.

Even in the dim light of my bedroom, I could see the glint of brass and the gleam of glass inspection panels over inner workings. Cogwheels, miniature pistons and springs. And even more disturbingly something that glowed an eerie lime green that looked like some form of battery like those Tesla devices use instead of steam.

The last of the glove she slowly pulled off, over her delicate brass fingers. They were fully articulated. Made by someone with astounding skill. Indeed they were in perfect proportion to her normal, and ever so human, left hand.

I'd seen artificial limbs before. They are, as I'm sure you know, common enough. Accidents happen, often because the many wondrous devices humanity conceives have the habit of biting the hands off their creators. Men have been losing the odd finger, arm or leg to mechanical devices for the whole of human history. In recent times we have just got better at making them. Not to mention those other devices mankind is so good at inventing, the ones that fire bullets, shrapnel or have a blast radius. And as long as we have been severing limbs one way or another we've been replacing them as well. Peg legs and hooks were common among sailors back in the days when the sail was king. In these days of steam, we have got a little more technical when it comes to putting people back together. Spring powered legs, the odd clockwork heart, and the occasional steam-powered arm.

I knew a quartermaster sergeant in my RAN days who had his left arm replaced after a tussle with Croatian freedom fighters a few years before. He was a ridiculously cheerful chap, seconded to the artillery stores at Baxley Hill. Swore his new arm was wonderful. After all, it allowed him to lift twenty pounder shells single-handed, and no one ever stood in his way when he was shouldering through to the bar. Also, the plus side was he was permanently grounded and worked in the stores. Which allowed him to earn a nice little slice for himself selling mislaid stock to the likes of yours truly.

The bulky, oily, and very noisy arm of Sergeant Hickson, with its large steam power plant strapped to his back, had, however, nothing in common with the delicately articulated mechanics of the young lady before me. His looked like it had been taken off a mechanical gorilla. Hers, on the other hand, if you will pardon the expression, had all the natural refinement of a genuine human arm.

I'd say it had nothing in common, but that's not strictly true. I suspected that her delicate digits had the same raw poundage per square inch strength of Hickson's gorilla fist. Possibly more so, for all the delicate finesse it displayed.

In a demonstration of the dexterity of her mechanical fingers, she probed them past my lips and pulled forth the cotton cloth she had stuffed in there earlier, telling me calmly as she did so, "You may well be tempted to cry out now, Mr Smyth. I would suggest, however, that you don't. I have no great compunction against silencing you once more, and doing so completely if I need to."

I took her at her word. Her metal fingers tingled against my lips as she reached in and pulled out the cloth, which turned out not to be undergarments at all, but my cravat. Which I suspected was now ruined. It could have been worse, I suppose.

Throwing it to one side, she returned those brass digits to my throat and ever so lightly squeezed. The implication that she need not squeeze so lightly was obvious. She smiled down at me, showing her teeth in the process. It wasn't a comforting smile.

"Now, Mr Smyth, when last we met I had some questions for you, do you remember them?" she asked. All the malice in the world seem focused in her voice right then, for all it was spoken gently.

"You wanted to know why The Ministry was sending me to India," I replied choking slightly against her fingers. My mouth was dry, either because the cotton used to gag me had soaked up all my saliva or because I was terrified.

I'll admit, it was a coin toss which.

"Very good, Mr Smyth, and what else?" she inquired, all sweetness, light and menace.

"Wells… You wanted to know why they were interested in Wells," I said. And felt her fingers tighten ever so slightly at the name. I wasn't entirely certain if she did so on purpose or if it was a subconscious reaction. But I remember being scared by it all the same. I couldn't think right at that moment of any worse than an emotional, angry woman not being completely in control of her vice-like grip. I had a feeling… no, truer to say I knew, she could crush my throat as easy as I could have crushed a tomato. With just as much spectacular oozing red stuff involved if she did, and I was rather fond of my 'tomato juice' staying in my veins where it belonged. Call me old-fashioned, but having my throat crushed and ripped out was something I wished to avoid.

"Very good, you remember. So am I to take it you're going to claim to know nothing again. Or are you perhaps feeling inclined to be a little more cooperative this time?" she asked, squeezing my throat just a little more to emphasise a point that needed no emphasis.

I want to say I was belligerent. That I made a sarcastic retort. Or, perhaps, that I said something witty and disarming. Or, even, that I exhibited a modicum of defiance. I wanted to, oh I desperately wanted to. I say this just so you understand that it pained me to swallow my pride. I wanted to do all the things you would expect of a hero at a time like that.

However, I just wanted to continue breathing a whole lot more.

"Yes, I'll tell you everything," I replied.

"Good," she said, relaxing her grip then taking her hand away from my throat.

I took a deep breath that was painful to inhale. I was certain she had left bruises I could already feel forming around my jugular.

She looked at me a moment, her eyes betraying nothing, then after tilting her head in a manner that seemed inquisitive, she turned her back to me and walked across the room. This afforded me a view of the back of her dress, which I had been admiring in the walk to my room from the bar. It clung ever so slightly to her in alluring ways, just as I remembered from stolen glances in the lift. I breathed hard once more, though this time it had nothing to do with gasping for air. The way her hips moved caused me to remember another source of pain, so recently inflicted, as it throbbed ever so slightly, a reaction I'd cause to regret almost instantly as the pain reasserted itself. My throat was not the only place growing bruises.

She poured herself a drink of water from the decanter on the dresser. Then turned to face me and leaned against it. I don't know if this was a deliberate ploy on her part or not, but it reminded me how arid my throat felt. Deliberate or not, thirst nagged at me as she drank, reminding me, if I'd been in any doubt, that I was completely in her power at that moment in time.

On second thoughts scratch that, I'm sure it was deliberate.

"You're not talking, Mr Smyth. Do I need to point out it would be wise for you to do so about now?" she said then swallowed the last of the water, looking at me with eyes with about as much humanity as that brass right arm of hers.

"Yes, yes, of course…" I said, trying to think fast. "They think Wells has something to do with all this, well, that Wells is leading a new uprising or something," I added with a certain urgency and sod all assurity.

I felt a momentary prickle in my left eye as I said it, which I tried to ignore. I tried to put it down to no more than a reflex on my part. At least I hoped that was all it was. I quickly turned to look away from her. The memory of the screens in Cairo was still fresh in my mind. The idea that lip readers could be employed to monitor conversations had occurred to me more than once in the past week. If I was betraying secrets and they picked up on it from her reactions, it didn't bear thinking about what they might make the blasted spider do to me. As if I didn't have enough to worry about right at the moment.

So as a consequence I didn't see her reaction, only heard it. She sounded disbelieving, however. "You expect me to believe that? How exactly do they think Wells is going to accomplish that?"

"They think he's behind the new Muldarin," I stammered slightly, feeling that same odd tingle behind my eyelid again.

"What? He?" The disbelief in her voice was more palpable now.

"Yes, he's up near the northern borders and raising an army of insurrection or something." I tried to explain, knowing that what I had been told was still only a sliver of the whole, and I'd a far from firm grasp on the whys and wherefores of it all. Right then I just hoped it would be enough to gain me a stay of execution from clockwork Annie Oakley in the corner.

"You said he…" she said. Her voice was tinged with anger once more, and I heard the sound of crystal shattering, which I assumed was the glass.

I was finding it hard to focus now, my eyelid seemed determined to flutter, and I could feel my eye watering. Worse, I could feel the damn spider moving, I was sure of it.

"He!" she said again. And there was a crash, which caused me to look back and see the contents of the dresser get scattered across the room.

Then the proverbial penny dropped.

"You're asking about Saffron, aren't you?" I said quickly. Wondering what possible connection there could be between the one-armed bandit girl and Miss Wells. Not that it mattered considering the way she was having a hissy fit. The next thing she decided to scatter across the room might well be me after all.

"Yes, Mr Smyth, Saffron. I want to know what The Ministry has got on her and why she is working for those bastards. Who the hell is this he you're talking about?" she snapped at me.

I noticed, surprising myself by doing so, there was something about the way she said Saffron. Her tone lightened a little. I only caught it because it took the angry edge away from her voice for a moment. There was definitely something there…

"Miss Wells's great-grandfather, H.G. He's the one they are really after," I tried to explain, trying to process what was happening and read between the lines. Wondering what Not-A-Maid's connection to Saffron was, what that odd lilt to her voice had meant.

"He's dead. He's been dead years," she said, a firmness to her voice. Whether it was true or not, she certainly seemed to believe it. There was something else again, I wasn't entirely sure what but her tone seemed to hold the same distaste about H.G. as it did when she spoke of The Ministry.

"Then they're sending me on a wild goose chase if that's the case. Because that's my mission, find him and infiltrate his army," I replied, feeling oddly safer now. Perhaps because I knew more than she did and now suspected a little of her motives. Only a slither, I should say, a fragment perhaps, but it was something to which I could cling and with it gain a little leverage. She cared about Saffron that was that odd lilt to her voice, cared or perhaps loved, I wasn't sure which. But it was something along those lines.

Yes, I will admit that may seem a bit of a leap, certainly to any of you who are of a more sheltered upbringing. I was, however, even back then, a man of the world. Those wonderfully reserved Victorian values which we hold so dear may make such a leap of logic seem surprising, but there are more things in heaven and on earth than are dreamed of in your… Well, actually it's perhaps truer to say that many things men have been known to dream of are actually centred in reality. Though, sad to say, in my experience such Sapphic ladies tend to care little for involving men in their trysts. No matter how much a man may dream otherwise.

So, while I did not know it for certain, I was reasonably sure right then, that my clockwork armed American friend was in love with Saffron, if not indeed her lover.

I was also sure that she held nothing but distaste for her lover's great-grandfather.

"Wild goose chase? I take it that's an English expression. Is that like a snipe hunt?" she asked after a moment's consideration, a note of calm about her once more. She was collecting herself as the conversation moved on a little. Remarkably quickly now I think about it. But Bad Penny was always one for swift mood changes, I would come to notice.

Bad Penny isn't her name, by the way, more it is my name for her. Let's just say she has a habit of turning up like one. But I'll not get ahead of myself.

"I'm unaware of the term, but I suspect so," I replied, thinking abstractly that old chestnut about the English and the Americans, two people's separate tongues, and all that...

"So they have Saffron looking for her great-grandfather too? That's their interest in her?" she asked me, her tone still levelling off. Indeed it was becoming almost conversational. Which was bizarre from my perspective, tied to a cast iron bed, still throbbing with unpleasant after pain, for none of the reasons I would usually be in such a position.

"I suspect so. No one bothered me with their whys. I don't know much beyond that," I replied. Though my attention was on spiders once more. My eye felt like it was streaming by this point. I tried to blink it out, for what good it did me.

It was only then I realised the damn thing had stopped moving and after a couple more blinks my vision started to clear. I was too preoccupied by what was going on to wonder why that was the case. Bad Penny was preoccupied too.

"It doesn't make sense. She hates the Empire and all it stands for. Why would she help them?" she asked, though I had the feeling the question wasn't directed at me and was merely rhetorical.

I kept silent, hoping to learn something useful. There are times discretion really is the better part of valour and my position was precarious after all. The more I could learn of my captor, the better my chances of seeing the dawn.

"And as for looking for H.G. that makes sod all sense either, even if the old bastard survived Washington. Why would he be in India, of all bloody places? Why the hell would he be working against the Empire? Damn it why is she helping them?"

'Washington? Had Wells been involved with the virus bombing? Christ, Harry, what the hell have we got ourselves into?' I thought. Though, that would explain why Penny was so sure he was dead. No one got out of Washington alive. Everyone knew that.

"She doesn't have a choice, any more of a choice than I do," I interrupted. Gathering information is one thing, survival is another. If she thought Saffron was helping The Ministry because she'd no choice, then I could use that. I could play the same card, that of the unwilling pawn, like her 'lover', Saffron. Play that, and I might just twist her emotions back on her, make it seem I was as much a victim as Miss Wells. It was a short step from there to convincing Penny I was willing to help them both.

'Convince her of that, Harry old lad, and we may still get out of here inside our own skin…'

I let the words hang. That's sometimes the real secret after all. Twisting words to suit your own devices. It requires a certain amount of talent and no little cunning. If I pushed too hard, she would assume I was trying to fool her. So you have to know when to hold your tongue as well as when to run your mouth. It was slightly ironic that I was telling the truth, and doing so by employing all my skills as a practised liar. But if it worked then it worked in my view, and, well, we all have our talents after all.

I'd had another thought as well. A brass arm shaped thought, one that said if she had access to someone who could build her an arm like that, then the same people may, in turn, be able to free me of The Ministry's spider. Something which was high on my list of desires.

In case I hadn't mentioned it, I was working for The Ministry and by extension The Empire because I'd no other choice. Not, as it were, out of loyalty to the crown and old child-bearing hips in Buck House. I'd mentioned it? I thought so, but just thought it worth repeating at this juncture. Just so you and I are on the same page…

Bad Penny laughed at me. It was a bitter kind of laugh, followed, in a bitter kind of tone by her telling me the following. "Oh but I assure you, Mr Smyth, my dear Saffron always has a choice. There isn't a way in blessed Hades they could hold that one against her will. She could vanish before their very eyes if she so chose, and be lost in the wind before they even realised she was gone."

I took a breath, dramatically if truth be told, as I tried to steer her into listening closely to me. Then I told her, "Not the way they are holding her. She can't hide from them… I can't hide from them…"

I added the last in order to put my own position in this firmly in her mind. It still seemed the best hope of winning her over to the idea I was not her enemy. And more to the point, that as I wasn't her enemy, it would be pointless crushing the life out of me.

I was quite certain I didn't want her to do that.

"What do you mean?" she said after a moment. She was curious now I could tell. I suspect she also had a modicum of desire in her question. Though it was only the desire to discover that her dear Saffron wasn't working for the enemy willingly. It was desire nonetheless, and you can always work with desire I have found.

"Come, look me in the eye…" I said, with a little hint of my old wit and charm returning. A little of 'blaze it out and let them feel your fire' if you will. "The left one," I added, just to make sure she understood what I was asking her to do.

She walked over to me cautiously. Then leaned across me, in a way that would have been alluring in any other circumstances. Indeed, even in these circumstances, as her brass arm was not the only thing about her that was well made. As she leant forward, I got a remarkably good view of a pair of her other assets. Regretfully. As in doing so she also unwittingly caused an accompanying painful throb in the wounded thing between my legs, I am somewhat ashamed to admit.

Penny peered into my eye closely. Close enough to see the bloodshot lines of red in my whites, I am sure. Close enough to see more than that as well. And what she saw, also saw her. I felt it moving over my eyeball or thought I did. There was a little star of pain, that same pain I'd felt before. I realised suddenly that I'd the distinct feeling the spider intended to defend itself.

'Is that the watcher, Harry, or the damnable spider itself?' I wondered and realised it was a somewhat chilling thought. 'Is the bloody thing capable of reacting to defend itself? Does it think? Or is it whoever is watching me? Watching in those damn porthole devices in Egypt. Or in London? Is someone controlling it even now? Damn Ministry, Damn Queen Lard Arse, Unamused, Iron Knickered, Brass Titted, Kraut Shagging, Bloody Victoria. Damn the whole bloody lot of them, and this blasted American Half Mechanical Bitch too.'

A mind of its own, or controlled by a watcher. I couldn't tell you which idea I felt was the worst...

The American Half Mechanical Bitch in question reached out the tip of her mechanical index finger, and with terrifyingly gentle control, she pulled down my lower eyelid. I tried not to shake with the sudden feeling of dread that washed over me. I was all too aware that she could pop my eye with the smallest of mistakes on her part. Spider or no spider, I was somewhat fond of my eyes. I had no desire to lose one.

"Oh, my," she said, and my world became just her inquisitive face and a nose she wrinkled up in a way I would have normally considered cute, as she peered all the closer.

"Gates or Jobs?" she asked me. At least it sounded like a question. I'd no idea who Jobs was, but I knew the first name obviously.

"Gates," I said, as calmly as I was able, which was not very. And then thankfully, she withdrew her face and hand. Then she took a step back, and I breathed out slowly. I had not even realised I was holding my breath at the time.

"Hum, strange. Jobs is normally the one obsessed with eyes. It's all eye this and eye that with him, obsessed with optics Steffen is..." she said, picking up an unbroken glass. She filled it with water from a jug on the side that had survived her temper tantrum. Then offered me a drink, or more exactly she started to pour it into my mouth. Which, all considered, I took gratefully.

"So..." she said and lightly dabbed a little spilt water off my chin with a handkerchief, "they put one of these... things in Saffron's eye as well, did they? I guess that explains why she is playing along with them and not off in the wind. Though she is probably just playing for time, I expect. Knowing her, and I do, she'll be trying to find out more by being on the inside. Yes... mmm." She lingered for a moment on a thought, then added, with a degree of certainty, "Yes. That must be the case, or she would have gouged her eye out by now."

"What?" I said, with genuine shock. More at the blasé way in which she made that statement than anything else. The thought hadn't occurred to me. Though I guess it would work. If, admittedly, you were willing to do it to yourself.

The thought of Saffron willing mutilating her own eye seemed absurd. And yet, perhaps because of the way Bad Penny sounded so sure of herself, I was suddenly certain that the American was correct. Miss Wells not only could do so, but I realised even from what little I knew of her, she would. There was something about Saffron that had steel all the way through. It was an alarming thought.

My mind raced to that odd conclusion, while Penny walked slowly around the bed to come to my left side. Looking at me once more in a strange and predatory way. Then she tilted her head a little as if considering something and I was certain right there and then I was not going to like what was going through her mind.

"Mathew 18:9, Mr Smyth. 'If thy eye offends thee…' Do you know your scripture? Yes? No?"

I shook my head in reply, not liking this turn of events. Something my mother once told me came back to me at that moment. 'When they start quoting the good book to you, Harry lad, it's time to run for the hills.'

I was tied to a bed, however. Running to the hills was not an option. "I know what I was taught," I said. Which is the world's most open ended statement ever.

Bad Penny just smiled at me, like a shark smiles at its prey.

"I assure you Saffron is quite capable of doing just that. I doubt she would even think twice about it in fact. If it came to it," the Maid-From-The-Psych-Ward said.

"Well, be that as it may, but I am sure you can see the situation I'm in, that Saffron's in, but maybe we can help each other," I said, with a hint of worry back in my voice. The conversation had suddenly taken a disturbing turn after all. I must admit that line of scripture had really got to me. Perhaps it's because I'm by nature a sinner myself although not a terrible one, you understand.

I'm actually quite good at it.

But still, as I mentioned, according to the wisdom of Old Mother Smith, which when not in her gin was fairly wise, when they start quoting scripture at you... Well, let's just say in my experience nine times for ten they're about to burn you at the stake, and I am not talking entirely figuratively here. There was this one time in... sorry, but I digress once more and that's a story for another day.

Suffice to say the turn in the conversation was making me a little nervous. As was the way she stalked around the bed and leaned over me once more.

"Help each other, why, Mr Smyth, you're being so very helpful right now. More so than you can possibly imagine, I am sure. But as you're helping me, perhaps I should return the favour and help you. Fair's fair, after all. Don't you think?"

Oh, the mercy of light at the end of a conversational tunnel...

"Oh, that would be very, yes indeed, if you could start by letting me up that would be a fine..." I started, but didn't get to finish. Mainly due to her clamping her right hand over my mouth.

And the light at the end of the tunnel, well it turns out to be attached to a locomotive. Of course it does...

She raised her left hand, the mechanical one if you remember and something about the brass articulations of her index finger seemed to twist in an unnatural way.

Rotating slowly anti-clockwise. I watched it turning, with, it has to be said, no little awe and a high degree of trepidation. Then as it turned some more, the steel-edged fingernail of that finger seemed to grow.

And it kept growing, until three inches of very sharp looking steel blade extended out of it. Scalpel-sharp steel. That moved towards my eye, in which I could feel the spider starting to move once more. Squirm is perhaps a better word. With little prickles of pain inflicted upon me as it did.

Bad Penny turned to look me directly in that eye, as if watching the spider moving over it. All the while bringing that overly sharp fingernail down slowly closer me. A look which in other circumstances I would have attributed to glee crossing her face as she smiled at me.

"Yes, you have been a great help to me, to us. I'm sure Saffron appreciated it too. So, in turn, I should help you," she said, whatever she meant by that.

All the while the razor finger moved ever so slowly closer, as steady as it would have been guided by a surgeon. Then, with the blade no more than an inch from my watering eye, with its unwelcome passenger wreathing about frantically, she asked me the most horrifying question of the evening.

"So how about it, Mr Smyth? Shall we, as Mathew says, 'pluck it out'?"

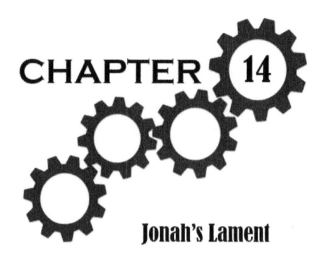

CHAPTER 14

Jonah's Lament

I've certainly seen many better airships than the Jonah's Lament. Sleeker ones, more impressive ones, ones which are better armed, and ones which were newer certainly. But I must admit it was a pleasure to lay both my eyes upon the Jonah the following morning.

I know, I jumped ahead, but it is important in its way to say this. The Jonah, with its inauspicious name, was a second-rate, second hand, ex-Royal Air Navy gunship that should've been decommissioned twenty years ago. Instead, it was sent to India to see service beyond its intended lifespan as a patrol craft for the East India Company.

And it looked like it…

In almost any other circumstances it would have been a deflating craft, if you will pardon the pun, to find as my berth for the next six months, or however long it managed to stay in the air. Looking at the multiple patches on the flanks of her air sack that might not be long.

Mostly it was small patches and some fairly new by the look of them. Patched which spoke of bullets being fired, presumably by those intent on bringing the Jonah down and unlike the modern ships I was used to flying in, there was a distinct lack of armour on the flanks. Worse, whatever had past for the minimal flank armour she'd once enjoyed had long been stripped away. Presumably, so the craft could gain the altitudes necessary for India's mountainous northern regions.

So, as I was saying, in most other circumstances it would be dispiriting to set both my eyes upon her. But, as it was, being able to set both eyes on her was a bonus after the previous night. So my relief at still having both my peepers helped cushion the blow a little. Not much, however, for in truth she was a truly awful looking ship.

Anyway, since you're no doubt wondering, it was moments after she spoke those inauspicious words from Mathew 18:9, with her scalpel-like fingernail poised by my eyeball, that the door to the room came crashing in.

There is it seems an upside to having The Ministry's spider in your eye. At least, if you're somewhere like Calcutta where The Ministry has one of its little hidey-holes. And of course if someone is watching you at the time. Gladly, in this case, there had been and they had watched the whole drama in my bedroom unfold. Luckily with a certain degree of haste, they'd also sent the cavalry.

I am, as I'm sure you will remember, less than enamoured of Sleep Men. With good reason, I'm sure you will agree. They give me the creeps like nothing and no one else on this earth.

On this one occasion, however, I was suddenly very, very pleased as the door to my room came crashing down and I saw two of them stomp into my room.

They burst in complete with those weird clouds of smoke I remembered from London, billowing out from under them. The same nightmarish visage, the blank gasmasks, the dark eyepieces, the tubes from strange devices, and the hulking size that made them seem inhuman. So while they were there to save me from optical surgery by a woman I suspect had never been granted a medical license, they still scared the crap out of me.

It's a profoundly ambivalent experience to be rescued by creatures that haunted your nightmares. Joy and terror combined. It's a heady mix.

My American friend, She-Whom-Was-Not-Now-Nor-Ever-Was-The-Maid, reacted to the threat instantly rather than completing the task at hand. Which was lucky in my self-preservation centric opinion. Not least because it would have taken her less than a moment to poke out my eye, a fact about which I remain uncomfortably aware. Perhaps she realised she didn't have one to spare. Or perhaps it had been a bluff to scare me in the first place, though I never doubted her intent at the time, it has to be said. If it had been a bluff, it was a damn convincing one.

Unlike me, whatever was in the smoke didn't seem to affect her. She just ignored it completely and leapt to her feet, before flinging herself into that fear-inducing poison. She moved quicker than I would've thought possible. I may have still been drunk, the shock of the door bursting in, the billows of smoke already clouding my judgment, but no one normal can move that fast. She stepped, with the speed of a sprinter, across the room from a standing start, hammering into the foremost Sleep Man and slashed at his mask.

Somehow in the intervening space between my bed and her target that single scalpel-edged digit of hers had been joined by three others. All as sharp, they appeared like the talons of a cat. And all in that fraction of a moment that it took her to reach him.

Four long slashes appeared down the left side of the Sleep Man's mask and gushed out what could have been blood. He, it, railed back from her. As his head came back up I could see tattered fragments of his mask hanging loose, and more blood. It must have been blood, what else could it have been? Despite the fact I had never before seen blood that was a sickly lime green colour.

I caught half a glimpse at what lay beyond the mask and wished to all that was holy that I'd not. Skin is not supposed to glisten that way, nor be that pallid. It was skin I have seen before. But only on corpses. And the mouth… Mouths are supposed to have lips, not be bared back to the teeth.

It was the gas, the Sleep Man's nightmare inducing gas, it had to be. As I have told myself so many times since. Else Sleep Men are walking corpses, enslaved to The Ministry by strange dark arcane acts, or the science of the insane.

It was the gas, I am almost sure of it.

The blow Bad Penny had inflicted bought her less than a second, no more than that. But that was enough for her to hot tail it across the room while the Sleep Men tried to follow, the first stricken one getting in the way of the second, who in turn blocked the doorway for the others that came behind.

Leaping, while still three yards way, a leap no one had any right to attempt, she dived through the window, which had been open due to the Calcutta night's heat. Luckily for her.

Not so lucky was the fact we were three floors up. She should, therefore, have been a nasty stain on the pavement by the time the Sleep Men crossed the room, clouds of smoke still issuing out from beneath their long heavy black coats.

The smoke took its effect, and I passed out for the second time in as many hours, which, I am sure you would agree, was definitely becoming an annoying habit.

When I came to the following morning, feeling none of the refreshment of sleep I may add, the door to the room had already been repaired. Nor was I any longer tied to the bed. Indeed the room was much as it had been when I first arrived at the hotel. Once I had blacked out, not only had the Sleep Men left, but others had come and repaired the damage. Untied me, and tucked me into the sheets.

All of which was creepy as hell.

Indeed if it wasn't for my memories of the night, there was no evidence at all. It really could have all been a dream, just a crazy dream.

But it wasn't. I knew it wasn't…

I got up and despite the odd tinge of cramp and a killer hangover, I managed to stumble across the room to the window she had left the room via. Looking out of it I saw the rock hard pavement below, knowing with all certainty that if the fall hadn't just plain killed her, it would've most likely crippled her. No one could have made that drop in one piece and while there were no bloodstains on the ground or anything obvious like that, if they could clean the room, they could clean bloodstains as well. So clearly my Bad Penny was dead or captured by the Sleep Men. About which I felt strangely disappointed for some reason.

What it did do however was spell the end of my American lady friend's interference in Ministry affairs and more importantly my own.

Okay, so no, I didn't believe that for a second either.

This mightn't be a penny dreadful story, a tale of the type which ignores common sense and logic. The kind of logic that says three-story falls from windows taken at high-speed head first tend to kill people. But all the same, I'd a feeling she'd turn up again like that proverbial, well yes, that proverbial Bad Penny. Whatever her real name was.

And just as I was sure that like a Bad Penny, she would be back, I was damn sure determined I wouldn't be taken unawares by her next time.

Well you have to be wrong about something occasionally, don't you?

Confused, muggy from the gas, and slightly nauseous, I dressed, skipped breakfast, paid my bill and hailed a taxi for the Company aerodrome.

I did that in the full knowledge I was going to commit the number one crime in the eyes of any captain that a new crew member could commit. I was going to be late.

"You're late," were my new captain's first words to me.

The captain in question was in his mid to late forties and sported a handlebar moustache with flecks of grey in it. He was weather-beaten and worn much like his airship. He also had a face that wasn't built for smiling. Which was lucky as he wasn't when he said those words to me. He was also a native, which did surprise me, as were all his crew, which didn't. Indeed, I appeared to be the only colonial on board. Which made me very much the outsider, which, I have found, is never the most comfortable of positions to be in.

Captain Jackson turned out to be a fifth-generation Anglo-Indian. The Anglo side of that equation had been somewhat watered down by successive generations. His first name was Mahatma, as I discovered later, and his family had converted to Hinduism in the second generation. His western surname was a gift from a Scottish great-great-grandfather. Technically, therefore, he was entitled to a British passport. It was this distant ancestor that had enabled him to rise to the exalted rank of Captain and have command of his own ship.

Say whatever you wish about British colonialism, but it's a broad church, and treats all men equally. Just so long as they can hold a passport stamped at the court of St James...

"My apologies, sir, there was an incident at the hotel," I said quickly, while not expanding to say that the incident in question was a mad woman with scalpels for fingers trying to perform major surgery on my eyeball. I had a feeling that would be an explanation that would get me nowhere.

"Waylaid by a veshya, I'll be bound. I'll not have it. Bad enough Company House forces me to take a bought commission Johnny on as the first officer. But you turn out to be a laggard as well. I won't have it, do you hear me, Mr Smyth? I won't have it. I have no time for laggards. Be late reporting to my ship again, and I will pack your arse back off to London so quick you'll have to run to keep up with it."

He was, as I am sure you can tell, following that fine service tradition of ranting. Indeed Jackson's accent may have been local, but his choice of words had Surrey Downs all over it. I kept my eyes steady on the wall and wondered what a veshya was, though it was no wild stab in the dark to assume it was the local word for a woman of negotiable virtue.

'Oh, but if only that was the case, Harry old son,' I caught myself thinking, then pushed the thought from my head and focused on the wall again while he roasted me for my lateness.

This wasn't the introduction to my new berth I had been hoping for. Getting off on the wrong foot with a new captain was a sure way to end up without a leg to stand on.

Of course, I personally would've welcomed being packed off back to Blighty with my tail between my legs. It was certainly a more inviting prospect than spending a tour of duty on this junkrat of a ship, or months of dull patrol duty in the arse end of India. However, I strongly suspected that The Ministry would have words to say if I was.

Words like, 'Back to the Bailey with you and have a nice short walk when you get there'. So, all considered that wasn't an option I wished to pursue.

"It won't happen again, sir. I will sleep in my cabin before I risk it. It really wasn't my fault, sir," I said, trying my best not to sound like an utter toady, while at the same time toadying for all it was worth. Which earned me a leer.

"See that it doesn't," he snapped, then made a passing impression of looking at the transfer papers before him. Though he didn't waste much time looking. Captains never do.

"Experience?" he snapped once more.

"I was a gunnery officer in the Royal Air Navy for five years," I replied, expecting this to buy me at least a little slack. It was clear enough to me that any captain of a tub like this should be all too happy to have a RAN officer on board. RAN officers are the best-trained airmen in the world and for all my foibles, being one had been something that I'd been inordinately proud of.

Captain Jackson looked me lazily in the eye for a moment or two, then spat on his own deck plates. It swiftly became apparent he didn't think that much of the Royal Air Navy or its officers.

"So, you hunkered down in a bomb bay for a few years and waltzed around in a shiny uniform on your days off trying to get laid by gullible young ladies. Doubtless, you know next to nothing about actually flying a ship like this. Let me take a wild guess, oh yes, I'd wager you got into some trouble back home, some lass or other, was it? I know your type… Or are you one of those buggers who think they want a bit of an adventure and thought to buy the better commission you couldn't earn in the Navy. Oh, I know your type only too well, Mr Smyth. Doubtless, you're a blaggard or a wastrel if I'm lucky. We get your sort down here all the damn time, Smyth. Thieves and philanderers, that's all the RAN ever sends us, because good officers get promotions and the shite have to buy them in India. And lucky me, office politics land you on my boat. Oh yes, because we have to have a white face around after all." He spat on the deck again at that point. "Well I'll see to it you shape up or I'll have you out, and sod anything the shit for brains clerks at Company House have to say about it. So take that as the only warning I'm going to give you, Mr Smyth. Your last warning…"

There was a venom to his words, as you can probably tell from reading them. I have no doubt it came from bitter experience. A story lay behind it, no doubt, but it was one I wasn't about to inquire of right then if at all.

Besides which he was uncomfortably close to the mark.

"Mr Singh!" Jackson shouted, and the officer who had first shown me into the Captain's office appeared in the doorway. He was a younger man, round about my own age, a native of the sub-continent and one with keen looking eyes. I also couldn't help but notice he had first officer's pips on his shoulders like my own.

"Yes, Captain?" he asked crisply as he approached the desk, before pulling off a salute that looked textbook. Something which I suspected was as much for my benefit as the Captain's. He knew who I was after all and why I was there. Well, that is he knew the reason they'd been told I was there. And it behoves a crew to show their captain respect in front of a new officer. Just to make sure he knows the captain has the crew's respect, while the new man himself has yet to earn it.

Captain Jackson returned the salute, and his tone changed from berating to apologetic as he told his man the news he undoubtedly already knew. In a pantomime also for my benefit, I was sure.

"Take the pips off, lad. Afraid you're going back down to second for a while. The Company has sent us another of their clowns."

Many a less experienced man would've protested this. A captain shouldn't start out by belittling his new first officer in front of his new crew after all. But I was all too aware how this game was played. I was being pushed to see when I would push back. The captain, doubtless, wanted a chance to chew me out some more, and to do so with his man present. So I let it slide by with barely a wrinkling of my moustache. But all the same, I suspect my displeasure was obvious. Hopefully, however, so would be the image of a man willing to work to gain his new captain's respect.

Of course, he might just see this as a display of a weak spine, but it couldn't be helped either way.

"Very well, sir," Singh said sharply, saluting once more before he unclipped the pips and placed them on the Captain's desk. Then he turned to me and nodded slightly before throwing me a salute which was blunt, half-hearted and a mere sliver above an open insult. So the games continued.

"Be about your business, Mr Singh. Keep the ship tight. We hoist in an hour. We are already running behind thanks to this fool as it is," the Captain barked.

So saluting Jackson flawlessly a final time, the newly demoted second mate turn and stalked out of the office seeking, I'd little doubt, men to yell at.

I stood before the desk awaiting orders while Captain Jackson carefully signed another couple of documents. Then he looked up from the papers and did a vague impression of being surprised to see me still standing there. Which of course he wasn't at all, he had just been setting up the next rollicking to come my way. Some moves in the game are as old as sin. He scowled at me and found his best bawling out voice once more.

"What are you still doing here, man? Get after Singh. If you're lucky he'll show you the ropes. Or else he'll get you slung over the guardrail at the first opportunity you give him," he snarled.

I was, despite expecting the first part, a little shocked despite myself. Games were one thing, but to hear a captain talk openly about his new first officer being ditched from a great height by his second? That went beyond games. I stared back at him trying to figure out from his expression if it was just the Captain playing up to see what shook loose.

"Sir?" I said a moment later, without meaning it to be a question.

"Mr Singh has been the first officer aboard my ship for seven years. And I shall tell you this, he is the best damn first officer in the fleet. Yet this is the fifth time a commission-buying fool like you has been dumped on me and taken his job. Yet, Mr Smyth, he still does that job, a job you blatantly can't. So if he has the crew ditch you out over the wilds, then I doubt I shall blame him overmuch as long as he does the paperwork for me. So, I would get after him and learn your ship if I was you, Mr Smyth. Might be you'll prove useful if you do. While I would be surprised if it was the case, you might actually be a worthy first officer if you let Singh do his job and don't get in his way. And if you are then maybe that will keep you alive a bit longer. So go learn the ship and don't step on any more toes. From what I've seen of you so far I'm not full of confidence you'll last a week."

"Yes, sir," I said, saluting in a hurry and all but running out the door after the newly demoted Second Officer Singh, winner of this week's 'Who wants to kill Hannibal Smyth' award. There is nothing as satisfying as discovering you've a new mortal enemy before you've even had chance to have breakfast I've found.

The second officer was hard at it, shouting commands in Hindi to a crew who to a man eyed me with suspicion. As for Mr Singh himself, he didn't even bother to hide his contempt when he caught sight of me. Then set about shouting some more and said something that made the crew laugh, and turn as one to look at me. It was a nasty gleeful sort of laugh at that. The kind of laugh that only members of an oppressed native majority can make when they are presented with an opportunity to indulge in some payback against one of their colonial masters.

Suffice to say, Captain Jackson had not lied once in his little rant, and stood on the foredeck of the Jonah's Lament, I felt as welcome as a case of the clap in a nunnery.

CHAPTER 15

A Blade At My throat

'W H E R E I S W E L L S'

I'll say this about painful, blinding, flashes of light burning into your iris, as a means of communication it has one overwhelming advantage over other methods. No matter how tired you are, no matter how long a shift you have just put in, no matter how exhausted mentally and physically you are, no matter how much your mind and body just want to shut down.

It grabs your attention.

'W H E R E I S W E L L S'

I was lying on my bunk just after a shift that stretched longer than twenty-four hours because neither the SO nor the Captain bothered to tell me I had drawn the dog's watch.

I say drawn, that is a tad misleading, it implies that the rota had been drawn up in some reasonably fair equitable way. Rather the Captain had just decided that his new first officer could do the overnight watch. While the SO, whose job it would normally be, got a good eight hours in the sack. So from sunset to sunrise yours truly had command of the ship. At least in a theoretical sense at any rate.

I had to walk the decks. Make sure the guys in the engine room were keeping the boiler stoked. Watch the pressure gauges, the alt meters, the lateral barometers and everything else, and make studious notes on the readings every half hour. It was dull, tedious work that I should have been able to delegate out to subordinates, only with the majority of the crew asleep, and the rest more than likely to ignore me if I tried to order them to do anything.

None of which would have been quite so tedious if the ship had been moving rather than tied up for the night as we were, in still relatively friendly territory, at a small way station just north of Surat. And, more importantly, had I not spent the whole day following the SO around, while being generally ignored by both him and the crew. Save of course for the occasional snide comment in relation to my competence to serve as the first officer.

In other circumstances, I would've put placing me on the dog's watch down to simple hazing. You know the kind of things, see what the new guy is made of, and all that. Push his buttons a little, shake the tree, make them pull the longest of shifts, and what not. But this wasn't a little hazing, it was simple vindictiveness. No one wanted me here, the SO even less than anyone else.

So after a long day learning, frankly, very little about the Jonah, and feeling somewhat resentful about the whole thing, I followed the SO to the cabin we were to supposed share. I'm not sure why I was surprised to see it only had the one solitary bunk when we got there. Even on the newest RAN ship, crew and officers alike were expected to share bunk space to save on weight. True on a RAN ship it was the junior officers who shared bunks, and the first officer would normally rate a cot of his own. But the Jonah was an old ship by any standards, and me and the SO were the only officers other than the Captain. So a shared bunk it was, and I wasn't going to get to sleep in it this night, clearly. I knew that even before he said the fateful words...

"You have the night watch, Chutiya," without even bothering to say 'Captain's orders' or anything to justify it. Indeed throwing his hat on the tiny desk by the wash basin he just climbed into our bunk. Turned over and proceeded to go straight to sleep. I'd no idea at the time what 'Chutiya' meant. But I guessed it was not a term of respect.

So ten long hours of the dog's watch stretched out in front of me, and while it was very tempting to find somewhere quiet to hunker down for a couple of hours in the middle of it, I could hazard a guess the Captain was a nightwalker. Particularly on this night if it meant he could catch his new first asleep on the job. I would not have put that past the SO either. So I made my way to the mess room and loaded myself up with what was probably coffee at one time but had since become watered down tar. And set about studiously following the rulebook as far as an officer of the watch was concerned.

At the end of the night, I handed the logs over to the Captain, saluted, and was more or less ignored until he could be bothered to dismiss me. Then headed back to the cabin, where the SO was still shaving and collapsed into the bunk.

I didn't even bother to listen to whatever veiled insults came my way as I was utterly exhausted by that point. Then about ten minutes later, just after the SO left the cabin and crashed the door shut behind him to wake me one last time, I dropped off into a fitful exhausted sleep, about five minutes before...

'W H E R E I S W E L L S'

The message burned into my iris one letter at a time and casting ghosts of itself everywhere I looked, ghosts that stayed when I closed my eye.

I shot out of the bunk somewhere around the second E and found myself leaning heavily on the sink for support by the first L, dry heaving as panic took me and my head pounded with an instantaneous migraine.

I'd been there before, if you remember, on the Empress that first morning. Let me tell you, it doesn't get any easier just because you have gone through it before. Luckily though this time, I wasn't trying to shave.

As I got the hyperventilating under control, I looked up into the tiny four-inch mirror that we were supposed to use for shaving and in the vain hope that whoever was watching me could lip read, I mouthed, "How the hell would I know?"

My stomach started to heave once more. I felt dizzy and not far from collapse. Blame lack of sleep, lack of decent food, the lack of half a bottle of single malt and the sudden need for a bottle of aspirins or something stronger. Blame all that, and the bursts of light setting my brain on fire.

I waited, in horrid anticipation, after the burning after image of the S slowly faded away but no further burst of light came. And slowly I calmed down, but the burst of adrenaline had woken me up once more, and I knew sleep would elude me for a while.

In the mirror, my reflection looked haggard. After all that had happened the night before in Calcutta, I'd had no time to shave that distant morning past. No time for much as I had been running late already. Now I had two days' growth of beard and the look of a man who was running on fumes. Which in fairness I was.

I remember muttering something into the mirror along the lines of "What the hell are you playing at? Why on god's green and occasionally pleasant earth would I know where Wells is? You sent me to find him. You put me on this damn rust bucket. What the hell do you expect me to do?"

If they had lip readers watching me, they deemed not to answer my questions. About which, considering the mode of communication, I was somewhat pleased.

A few minutes passed and I poured water into the sink, deciding I may as well have a shave, and generally clean myself up a bit before I crawled back into the bunk. Tired though I was, I was wide awake now.

So I lathered up and commenced carefully guiding my cutthroat around the handsome ridges of my face. It's remarkable how a good shave can make you feel human again no matter what the circumstances. By the time I was half done I was feeling a little drowsy once more but a whole lot happier. So I was almost cheerful by the time I lifted my chin and started to scrape the blade up the line of my throat...

'F I N D W E L L S'

I dropped the razor and stemmed the blood from the nick I had just given myself before the N. By the W, I was cursing The Ministry, Gates, Queen Brass Corset and the entire population of the bloody Empire, rather loudly, a wave of nausea sweeping over me again.

Minutes later, I silently and calmly forced myself to finish shaving. Because nothing looks worse on a man than a half-finished shave.

'Find Wells'. 'Where is Wells?' Well yes, I would love to find the damnable man, and when I did, I was going to punch his lights out and give him a good kicking for putting me in this position.

"Where is Wells, indeed..." I muttered as I finally climbed back into my bunk.

In fairness, it never occurred to me specifically which Wells they wanted to know the whereabouts of that morning after the dog's watch, and why they thought I might know. Looking back on it now, knowing all I know about what was happening elsewhere at the time, I have a suspicion it was not the one I was thinking of.

The only firm conviction I'd come to that morning, however, was as long as they could blast messages at me in that fashion, sod shaving, I was going to grow a bloody beard. It seemed a safer bet all-round.

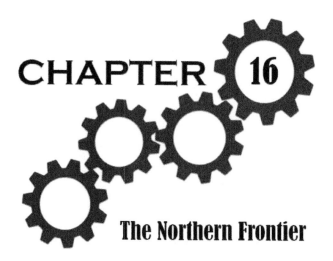

CHAPTER 16

The Northern Frontier

Three weeks passed without me plunging to my doom.

They also passed without me passing out. No blows to the back of the head. No mad women with scalpels for fingers tried to slice out my eye. No Sleep Men came along to gas me into unconsciousness. No former friends tried to have me arrested. Screaming hordes didn't charge over the hill. Angry cuckooed husbands didn't challenge me to duals when I was strung out on LSD. The 95th Cossack regiment didn't start shooting in my direction. No one tried to stake me out over an anthill and cover my unmentionables with strawberry jam. No more bright lights burning messages into my skull either, thankfully. Indeed, no one, in fact, tried to kill me, arrest me or stick mechanical insects in my eye.

You'd think I would be bored, wouldn't you?

I would have taken bored. Instead, it was three weeks of something akin to a living hell. One in which I lived on shredded nerves alone.

That said the beard was coming on a treat.

I was First Officer of the Jonah in name only. No one obeyed a single order that issued from my lips, or would've even if they understood them. Which it is perfectly possible they didn't, as no one aboard spoke English other than me, the Captain and the newly demoted second officer. At least, that is, they never did so in my presence. All I heard from the crew was Hindi, and my ear for languages had managed to pick up all of three words. None of which were the kind you could use in polite company.

The words in question were 'Lanata hei' and 'Veshya', which if I understood them properly meant I was capable of asking for sexual congress with a lady of negotiable virtue in broken Hindi and that was about it. There were other words I also came to recognise but not understand. 'Chutiya' for example. Which I am reasonably sure either means 'yes sir' or 'wanker', I suspected the latter.

The language barrier did nothing to help with the sense of isolation I soon started to feel. I am by nature a sociable man. I like a game of cards or a push of dominos while I partake of a nip with fellows of the same strip. Being a social pariah was something new to me. I laugh easily and have been known to take a good-natured ribbing as well as the next man. Even at Rudgley, while I was never what you could call popular, at least I'd had friends. I may have hated that bloody place, but soon recalling my school days seemed like memories of paradise compared with life aboard the Jonah.

As the only Brit on that fine ship of the Empire, I guess I represented a symbol of the resented Imperial authority.

Which was somewhat ironic as I found myself lacking even a modicum of authority among the crew.

The chef spat in my food at every meal. He didn't even pretend to hide it, just dredged up a gob full from the back of his throat as he served me. I could by rights have put him on a charge right there and then but what good would it have done me? At best the Captain would make his disapproval known, for the sake of face at least. Then snicker about it behind my back with the rest of the crew, and slip the cook some rupees to do it some more. So I put on a brave face, pretended not to notice, and let it go.

I know what you're thinking. You think this sounds ridiculous. You think that no ship of the Empire would be run in such a way. But this was a Company ship, not the Royal Air Navy. Here, I was an interloper, as the Captain had made plain from the start. Unwanted and unneeded. So, if the chef's insults ran me off the ship, it would be all the better to the Captain's mind and the chef wasn't the only one to hurl phlegm in my direction. Let's just say I took to avoiding walking below gantries as much as possible if only to preserve my dignity.

Such as it was.

I felt I was walking a tightrope, and there was no net. Literally in this case, given the ship cruised along at two hundred feet up most of the time. We were in the backwaters of the northern frontier, running supplies and mail between the scattering of small forts that littered the line. There was little else up there. So I could be 'dropped off' at any point, or thrown if we're being accurate, and if I was... Well, I'm sure the Captain's report would read something like...

I regret to inform you that first officer Smyth while undertaking an inspection of the lower gantries, lost his footing and fell from the craft. I send you his personal effects including the half-drunk bottle of scotch

that was found on the gantry… Please forward my regrets to his family.
He was an exemplary officer when not in his cups.
   Captain Muhatma Jackson
   The Jonah's Lament EICAN

Well, that would be if he even bothered to file a report. Given his 'paperwork be damned' attitude, he may not even have done that much. Instead, I imagine, he would draw my pay and split it with his newly promoted first officer Singh. Lord knows it would hardly be the first time a ghost drew pay from the Company coffers for a while.

The worst that could happen from their point of view was probably the chance I might land on a yak or something when I hit the ground and in doing so annoy a local farmer. The chances of my body being found by anyone who gave a damn were slim to the point of anorexia, but more importantly, in my opinion, I'd be dead. Frankly, I couldn't give a damn how much trouble it did, or didn't get them in afterwards. My ceasing to be among the breathing was the bit that concerned me.

Of course, there were worse fates than a swift death from a two hundred foot drop. I suspect all of them occurred to me during my time aboard that ship, generally, while I was failing to get any sleep.

People had been known to survive falls like that in the past, not very often, but it did happen. Catch a few tree branches on the way down, and it might be enough to slow your descent. Slow it enough so that the impact doesn't kill you. Just breaks both your legs or leaves you crippled in some other way. Then it's just a matter of waiting for a tiger or something else with sharp teeth to come along and make a meal out of you. Or you could just bleed out slowly over several agonising hours. Even if you survived that, the best you could look forward to was likely a death from starvation and exposure. This is discounting gangrene setting into your wounds, maggots and blowflies slowly eating away at you or the vultures getting bored with waiting for you to die.

If you believe I've put too much thought into this, you need to understand that this is because it was the favoured subject choice for my rare conversations with SO Singh. Well, I say conversation, that's misleading. What actually happened is he spent a playful half hour each morning recounting all the ways a man could die if he survived such a fall. Generally, while he was shaving around his pencil thin moustache with a cutthroat and I lay on the bunk next to him, trying in vain to catch some sleep after pulling the dog's watch.

Sleep was something that singularly failed to come whenever my fellow officer was about and playing merrily with his razor.

My best course, I decided early on, was to take the jibes and the insults in a pretence of good humour. So I took a page out of the current Viceroy's book and played the harmless bumbling fool for all it was worth. Even Boris's worst political enemies would admit that Mr Johnson had the common touch. His appeal among Indian's and ex-pats alike was legend. How a multi-millionaire, old Etonian, who read classics at Oxford, managed to convince people he had the common touch, I will never understand. But it seems if you fall off the odd elephant, have floppy hair, and bumble about in public giving off the impression you're nine parts idiot, you can convince people you give a crap about them and not just your own pocket. But if it worked for him, then perhaps playing the bumbler would help keep me alive a while longer.

So that had been my plan, at least, until I had a chance to gain a little respect from the crew. A chance I knew could be filed under 'slimmer than the aforementioned anorexic'.

At least, while I played at being a bumbler who didn't realise the threat he is living under, the crew were enjoying themselves. Therefore, I reasoned, as long as they continued to enjoy victimising the colonial, I was probably safe from the long drop. Though I knew only too well such a respite was limited in its nature, and the crew would just follow orders, other than mine, of course, so they were not the arbiters of my survival, that was the man I shared a cabin with.

Sharing a cabin with the SO was the cause of a daily gauntlet, which had so far included everything from my shoelaces being tied together while I snoozed between shifts, to a razor blade in the soap.

"Oops sorry, old man, how did that get there?"

We didn't speak much beyond the morning's litany of doom beyond the guardrail. He didn't listen to my orders such as they were, not that I issued any. And most of the time I couldn't make sense of a word he said in any regard, as he conversed with the crew and Captain in Hindi. A language I was readily growing to despise.

Even the soldiers at the little forts we visited were almost exclusively by Hindi speakers, so I barely heard a word of the mother tongue from one day to the next. The occasional white officer in command of those forts, as it was always a white officer, would speak with Captain Jackson in their own offices and inevitably the Captain invited the second officer along with him. So usually when we moored anywhere, I was left aboard ship, figuratively in charge, as long as I didn't try to do anything rash like issue an order. As such, I didn't even get to hear a few relished words of English on our travels from my fellow Brits.

The Captain occasionally would deem to see me in his cabin. But that was mainly when he felt like shouting at someone. Inevitably he would call Second Officer Singh in shortly afterwards and give him the orders for the day in Hindi while dismissing me, which no doubt added to the contempt I was held in by all aboard. After all, if the captain doesn't care to send his orders through you, then who gives a damn what you say.

If there was a plus side to all of this, it did mean I'd little to do and could walk the ship at my leisure, all be it with a degree of fear inspired caution. I'd avoid crossing another shipmate on the gantries for a start. It did, however, allow me to go poking my nose here and there in all the nooks and crannies of the ship. A nasty habit I shared with scoundrels and policemen the world over, not that there is generally much between them in my experience. It has however always been a firm belief of mine, stemming from my childhood in the East End, that you should always endeavour to find the best places you can stash things. Or failing that find the stashes belonging to other people. This may have been foolish as an exercise given my circumstances. Sometimes it is better not to know something after all. But foolish or not, these little searches of mine did at least prove to be rewarding.

Our good Captain Jackson or the Second Officer Singh, and I suspected both, had a little side operation going. Stacked at the very back of the cargo hold, behind a bulkhead panel, were several crates of the local Indian scotch, as well as a dozen or more bottles of the good stuff. They were clearly selling it on to the dry northwest for a tidy profit.

There was other contraband as well. Stuff that they were picking up from the hill tribes, I suspected, and shipping south for a fee. All fairly run of the mill stuff, to be honest. I strongly suspect that every boat in the air is carrying something it shouldn't be to somewhere while not asking too many questions about it. If it's not the captain running it, it's the first officer or come to that it's the gunnery deck officer who is responsible... So all told it was hardly a surprise to discover it happening on board the Jonah.

There was a plus side to being party to this information from my point of view, however. That being that I could try my hand at blackmail if I needed leverage to stay alive. Though I'd no illusions about my chances of survival if I did.

I'd a stark choice, you see. Make myself useful somehow, indispensable if possible, or expect to get the drop once they were tired of ribbing me. The main reason I was still alive was probably because kicking me off the ship in literal fashion too soon would look bad if anyone came snooping. Which would do me no good in any regard if they did, and I didn't see my masters at The Ministry as the overly sentimental types.

So for three weeks, I took what contempt came my way and tried to shrug it off as much as I was able. Public school education, you may be surprised to learn, does have some benefits, and the development of a thick skin is one of them.

Then after our third Sunday in the air, our patrol took us south again to restock, and no doubt drop off the nose powder for the discerning that was hidden down in the hold.

It was then things came to a head, and when they did so it was in a way I didn't expect.

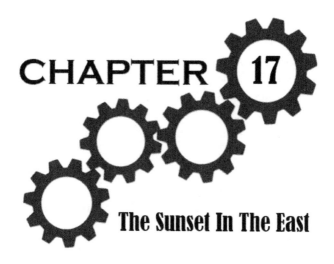

CHAPTER 17

The Sunset In The East

We put down for the night in a little town call Sangura northeast of New Delhi by a couple of hundred miles. It was a fair ways south of the foothills of the Himalayas and the uppity hill tribes we were supposed to be keeping an eye on. A safe enough place, you would imagine, to compress the gas sack and pump air into the bladder thus making the whole ship heavier and sinking us towards the ground. Not an unusual manoeuvre in safe territory.

The ship dropped to about twenty feet, and the cargo winch started up. I was on duty at the time, but the Captain was the one issuing the orders. I was doing my best to stay out of the way on the aft deck of the gondola. The aft was open to the elements and housed the airship's main gun, a battered old howitzer on a pintle ring mount that allowed it to be swung port or starboard. The deck to either side sloped away allowing it to be depressed low enough for a fair old shot at ground forces. The baffle springs looked shot to me. So much so, that if you tried to fire the thing, there was a chance the recoil would rip it free, sending the gun and its unlucky crew off the other side. It might, at a pinch, have taken one or two shots before it wrenched free, but in the condition I found it I'd be damned before I was the one taking them.

If there is one thing I know, it's gunnery. More precisely I know how to make sure that the guns are safe to use. One of the first things they teach you at gunnery officer school is how to keep your boat's cannons up to scratch. Mainly by telling you horror stories about guns ripping open their own ship's air sacks or blowing the magazine. If that happens, then the one officer who was bound to become surplus to requirements is the gunnery flag, because there is not much you can do anymore when you're reduced to a brown stain on the deck plates.

The wisdom that they impart to you is twofold. Firstly you need to know your boat's guns like the back of your hand. Secondly, you need to have a good gunnery sergeant maintaining them.

Or to be more exact, you need to know what a gun in good repair should look like but for god's sake don't try and fix them yourself.

There was no gunnery officer aboard the Jonah so I'd taken it upon myself to inspect the guns on my first day. Old habits, I guess.

The forecastle had twin link 3/8th's in good repair. The two pintle mounts on either side had Vickers guns similarly well maintained. The howitzer on the other hand, as I said, I wouldn't order fired for love nor money. Mercifully it only had five rounds in the locker. It would have been more merciful to have none though just to be safe.

I submitted a report to the Captain about the gun's condition and got told to 'Lanata hei...' for my trouble, before he somewhat begrudgingly explained that if the ship did come across something it needed to use the howitzer on, then it would be high-tailing back to Delhi as fast as it was able. A sentiment I could only agree with. The gun, therefore, was there for show, nothing more. So unless I 'wanted to fix the damn mounting myself', it would stay that way.

Which was why I was up in the aft deck looking at it when the Captain shouted me. As I said old habits. I really hated having an unusable main gun on my berth. Pride more than anything. Not that I had that much of a sense of pride in the rusting hulk I was billeted on. But, you can pull the gunnery officer off the burlesque dancer, but you can't stop him playing with his weapon. Besides which, if I could get it in workable order than I would at least prove to the Captain I had some worth if only a little.

Small victories and all that.

Of course, it also gave me an excuse to keep out of the way for a while every couple of days, while I tried to figure out how to fix it, which given the crew's general attitude towards me was a reward in and of itself.

"Mr Smyth, you have the ship. We are going to ground for the evening," the Captain shouted up to me, without bothering to turn, salute or extend any of the other niceties that I would've expected on a RAN gunship. Having proclaimed his intent, he just turned and walked towards the winch, where more than two-thirds of the crew seemed to be gathered.

"Aye, sir," I shouted back as he departed. I even saluted, god only knows why as he had no doubt forgotten me already as he went to ground.

It was going to be another one of his little jaunts. I was getting used to them. They seemed to happen about once a week when the ship was anchored somewhere safe, normally above a hill fort he knew the commander of or a small village in friendly territory like this place. He, Singh and a goodly portion of the crew would go on ground leave, while muggings here would be left to mind the ship with a couple or more unlucky sods who had drawn the short straw. That or men who had earned themselves a black mark from the second officer that day I didn't doubt. So they left the dregs and me while they went to enjoy whatever hospitality could be found below.

Regulations in Old Iron Knickers's Air Navy state that one senior officer and a third of the crew must remain aboard ship at all times, even when in its home port. In theory, they are there to see to the basic maintenance and upkeep of the craft. As well as to set a watch over it, and if needs must to get ready to be underway should trouble of some kind break out.

I suspected the regs were much the same in the Company fleet. Captain Jackson played loose with them regardless and only left two or three 'trusted' men aboard on a night in a safe anchorage. Well, four if you included the officer left in charge. But as I was far from trusted, I don't think that I counted.

If this was a RAN ship and I had drawn ghost watch, I'd have had two men posted sentry, making a circuit patrol of the outer walkways, in opposite directions. Another man in the flight cabin and one watching the boiler house. The remainder doing whatever little jobs needed doing or taking shifts for the patrols. Having sorted out the rota, I'd probably have sloped off for a kip myself of course, or joined the spare men in a game of cards in the mess. I was a layabout and a laggard after all. I was, however, a good enough officer to make sure I kept the ship secure all the same.

As it was, however, there were four men on board including me. No one was expecting trouble. This was a safe port, and the Captain had business ties with the village. Judging by the crops being grown in the fields we had passed over, that business was by way of bribes and illicit goods. So it was unlikely we would come under attack by bandits, in a village of drug smugglers who were also trading partners of the crew. So the Captain wasn't worried. If he had been, I doubt he would have left me in perfunctory charge.

It came as a surprise to find growers this close to New Delhi, but I suppose we were in the last of the foothill valleys. The only access to the place was by air as far as I could see. I suspected there was an arrangement. One that involved most of the crew getting blind drunk and partying with the locals, so the best men were all below.

So there I was, the Captain gone for the night and the barrel-scraping crewmen who were left, without a word of English between them, were playing cards in the boiler house. Which at least meant they would be keeping an eye on the steam pressure and such.

That was one job that definitely had to be done. Lax Mahatma Jackson might be, but he wasn't so lax as to let his boilers go untended. So the given order of the night was that's where the card game would be. One of the crew would walk the perimeter every hour or so, for the show of it. But as long as the boiler was tended, the Captain would be happy, and the crew knew it. So damn all need for me to issue any orders myself, not that they would be listened to or understood if I did.

Set, as I was, for a night of relatively safe boredom, in contrast to weary terror and looking over my shoulder every five minutes as was my usual evening, I took it upon myself to liberate one of the Captain's contraband scotch bottles from the forward compartment and retired myself to the aft deck again for the evening.

The Indian night was hot but dry and a cooling breeze was starting to blow down from the mountains. It was a damn sight more comfortable up there than down in my cabin. Probably safer as well as I half expected a scorpion in my bed one of these nights.

Oh but the SO does like his little jokes…

There was a chance the bottle would be missed, but like as not the crew would get the blame. It was the cheap Indian stuff anyway rather than the good single malt. Sure, I would have preferred the single malt, but chances were Captain Jackson would know exactly how much of that was down there, and the crew would know better than to get caught with a liberated bottle of the good stuff. So rhaki it was.

I whiled away an hour drinking the clear Indian fake scotch. It's the kind of stuff to send you blind in excess, but sometimes needs must and I needed a stiff drink for my nerves, don't you know.

I just propped myself up against the howitzer and drank, while wondering how the hell my being on this rust bucket of a ship was supposed to get me into H.G. Wells's good graces. As plans went, this seemed a remarkably haphazard one to me. I'd gotten past the point where I thought The Ministry knew what it was doing. I'd tried to piece it together of course. One does not like to be heading towards danger, blind and ill-informed. Mainly because if the one in question is me, I don't particularly like to be heading into danger.

Let me dissuade any false impression I may have accidentally given you. I'm not merely self-effacing. I really am not the dashing hero I might otherwise pretend to be. I am merely dashing, and it takes all my energy to be so.

An hour or two must have passed this way. With me slowly getting drunk and starting to feel the chill in the air as the day's heat evaporated, when I saw an unexpected glow in my peripheral vision. Like the red glow of sunset to the east. An hour after dusk.

It took me a moment or two to spot the problems with that proposition, for which I blame the rhaki.

East, sunset, after dusk.

I jumped up and almost banged my head on a beam, and found myself a little unsteady on my feet. Looking at the bottle in my hand, barely half drunk. I was surprised and figured drunkenly that the local Indian scotch might taste like rubbing alcohol, but it was damn strong stuff.

Stumbling slightly as I moved closer to the rail, I peered into the darkness and discovered the source of the glow and smirked. One of those suspicious-looking fields was ablaze. The smoke billowing up into the night sky might be all but invisible but the fire itself was glowing bright and angry. It was pretty too, after a fashion. So I smirked some more, thinking of my Captain and his profitable sideline burning down there.

Again I would blame the rhaki, but in truth, it was just a little bit of vindictive humour on my part. I'm not proud of it. But on the other hand, I wasn't going to lose any of the sleep I wasn't getting over it either.

Soon enough I wasn't the only one to notice the fire, the village below was suddenly like an overturned anthill, the locals and my wonderful crewmates running around like headless chickens. In minutes they were streaming out towards the fields with buckets, shovels and anything else they could use to put out the fire. More than one of them was stumbling drunkenly as they did so.

From my lofty position, I could already see it was going to be a fool's errand. The fire had caught hard and was blazing down both sides of the main field, as well as in a couple of the smaller ones. I found the whole thing hilarious, truth be told, for which I also blame the rhaki. I started shouting encouragement to the firefighters and felt like I was cheering on a rugger match. All the while I was swigging away at the rhaki between hollering advice. It may have been just due to how highly strung I was at the time, but the evening was turning out to be the most fun I'd had in an age. I probably made quite a sight when one of the crew came up to see what all the turmoil was. I remember shouting after him as he turned and bolted down the gantry.

Something witty no doubt, to me at any rate. So I burst out laughing once more.

The crewman didn't care what the mad English officer was doing by the main gun anyway. He was too busy shouting in Hindi down to his crewmates in the engine room. Doubtless, he was trying to organise them to go help fight the fire. Later when I was in a better state of mind to think about such things, I realised that the Captain probably cut his crew in on the profits of his illicit trade. The best way to buy a man's silence is with a few rupees, after all, so the way the remaining crew rushed to the winch room to go down and help fight the fire that was eating up their slice of the profits made perfect sense. Only two types of men run towards a fire. Professional firemen and those who are seeing their money go up in flames.

I was still laughing hard after them as I heard the winch descending, I didn't care a boiled fig for my Captain's sideline, so their panicked looks just added to my entertainment. After all, he had not offered to bring me in on it, and as he was running a sideline, it made ditching the inconvenient white officer over the side only the more likely. The last thing they'd want is someone like me spoiling the pot.

Hell, in their position I would be thinking much the same. Though I would have tried bribery before murder myself. No matter what had got me into this mess in the first place.

So laugh and drink a little more I did.

My laughter stopped about the same time the winch hit the ground, and a volley of shots rang out. Even drunk as I was, the fire suddenly made an unnerving amount of sense, if that was, it was a diversion and someone was making a play for the ship. Someone who knew the patrol route well enough to stage the whole thing.

Another round or two of weapons fire cut through the general hullabaloo of the fire. And I heard the gate of the winch platform crash open and shut. Boots on the metal platform, and more shouts that had nothing to do with the fields burning on the hillside.

Rhaki or not, I realised quickly the Jonah's Lament was being hijacked. And there was I, drunk on knocked-off scotch, the last officer on board.

Hell, I was the last man on board come to that. As such all my RAN training told me I was behoved to defend my ship with my life and do all I could to see the dastardly hijackers off.

I was the last line of defence.

I was the thin end of the wedge.

This then was an opportunity to prove my worth to Captain Jackson. To be the man to save his ship from would-be hijackers. After this, I would no longer be that bastard British officer foisted upon the ship's captain by the Company, but the brave, stout fellow who saved his ship. The man he doubtless would recommend for his own command. The one he would be sure to mention in dispatches. The fine, upright fellow, the captain, and God damn it, his crew would both admire and trust.

No more phegm in my food for me, 'oh no, sir, only the best for you, sir…'

The last officer, holding the line. A dashing blade in one hand, a stiff wrist holding his pistol firmly in the other, defending his command with his life's blood. Denying the laggards their prize and standing front and centre to greet them with defiance, saying, "No, sir, not on my watch, you don't. Have at you, sir, have at you and be damned."

So, with all this in mind, I did exactly what you would expect from a man in my position.

I ran for the forward cargo bay and hid myself in the stash.

CHAPTER 18

Captured By Jove...

Okay, I'll be the first to admit that as plans go, it had its faults.

So yes, I was stuck in a cargo compartment hidey-hole. With no idea who'd taken over the ship. I was alone, only lightly armed, and had no access to food or water, so hiding out for any length of time was a non-starter. I'd no idea how many of them they were, or what their intentions were. We were somewhere over northern India, heading gods only know where. To top it all off, I knew, in all likelihood, I was going to be found the moment they started to take an inventory of their ill-gotten gains, because depressingly I also knew exactly how long it had taken me to stumble across Captain Jackson's 'secret' compartment in the hold.

In case you're wondering it had taken me about five minutes from the first time I entered the hold. That was on my first day on board, well the first night, when I went looking around on the dog's watch I'd endured.

True, I had been looking for some kind of stash at the time, because I am a suspicious sod who knew the captain of every airship has a stash hole somewhere in his hold. But that was scant consolation because I worried, nay suspected, that people who went around hijacking gunships were suspicious types themselves. Exactly the types to go looking for hidden compartments and checking that none of the crew were still aboard. So I doubted it would take them much longer than it had taken me to find my sodding hidey-hole.

This didn't please me, as thoughts go.

After I'd heard the hissing that could only be the ballast air being blasted out, followed by the rumble of the main engine firing up, and felt the tugging at the belly that only a sudden uplift can cause, I'd known we were underway. That had taken all of five minutes from the moment I got myself securely hidden in the cargo locker. So I knew whoever these pirates were, they knew their airships. Which also didn't bode well for my chances of staying hidden in the hold very long.

As such, I found myself taking stock of my situation, and it seemed grim.

However, one of the things they teach you in officer school is evasion and escape. It's your allotted task, indeed your duty, should you get downed in enemy territory, to make it home in one piece. That and a general understanding that you should try to cause as much disruption to the enemy as you could in the process. They ship us up to Bodmin Moor, and all the cadets have to go through the training exercises. It's something akin to cross-country running from my school days. Well, cross country running with a pack of dogs on your tail and men with ballast guns ordered to shoot any cadet they set eyes on.

In theory, a ballast gun will only knock you on your arse with a splitting headache. Airmen of the ranks often volunteer for 'shoot the cadet' duty. Presumably on the grounds that if they are going to have to take orders from the cadets once they pass out, they might as well get revenge in first while they have the chance. So for the hunters, it's a bit like a pheasant shoot if the pheasants are snot nosed bastards you will have to obey in a couple of months' time no matter how stupid the orders they give you are. They 'the rank airmen' look forward to it, so I am told.

For a cadet, however, being chased by men with ballast guns, dogs, random patrols of 'enemy troops', across miles of boggy moorland, in thin fatigues that do sod all to protect them from the weather for three days is utterly terrifying. So, as I said, very much like cross-country running at Rudgley School.

The first lesson of the evasion and escape course is 'take stock of your inventory'. What do you have to help you evade the enemy, and if at all possible make his life difficult in the process? So let's do that then shall we...

I had one pistol, my standard service revolver, five chambers loaded with rounds and one empty, because only an idiot keeps the trigger barrel loaded when he is walking around on an airship. I also had a couple of spare cylinders on my belt. So seventeen rounds in total.

My sabre was in my cabin. Leaving it there is technically against regulations as the officer of the watch, but only an idiot walks around with a sword hanging by their legs when they're drinking rhaki on an open decked airship.

On the plus side, my cutthroat was in my boot, because only an idiot doesn't carry something sharp and dangerous with them when they're on an airship at night full of unfriendly crew.

So when I did this little exercise, all I managed to establish with my inventory was that I'm not an idiot.

Not completely at any rate. But given that the man saying this is hiding in a small, not very well concealed compartment… In the cargo hold of an airship in the process of being stolen… With no food, no water, but enough rhaki to knock out half the population of Madras…

Well…

Anyway, added to this I was also facing unknown opponents. In a country whose language of choice, I didn't speak. Oh, and I was very obviously an English officer. It was a reasonable bet therefore that for all my own crew didn't like me very much, that would be peanuts compared to how much the hijackers were likely to despise me.

If I'd had any sense, I'd have slipped down a mooring line before the ship had lifted. True, with my luck I would probably have hung myself by mistake, but that could well be merciful compared to anything my soon to be captors were likely to do to me.

The infamous Muldarin, remember him? Well, he liked to skin English officers alive, very slowly.

I'm also told that he was rather fonder of the odd crucifixion than you would have suspected as a Hindu. A fate which, I'm reliably told, is far from a doddle.

Then, while we are on the subject, there were these Thuggie strong men who Muldarin used to take along for the ride. They apparently consider it a test of strength to crush a man's skull with their bare hands. If, so they tell me, you were really lucky, you got one of the ones who were actually capable of doing this feat of strength first time. If you were unlucky, the lesser Thuggies would take it in turns to try to do so, until your head went pop.

None of these fates, or the numerous other nasty ways to dispose of British officers which rebels have come up with over the years, held much appeal to me.

So there I was, cramped up in that little secret hold. I'd followed my evasion and escape training to the letter and taken stock of my inventory. So I decided to make the best use of that inventory I could think of.

I started drinking the rhaki.

My reasoning was simple enough. If I was going to die a painful, slow and nasty death at the hands of the hijackers, I might as well be blind drunk when it happened.

Say what you like about rhaki, it may not be real scotch, but it will get you drunk quicker than it will rot your insides. Only marginally, it's true. So by the time I'd finished the first bottle, I'd ceased to care about the taste and any lingering effects it might have on me.

I was on my second bottle, the world by this time a blur, when I heard footsteps in the hold. Heavy booted ones and more than one pair.

I tried to focus on how many I could hear and picking out the individual ones. Which was harder than you may think as it was hard to focus with my head swimming with booze the way it was. However, by listening very carefully, I figured out there was a heavy-footed big guy, another heavy-footed big guy, the big guy in boots with steel nails in the sole, and a light-footed one. So maybe four hijackers, maybe more.

Thinking on this, I took another drink.

In my defence, getting drunk may have been a damn fool idea, but I was out of good ones. This way, at least, I might die with a smile on my face.

My stomach lurched a little as the ship gained altitude again. I didn't feel too good, and the footsteps on the deck plates were only getting closer. So I took another swig of the paint stripper that masqueraded as liquor and fumbled with my revolver. I'm not sure why. Perhaps my drunken logic told me if I had a gun in my hand they would probably shoot me and it would be over quick. I might even take one with me though I personally doubt I considered that. Not that I'm not capable of being vindictive, you understand. But I wasn't sure at the time that I knew which end of the gun I was holding.

I think I cried out at some point, as my gun stuck in my holster and I got myself in a tangle. "Bloody arse briskets." Or something equally absurd. Realising that these could possibly be my last words got my gander up a tad.

I've always wanted my last words to be more like, 'That's it, dear, suck harder.' Uttered in my dotage to some girl a third my age at the time. It's a vulgar idea, I know, but there you are, a man can dream these idle dreams.

"Behind there," I think someone said, though it may not have been those words or in English. I just knew with dreadful certainty what the sounds meant for me.

The deck plates rang out with further footsteps. Then there was a scraping of metal, and the flimsy plate covering the wall was pulled away. Revealing my good self in all my somewhat worse for wear glory.

I looked up into the light of hand torches, fancy Tesla power things that shone in on me, making it impossible to see anything but their light.

'Bravely' for want of another word, I levelled my pistol in what may have been the right direction and uttered something that probably sounded incomprehensible to them. But, I reasoned at the time, if you can't have a whole dream, you can, at least, have a bit of one.

"That's it, dear, suck harder."

All the while trying to remember how to pull the trigger.

Which was when I heard the words… "Mr Smyth, so that's where you're hiding…" spoken by a voice I recognised, even through the fog of the rhaki. An impossible voice in the circumstances, but having said my desired last words or not, it led me to say something else.

"Miss Wells?"

The fog of the rhaki cleared long enough for me to recognise her face peering down at me with, of all things, a black eye patch over one eye. It made her look like a pirate, which I suppose she was right at that moment. She smiled down at me, nodded, then offered her hand towards me. No doubt in an effort to help me out of my ridiculous hidey-hole.

It was at that point the rhaki in my stomach finally rebelled, and I lurched forward, catching myself on my hands before my head hit the deck plates, and in utterly unheroic fashion vacated the contents of my stomach all over them.

And as my ill luck would have it Miss Wells's well-polished, black boot.

It wasn't my finest hour.

CHAPTER 19

The Famed Shangri-La Or Some Other Mythical Place

So, I've had better moments. Let's leave it at that, shall we? Instead, let's jump ahead a little. If only to preserve a little of my dignity.

What happened next was I spent the next several days or more, a week perhaps, locked up in my cabin. Not that they needed to lock the door all things considered, because I was nursing a stomach that rebelled every time I ate food, and had cramps worse than needles the rest of the time.

On top of that little indignity, I also had a recurring case of the runs on the rare occasions I actually kept anything down. And of course, nothing but a bucket to squat over that was emptied once a day by an angry-looking man. He looked like he considered bucket duty an insulting task, and that he would be more than ready to vent his spleen on the subject by way of giving a good kicking if I gave him any gyp. All things considered, not least how bad I already felt, I kept my mouth shut for once. Perhaps that's a sign of personal growth on my part. Or just a healthy sense of self-preservation. Either way I spent most of the time curled up on my bunk and lying to myself, "Never again…"

It was, at least, three days, but could have been more like five, before I was fully in charge of my faculties once more. A bout of severe rhaki-induced alcohol poisoning on top of the spicy food I wasn't used to, were not the only things that had laid me low. I believe I was suffering from mild hysteria as well if I'm honest. I had been very out of it, such that it all felt a little akin to a near-death experience. Combine this with seeing the delightful Miss Wells in all her glory, like the light of heaven, coming to my rescue bathed in a halo of light. Though that could have been just her framed in the torchlight.

Of course, I then threw up on her, which spoiled the mood somewhat. I suspect she was the one that gave me a nasty little kick to the head at that point. Payment for the insult done her. Judging by the bruise I had on my temple she had meant it too, though that could just as well have been caused by me falling down.

Most of those first few days in my cabin were a bit of a haze, truth be told. I have a vague recollection of Saffron coming in at some point and strapping an odd monticule thing over my head, which covered my left eye. It had a green tint to the lens that made my vision seem strange. One eye normal, while one had this green sheen to everything.

When I examined it in the mirror, I noticed it had an odd design on the lens. One I could not see from inside it. The design was made with lots of little wires and odd components. I wanted to remove it to take a closer look, but something told me that would be the definition of unwise. Uncomfortable though it undoubtedly was, it was definitely doing something. I could no longer feel that almost constant itching I'd hated but grown so used to. Whatever she'd made me wear it seemed to have put the spider in my eye to sleep. A little discomfort was a small price to pay for that, all considered.

Besides which I was not the only one wearing strange devices. Miss Wells had one much the same as mine. It was this I'd mistaken for an eye patch in my drunken haze. It didn't take too much of a wild guess to figure out the device was some way to subvert The Ministry's control of its little spider. I was, as I said, all for it.

After a few days, I was feeling my more robust self again. Enough that I asked the bucket carrier to bring a tub of water for the sink in my room so I could clean myself up at the very least. The ship didn't have running water in the cabins. It was, after all, no liner, just a tatty old gunship that should've been sent for scrap years before. But it did have a little sink with a drain, and a mirror which showed me a stranger whenever I looked in it. A haggard mess with a month's worth of beard, which made it look all the worse. I hadn't looked that bad after my stay in the New Bailey.

The bucket fetcher growled something in Hindi at me that I vaguely recognised as an insult when I asked for water, but he came back an hour later all the same with the second bucket of relatively clear stuff. I didn't ask for a razor despite the beard getting the better of my chin. It was, after all, an unlikely request to be granted. Whatever else was going on here, I was reasonably certain I was a captive. I hadn't tried to leave the cabin, at any rate. Some things are clear without words needing to be spoken, and I wasn't sure I wanted to find out what happened if I did.

Besides I had a razor already. Surprisingly my stubble slicer was still in my boot. These pirates, or whatever they were, had been somewhat lax when it came to searching my person. Possibly that was due to me vomiting everywhere at the time. So something good came from my disgrace as. Small victories and all that. Yet I thought it wise not to give the secret of my razor away and went without a shave, no matter how tempting it was.

I did my best to make myself presentable. Partly this was just a pride thing, and a desire to straighten myself out a bit. Even the beard didn't look too bad once I had scrubbed at it a while and forced it into some kind of order. If I am honest it wasn't just a pride thing; it was also partly in the hope Miss Wells might come back to see me now I was a tad more human again. It wouldn't do to be unpresentable in that event. Vain of me, I know, but one must keep up one's appearance. Even if, as I suspected, the impression I left in the cargo hold was one I would never quite live down.

The days dragged past slowly. The deck plates vibrating with engine noise. The air growing thinner. Wherever we were headed, it was at high altitudes. Up in the mountains, I suspected. Not that it was much of a leap of deduction to make. The Himalayas have always been the haunt of bandits and brigands. It's all those hidden little valleys offering such fine places to retreat to when things got nasty. For your Johnny come lately insurrectionist, they were just too damn inviting.

What little I could see through the tiny porthole in my cabin seemed mostly cloudbanks and mist. From the glow of the sun, however, I'd gathered we were predominantly heading east. What little I recalled of sub-continent geography from my school days made me suspect that meant Nepal, which is, after all, a kingdom of those nice little hidden valleys. It was that or we were going to turn north at some point to cross the whole range over to China. Either way, it mattered little as I had damn all say in it. But wherever we were going, it was away from Imperial India. Which made sense, as you don't go stealing British gunships and hang around where they might find you, but it didn't bode well for me. The British haven't been popular in

Peking since before the boxer rebellion. While the Nepalese have been staunchly independent for the last century or so, and were left to it as they didn't have much of anything anyone wanted. Indeed the mountain kingdoms made for perfect buffers between the great powers, and neither us nor the Chinese wanted each other for neighbours. Each empire had enough to keep themselves busy between our African adventures and China's continued attempts to annex what was left of Japan.

I always felt a little sorry for the Japs. Tying themselves so closely to the Americans had cost them dear when the US fell to its inner turmoils just as the Land of the Sun had started to rise. Of course officially we British disapprove of China's empire building across the Sea of Japan.

'Going around invading a sovereign nation and sticking your flag in the ground is dashed foul play, don't you know?' says the greatest empire builders the world has ever known.

I may be a tad cynical, but I've long suspected the main cause of British disproval of Chinese foreign policy in this regard was not due to outrage at Japan's invasion, but because the Chinese got there before us…

But regardless of my opinion on such trivialities as foreign policy, Nepal, buffer though it may be, was no place for an Englishman. Not since those couple of lackaday adventurers, Dravot and Carnehan tried to set themselves up as kings around those parts a century or so ago.

But as I didn't have much say in the matter, I tried not to let it worry me too much.

I spent most of my time sleeping, eating what they gave me as slowly as I could in the hope my stomach would retain it and wishing I'd a book or two to pass the time, not that I'm much of a reader as a rule. Mostly though, despite my predicament as a captive of some unknown force of rebels or pirates, who in all likelihood just hadn't gotten around to killing me yet, I was bored to tears.

Odd I know, but I can tell you from bitter experience that being a prisoner awaiting your death is one of the most boring things imaginable you can live through. Death cells don't go in much for entertainment, either in the Old Bailey or locked in a cabin on a stolen airship. Either way, the end result is much the same, boredom then death.

I'll admit I was feeling a little morbid at the time. Though as the days stretched on, I felt there was at least a little hope that I wasn't for the chop straight away. They kept feeding me for one thing. Though that could have been them using a weird way to kill me off considering the quality of the food. Rebels and pirates never seem to have good chefs in my experience.

That I know this to be the case, says a lot about my experiences…

If anything, however, I realised after a few days I was probably safer now than I'd been with my actual crew. The realisation of this led to me even cheering up a little and made me look at the bigger picture. Mostly the bigger picture I looked at was imagining Captain Jackson and Second Officer Singh trying to explain how they lost their command. Which I suppose is a tad petty of me. But, thoughts of those who did me a wrong one suffering, well such thoughts always brighten my day.

Small victories and what have you…

In any regard, somewhere around the seventh day or so by my reckoning, which was shaky at best, I felt the ship sinking for the first time in what seemed like an age. Investigating through the little porthole, I could see little. Just a veil of cloud which enveloped us as we descended and obscured my view of what lay beyond the ship. We started being buffeted by the turbulent mountain air pockets, and I will admit I started to worry a little.

Only two kinds of pilots take a ship down through clouds in a mountain range. Though who know exactly what they are doing and where they are going, and utter morons. The way the ship was being swung about I had to hope it was the former, because the latter was going to get us all killed.

There was one thing for certain, however, we were definitely going down into some kind of valley.

What should have happened next I realise, at least for literary merit, is that the clouds should have parted to reveal the wondrous valley into which we were sinking. Some kind of remote nirvana, high in the Himalayas. The famed Shangri-la or some other such mythical place.

Sadly what actually happened was the ship stopped going down suddenly, and a few minutes later I heard the winch start up. At which point I realised the clouds we were descending through were more like a dense fog, and I still had no bloody idea where I was.

On the bright side, the ship had not been torn apart on rocks, and we seem to have made safe harbour, wherever we were. Having avoided being involved in a god awful crash, my day could have been going a lot worse on the whole.

I stalked around the tiny cabin for a while. Listening for footsteps on the deck plates outside. Then popped open the porthole in the hope of hearing what was going on outside. It was of course way too small to climb through. Not that it would be a wise course of action if it were. I may not know where I was, but I could hazard a guess that there would be no one friendly about. If I started trying to escape the most likely thing to happen would be capture and chains on my legs. That or something sharp in the guts at any rate.

I could hear muffled voices outside, much as I expected, however, they weren't speaking English so even if I could've heard them properly, I'd a chocolate fireguard's chance of learning anything.

Somewhere a dull ringing sound came out of the fog. Deep and low sounding, it took me a moment to realise it was from some form of a bell. A slow deep ring more like a thud than a peel. I realised we were definitely at some place with people and not just hunkering down for the night. If I seem surprisingly keen to find out where, possibly it was just because I was bored sick of looking at the inside of my cabin.

An hour or two must have passed before they sent anyone for me. My guess was the crew were reporting in first. Your guess as to with whom was as good as mine at that point. I was, however, hoping that I was missing with my guess. Coincidences seemed to be piling up, you see. Maythorpe on the liner, Bad Penny in the hotel, Saffron and her pirates just happened to steal my airship. There was an air of the inevitable about it all. As if a story was being written and I was just being pulled along by the narrative.

I know that sounds ridiculous, but a week of isolation at thin altitudes can give you all kinds of odd ideas…

I had been sent to India for a reason, after all. Not that The Ministry deemed it wise to explain a damn thing to me. But I was placed on the Jonah's Lament for a reason as well. The Ministry had manipulated things to get me a berth on that particular ship. Then of all the ships to get half-inched by bandits, it's the Jonah that gets hijacked. I may be a little slow at times, but that seemed too much of a coincidence to me. The Ministry must have known it to be a likely target at the very least. Or they had set her up, a lost flight plan here, rumours of goods it was carrying, whatever. I knew full well there were people who bought such information, as there were people who sell it. It is no great leap to guess The Ministry's hand at play. It was a set up plain and simple, feed the pirates the right information and Roberta's your father's cross-dressing brother.

So the pirates, bandits or whoever they were take the ship and take me prisoner into the bargain. Which led to another set of questions entirely, the same question I kept on asking myself.

Why me?

Why did The Ministry think they would take me prisoner, and not just lump me over the side or run me through.

I still wasn't sure I would like the answer to that particular question. If I ever found out, and even that wasn't the end of it. Because of all people, look who turns up with the pirates. The ever lovely Miss Saffron Wells, whose great-grandfather was the whole reason I had been sent to sodding India to start with. A fellow mole of The Ministry's, or stalking horse, or whatever they thought she was. Though I wasn't sure that was the case anymore. If the monocular thing I was wearing, we were both wearing, was any clue at all, she had managed to escape their tender charms in some way and had found a solution to the whole spider in the eye problem.

Yet even that wasn't straightforward, was it? I mean, well, my guess was that The Ministry knew that this ship was the right kind of target because they probably knew about Captain Jackson's sidelines and when the ship would be vulnerable, setting him up and me at the same time. But the only way they could know what kind of targets were likely to be the right kind of target would be to get that information from someone who knew. Someone they have some element of control over, who also had connections to the pirates. Someone very like Miss Wells.

Which begged the question of why Saffron would go through with it when she found a way around the whole Arachno-Oculus problem? If you're no longer playing the bait, why go through with the trap. Unless she was playing a longer game than I suspected? A worrying thought I'm sure you'll agree.

But the possible duplicitousness of Miss Saffron Wells aside, it was no great leap of logic to suspect I had now found myself landed in the clutches of her great-grandfather H.G. Another worrying thought. Not least because if Saffron was now batting for the other side, she'd likely throw me to the wolves in a heartbeat. She knew why I was in India after all. So when I heard the clang of boots on deck plates in the corridor outside a while later, I was certain that I was about to come face to face with H.G. Wells esquire. A meeting I had every reason to suspect would not go well for me.

CHAPTER 20

At Least It Wasn't Bloody Snowing...

The door of my tiny cabin opened, and as it did so, I took a step back. Which given how small the cabin was put me up against the wall. I suddenly felt very hemmed in, and found myself crouching slightly. My hand must have nervously been hovering towards the top of my boot and my trusty cutthroat, just on the off chance I would pluck up the courage to actually grab it.

My heart was racing by this time. I had passed the last hour or so worrying about all the whys, and the whos, and the 'what the hells'. I'd gotten myself a little tightly wound if I'm honest. After all this I was finally going to get some answers. I was still not sure how much I wanted to know what they were.

In the doorway stood something utterly unexpected. Well, not that unexpected, it was a man after all. Unexpected would have been something else entirely. But all the same, it was a man dressed as a Buddhist monk, which was not what I expected.

When I say dressed as a Buddhist monk I mean the whole works. The orange robe, shaved head, prayer beads, wooden sandals, the whole shebang. Which threw me off my stride somewhat. He didn't look quite right though, and it took me a moment to realise what was wrong about him. But when I did see it, it became obvious. The man in front of me. He wasn't Nepalese, or Chinese, Vietnamese or any other 'ese', he was in short no one you would expect to find in a Buddhist robe, because he was in fact European.

Northern European at that, for all his skin had the tan of a man who had spent some years away in sunnier climes. He also had little horn-rim glasses and a bushy moustache. A civil servant, bank manager of a moustache. Which was quite a surprise on a Buddhist monk, as I'm sure you can appreciate. That should have been a clue, but I was still been slow on the uptake. So it took me a moment or two to recognise him.

In my defence, the picture I had seen him in before had been a faded old thing, not quite in focus as a lot of old photos aren't. But it was still him, the man in M's picture. Shaved head and mantra chanting robes aside it was him. Mr H.G. Wells Esq. Formally of some Church of England parish in the Cotswolds. Now as far from a man of the Church of England as you could get.

The blighter had apparently gone native.

"Mr Hannibal Smyth, I presume?" H.G. Wells said with a certain calm self-assuredness in his voice. He was a picture of calm right then. This, The Ministry's most wanted man in Queen 'Face Like A Slapped Arse When She's In A Good

Mood's' Empire. Calm as you like, far calmer than I felt at any rate. And, he said my name in an 'I know all about you' kind of way, if you get my drift. This, all things considered, did little for my confidence in the possibility of a prolonged existence.

The thing is I know all about myself. In his position I'd have killed me on the spot. Occasionally, in my wistful moments, I thank God almighty that I've never been captured by myself.

I tried to force myself to relax, and straightened myself up. Even if that meant my hand was so much further away from the cutthroat in my boot.

Trying to hide my racing panic-stricken mind, I coughed loudly, as if clearing my throat, while wondering if I should offer him my hand. Whatever else he was, he was still British after all. There are, after all, certain forms to be maintained when two Englishmen meet abroad.

I coughed once more for good measure before I replied, still trying to gather my wits.

"And you would be Mr Herbert George Wells, I suspect," I said, trying not to be outdone on the 'I know who you are' stakes. I suspect, however, I didn't sound as calm as he had or I wished to. Something else was still bugging me though I was a little too strung out to know what.

"You suspect correctly. Now Mr Smyth, I am afraid I have to ask you, have you been sent to kill me by my old friends at The Ministry?" he asked, his voice betraying nothing at all. It was still just as calm and level. I'll say this much, whatever mantras he was saying for inner peace they seemed to be working. He was utterly unruffled by the idea that I might be an assassin aimed at him by a shadowy branch of the British government.

He was a damn sight more unruffled than me that was for sure. But not to be outdone I was determined to brazen it out if nothing else.

"I have no idea," I replied after a moment, which was the absolute truth. "My brief was just to find you and infiltrate your… whatever you have here," I added, deciding in an instant to stick with the whole truth-telling plan, which did not come naturally to me, truth be… well, you know what I mean.

I was still feeling that itch that something or other that wasn't quite right as well. Something important I was still missing while I discussed the possibility with this middle-aged, middle-class Englishman, come Buddhist monk that I had been sent to kill him. It was nibbling at my paranoia.

"Hum, yes I am sure. Big Mac predicted as much I am told. The Ministry does like its secrets. Even when they are keeping them from their own cat's paw. Still, you're here now. I suppose I could even congratulate you on your success. Finding me was, after all, your mission. But it does rather beg the question does it not, what am I to do with you?" he asked.

I found myself wondering who in God's name Big Mac was. All I needed on top of everything else was some Jacobite mystic to deal with as well. But that was a question that would have to wait a while. And I was none the wiser when I found out. Bloody thing that it is, it remains a mystery to me how all the cogs and gears on it manage to come out with answers to questions because you feed the right piece of cardboard into it. But let's not get ahead of ourselves talking about Mr S Jobs's contraptions.

I put it out of my mind and carried on with the bravado and brazen plan of action. What was he to do with me indeed?

"You could… I don't know, let me go, drop me off in Shanghai or somewhere else out of the way. I'm no fonder of The Ministry than you are. I'd be quite happy to just disappear, as it were," I replied after pretending to give it some thought.

Some hope of that, but it was worth a try. It wasn't like I'd many options before me. I probably sounded more puzzled than bullish anyway, because try as I might, that itch at the back of my mind was not going away.

Wells laughed. On the whole, it was a more pleasant laugh that I would have gotten out of M I am sure, but still I wasn't sure I liked that laugh, and what it might mean for me.

"I think not, Mr Smyth, I think not," he said, turning his back to me, quite unthreatened by the possibility I might attempt to do him harm when he did so. Then he just walked away past the two burly guards he had brought with him. I forgot to mention them, I know, but did you really think he was alone? They were big men, thuggie cultist kind of big.

Remember them, the head squeezers? I did. So as they stepped in and took hold of me, I came to the swift conclusion I was going to let them escort me out of the ship. I wasn't going to make any trouble, and I was going to hope that while I wasn't getting dropped off in Shanghai any time soon, I was probably not going to get killed right there and then. At least I bloody hoped not…

It was while they were, without too much in the way of nastiness, marching me through the bowels of the Jonah's Lament that what had been bugging me about Wells struck home.

It wasn't that I recognised him from his photograph, or even that he looked like his photograph. It was that he looked just like it, in fact. I would venture he didn't look a day older than he had in that picture. Oh shaven head, orange robes, a decent tan, yes. But not a day older.

And that photograph had been taken over a hundred years ago.

The guards gently marched me out of the ship, across a boarding ramp and into the icy cold mountain mists. Snowflakes were falling in the gloom like they were forming in the very cloud that hung around me. They marched me a good hundred yards or so across barren ground. Then shoved rather than threw me into a cell.

The cell was one of a type achingly familiar to me. Oh, the steel bars were a bit rustier and the stone walls were of a rougher hew. But it was still exactly the type of cell I should have expected. I could tell this because of the view through the shroud of the mist beyond the bars.

An upright frame, a heavy cross beam, and a loop of rope dangling down. I recognised it straight away. I mean, what else could it be? Standing there, a short final walk away. A mist-wrapped gallows across the yard. All but calling me to my fate.

I had travelled across half the world, been beat up, knocked out, tied up, assaulted by mad Americans with brass arms, gassed, threatened, poisoned (though admittedly that had been by myself with the rhaki). I'd had insidious mechanical spiders inserted in my eye and become the cat's paw of powerful bastards who don't even bother to tell you what you're doing in the first place and at the end of all that I'd ended up in another death cell staring at a gallows.

And why? All because of some mad bastard who was walking around in an orange dressing gown who was just as bloody mysterious as my damn employers. And just to top it off, the mad bastard in the orange dressing gown playing at being a Buddhist monk was running around with airship pirates and upsetting the apple cart.

A mad bugger called Herbert George Wells who just to cap it off wasn't ageing. Just like Queen Iron Knickers, Brass Brassiere'd, Seldom Bloody Amused, Clockwork, Bun-Haired, Empress Of Every Pink Bit Of The Globe, Pieced German Sausage Loving. Bloody Victoria herself.

As I sat there, while icy flakes came through the open bars of my cell, staring at that gallows across the yard, I whispered to myself.

"Well Harry old lad, you might as well have stayed in the New Bloody Bailey. At least it wasn't bloody snowing there…"

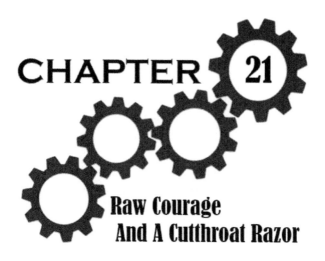

CHAPTER 21

Raw Courage And A Cutthroat Razor

The cells of a Nepalese mountain monastery aren't somewhere they take you to. Rather, they're a place they throw you, because once they put you there, then they're finished with you.

It's the last stop but one. The last stop, the very last stop, is the mist-shrouded gallows across the courtyard...

Stop me if this sounds familiar...

Or if I just sound maudlin come to that.

Suffice to say I wasn't at my happiest that night. After all, they had just marched me off the Jonah's Lament and thrown me into that cell that looked out on a gallows. Well, okay, prodded me in there, if I am being entirely accurate, but the effect was much the same.

As the door slammed shut and the heavy bolt was locked off, I stood for a while staring out through the bars, and watched as snow fell lightly through them, into the mist which still hung heavy, staring at the shadow across the courtyard. The shadow of those gallows seemed to be beckoning me.

Eventually, I resigned myself to a night shivering in the darkness. So I huddled under a blanket that I'd found in the back of the cell. Its three solid walls, stone floor and roof were, at least for a short time, now my home. Rusting steel bars formed the fourth wall, dear reader. Bars that ran the full length of the wall and formed the door as well. This also left it a wall open to the elements so, just to add to my bitterness before long the snow came drifting in.

That my re-found bitterness, not that I had ever lost it, and the bitter cold of the mountains were likely to last only a short time was of little consolation. Looking out across the yard at that shadow, it would be all too damn short, for my liking.

I must have fallen asleep despite my nerves and the buggering cold because I woke later to find someone had put a small coal brazier into my cell. It was smouldering happily and giving off enough heat so while I wasn't actually warm, I at least wasn't going to freeze to death.

I huddled a little closer to it and found myself musing that if ever I wrote 'The Good Death Cell Guide' at some point in the future, a future I suspected I didn't have, then this place was going to get at least one more star than the New Bailey.

Open Sided Cells in the Hidden Valleys of Nepal

Not entirely unpleasant places to spend your final hours on this earth. It may only be because they want to keep you alive long enough to hang you, but at least, they have the good grace to keep you warm.

A reasonable five out of ten, (point added for ample fresh air)

Highly recommended if you happen to be looking for a place Asiatic mountain regions to spend your final hours of incarceration.

I suspect there'd never be much of a market for that particular travel pamphlet. I don't see it replacing the good pub guide on the best sellers list. So while the thought amused me for a passing moment, it was a swiftly passing moment. Besides, I suspected right then I'd have little chance to write it anyway, though as it so happened, I was wrong about that.

The uncomfortable night passed and the morning sun slowly burnt away the mist, and with the dawn came a lifting of my mood.

The gallows which had so haunted me in the small hours, revealed itself to actually be a block and tackle winch on an L frame, which hung out over a ravine. Doubtless it was used for hoisting god knows what up and down from the level plateau I'd found myself on. While I'd no doubt it could also have been used as a gallows at a pinch, it seemed to me now unlikely that was the case. As such it was just possible I'd have to drop an entry from 'The Good Death Cell Guide'.

My publisher doubtless would be gutted.

As the mist lifted, the valley beyond slowly revealed itself. Not that I could see a great deal of it with my singular viewpoint. I reasoned my cell must be at the foot of the main buildings because all I could actually see was a barren valley with a few terraced fields on the mountain slopes. Presumably, those fields got more of the sun as these were on the south-western side of the mountain. Though god knew what you could grow up here in the mountains. I admit I've little idea when it came to agriculture. A city boy to my back teeth and I wouldn't know a plough from a scythe in all honesty, but the gritty grey soil of the mountains seemed far from ideal for farming. Yet despite this those who knew their business better than I had a healthy crop of something growing on those slopes.

'Probably beans,' I remember thinking, for no real reason, save a personal loathing of such things that stemmed from a childhood in the East End where I was raised on sporadic vegetables and the myth of meat. Something akin to worldly knowledge only by the broadest of definitions had sunk into me long ago, so I was more or less aware that half the world lived on beans or rice, and I knew enough to know that the terraces weren't paddy fields.

There were, it has to be said, more interesting things to see in the valley than the bean crop. To start with, apart from the not so good ship Jonah's Lament, there were three other airships moored in its shadow, or to be exact it was moored in theirs.

Two of them were, or had been at least, grandiose passenger liners. Doubtless, I reasoned, they were steadily being stripped of valuables. It was the fourth airship which drew my eye, however, due to the twin headed black eagle emblem on its iron-plated flank. It was a Russian gunship, and one that was considerably larger and newer than the Jonah.

Staring at the Romanoff Imperial Eagle on its side, I found myself recalling some snipping I had read in The India Times back in Calcutta some weeks ago. Some minor report of a Russian airship vanishing along the Afghan border a month before, but that had been a liner according to the ever unreliable Times, not a gunship.

Was it possible, just to add to my problems, the Imperial Russian Air Navy were in cahoots, to quote my employers The Ministry, 'that most despicable enemy of the British Empire H.G. Wells'?

Or at least that is how The Ministry would describe him if they were pantomime villains, which I can assure you they're not, very much not. Just in case you were labouring under any illusions on that score.

Pantomime villains are set up to lose and played for laughs and jeers from the cheap seats. The Ministry, it has been my experience, don't care for laughter…

I thought about that for a moment. The thought that the Imperial Russian Navy might be in cahoots with that former writer of incredulous fictions. It seemed unlikely, but by now little in all this would've surprise me.

Well, I say that, but considering the number of times I'd suffered mild concussions of late it possibly isn't true. People seemed to have developed an irritating habit of surprising me, normally from behind with something heavy, but I digress…

I suspected rather that H.G.Wells merry bunch of pirates, which as you know took the Jonah so easily, had taken this Russian craft too. Though exactly how they had managed that little trick was another question entirely, because it was no out of date steamer consigned to the back route patrols in rural India like the Jonah.

If I can be clear about this, the Russian craft was a beast, a real bloody big bastard of a beast at that. If it helps you picture it, let me say it bore some similarities to our own Dreadnaught class, and by our own, I mean Queen 'Iron Knickers' Victoria's Royal Air Navy's. The organisation in which I'd formally served, so vaingloriously.

I guess it says something of me that even after all that had happened, I still more or less considered myself a RAN man. As such I still tended to think of Dreadnoughts, the super heavy airship of the British fleet, as 'our own'.

What it says about me, I am not entirely sure.

Dreadnaughts are the backbone of the British fleet, flying the flag for old Britannia herself, and putting the fear of god into anyone, indeed everyone, who would cross The British Empire.

I've long suspected the sight of a RAN Dreadnaught in the sky would be enough to take the fight out of all but the most committed of the crown's enemies. So when I say this beast of a Russian airship reminded me of those fine craft I say so with some admiration.

Except, that is, this big bastard of a Russian ship was half as big again as a Dreadnought, and sported more guns than any air-ship had a right to carry.

As such it was hard to believe Wells's ragtag band of bandits could have taken her. I say this even while bearing in mind how easily they'd taken the Jonah from my former captain and his crew. Not to mention from me, for that matter…

The Russians, if I recalled my old RAN intelligence briefings correctly, called this class of ship their Iron Tsars. Though, as the military intelligence boys told us, with a rye smile and what for them was an attempt at humour, these were no pampered Romanoff princeling air-ships, like the Russian Tsars who routinely got pictured in the scandal sheets and tabloids. These weren't ships named for those pamper playboy peacocks. These were Ivan the Terrible air-ships. The old-fashioned kind of Tsar. The kind of Tsar known for angry rages and occasional bouts of mental instability. RAN briefings had a habit of verbosity when talking about our Russian 'friends', as I recall this particular comparison drew quite a few laughs in briefings.

As I stood in that cell looking at her I realised just how apt that description really was. Any craft with that many guns on it was bound to have stability issues for a start…

As far as I was aware, no Dreadnaught had ever gone toe to toe with an Iron Tsar. The British and Russian fleets tended to dance around each other almost as much as their respective political masters. A damn good thing in my opinion, for if the Lion and the Bear ever came to blows, it would surely be a battle of stamina over strength and both empires would end up weaker for it.

Of course, as far as the Iron Tsar's were concerned, as a British airman, I'd long been assured fleet intelligence briefings a Dreadnaught would win out in any such engagement. Though looking at an actual Iron Tsar from that cell it struck me those briefings mightn't have had the right of it. A broad side from that bear of a ship would likely rip through anything. I knew there and then that I for one wouldn't want to be facing it in battle. Indeed, if I'd anything to do with it, I wouldn't want to come within a hundred miles of one of those buggers, let alone the whole Russian fleet.

What it did confirm to me though was this. If Wells's little army was up to the task of taking a ship like that, then I could understand The Ministry's concern. You could, after all, start a small war with one of those bastards.

More to the point, you could win one too.

I was also struck by another unpleasant thought. I doubted there was a single British Dreadnaught in the whole of India. The air superiority of the East India Company's rag tag navy had always been enough to put down rebellions for the last hundred years or so. When your enemies are peasants crawling in the mud, any old rust bucket ship will do. But I was fairly sure none of EIC's old rust buckets would last more than a few minutes against that Iron Tsar.

You'll have to forgive me somewhat if I sound like I'm drooling a little but I'm an airman after all. The big Russian may've been a beast, but it was a magnificent beast. It made the Jonah and those old Fearless class ships I used to fly in RAN look like… Well, I'd venture the nautical equivalent would be paddle boats.

Eventually, when I dragged my eyes away from the Russian death and thunder machine, I took a closer look at the two liners. It's not like I'd much else to do while stuck in that cell. If you remember my first thought was their captors were stripping them of valuables. But as I looked again I realised I was only half right. They may well be stripping them of their tacky interiors, but they were also making alterations to the airframes and the sleek-looking gondolas that hung below them.

Work gangs on rudimentary scaffolds were welding this, or cutting holes in that, in the early morning sunlight. Turning those sleek passenger craft into something else entirely. Slow though I may be, it didn't take me long to figure out what they were up to. I knew what to look for, after all. I'd spent enough years around navel craft to figure it out.

They were adding armour to the flanks and building in gun ports. They were, in short, weaponising the big liners. Which could only mean the big Russian and my own little gunship weren't going to be the only fighting machines moored on this mountainside before long.

It came horrifyingly clear to me then that H.G. and his merry band of cutthroats weren't hijacking liners for funds, though I'm sure the money did them little harm. They were instead building an air armada, a war fleet, and that, in case you can't guess what that's means, let just say it didn't bode well for anyone. Peasants throwing mud at red coated soldiers was one thing, but peasants in a fleet of gunships, well, that could set India aflame, and that was the least of it.

Even with my slim grasp of politics, I knew there was more to it than that. Given that beast of an Iron Tsar his men were busy with. Wells didn't care if he made enemies of the Russians as well as the British. In which case, I reasoned, he was preparing for something more than just an

Indian insurrection. If you wanted to free India from its benevolent overlords you would want the Russians to stay neutral rather than set them up as your enemies. Whatever he was up to, up there in the middle of nowhere, it was something big. Something that, it seemed to me, was all too obviously also likely to end badly for someone.

I decided there and then to try to make sure that someone wasn't me.

That realisation of what appeared to be underway in that remote Himalayan valley sent a shiver running down my spine that was nothing to do with the light snowfall drifting in through the open side of the cell. Britain and Russia were probably the two most powerful nations in the world. Certainly they had the two largest air fleets in the world. Yet here in the mountains of Nepal a mad scribbler of fatuous fictions come want to be rebel overlord was, one way or another, spoiling for a fight with both of them. Whatever Wells true aims were, he was going to set off a powder keg. But more than that, when the fighting started there was all the chance in the world it would only be a matter of time before the superpowers turned their guns on each other.

I mightn't be the sharpest political knife in the drawer, but even I knew that the peace between the two empires was fragile at best. Alliances had long been drawn on either side. Plenty of lesser nations hung to the coattails of that delicate balance. The wise ones were of course pro Britain. But others, foolishly, had strong ties to Moscow. Then there were the other big players as well, Japan, Spain, Greater Mexico and others all had treaties tying them to Russia. While the Canadians, the Brazilian Confederacy, the tattered remains of the North Eastern American States all depended on British strength to keep the Russians and their allies at bay. Even those nations which chose to not chose a side like France and China leaned a little one way or the other. If Wells started a shooting war in India with a fleet of gunships the whole house of cards that was Imperial diplomacy could come crashing down.

I read once about a failed politician called Churchill or something. He'd been nothing much, just a half-baked foreign secretary at best, but he'd famously warned that the world always stood on the brink of disaster. According to him the long peace between the great nations was nothing more than a convenient fiction. The hundred year detente was 'A powder keg waiting only on a single flame.'

As I recalled he'd been laughed out of the commons at the time, what was that fifty odd years ago, more, seventy perhaps? No one, they'd all said, would be mad enough to start a war between the great powers. 'They' in this case being the powers that inevitably be, those with the most invested with the status quo. But, I realised on that mountain side, for all mad old Winston had been seen as a flake, he was right about that one thing. It wouldn't take much to bring everything crashing down. This fleet Wells was building on a Himalayan mountainside, might just be the spark the powder keg needed…

So, let's recap a moment shall we. Just to take stock of all this. There was I, in a cell on a Nepalese mountainside, looking at a rebel air fleet in the making. Me, the man The Ministry sent as their foil. The pawn they'd moved to counter whatever Wells was up to in the back of beyond.

Me, Hannibal Smyth, a man happy to admit, with a certain degree of self-loathing, he is at best a liar, a thief and on occasion a murderer. A condemned man loathed by everyone, and as you may have surmised by now, one with all the moral fortitude of a tory politician with a bag of cocaine in his pocket, stood in the doorway of a Whitechapel brothel.

I said at the start I would be honest with you, I never said that honesty would be pretty…

Meanwhile, here we have Herbert George Wells, a man who it seemed to me as I stood in that cell on the mountainside was bent on bringing the whole world to its knees. And one who despite all the odds you'd have expected against such a thing, might well have the means of doing just that.

I will not lie, what after all would be the point in doing so. I found the idea of all this terrifying.

I may have muttered something to myself as the realisation of the scale of everything I'd been dumped in the middle of dawned upon me.

Something ungentlemanly.

Something that rhymed with duck.

For what dawned on me right at that moment was this. The Ministry had sent me right into the heart of a mad man's base. They had made me no so much their pawn as their only move. Their agent charged with stopping this maniac H.G.Wells in his tracks.

Me, Hannibal Smyth and me alone, Great Britain's only line of defence against the madness of this man. On balance things weren't looking good, to be frank, I no idea how I was going to get out of this alive… I was after all alone, and armed with nothing but the cutthroat razor in my boot and my own raw courage.

So let's face it…

Just the cutthroat then.

THE END

Not bloody likely!

Hannibal Smyth will return in
'From Russia with Tassels'

ABOUT THE AUTHOR

Mark writes novels that often defy simple genre definitions, they could be described as speculative fiction, though Mark would never use the term as he prefers not to speculate.

When not writing novels Mark is a persistent pernicious procrastinator, he recently petitioned parliament for the removal of the sixteenth letter from the Latin alphabet.

He is also 7th Dan Blackbelt in the ancient Yorkshire marshal art of EckEThump and favours a one man one vote system but has yet to supply the name of the man in question.

Mark has also been known to not take bio very serious.

Email: darrack@hotmail.com
Twitter: @darrackmark
Blog: https://markhayesblog.com/

Printed in Great Britain
by Amazon